TIME TRAVELING WITH A HAMSTER

ROSS WELFORD

TIME TRAVELING WITH A HAMSTER

schwartz & wade books · new york

Copyright © 2016 by Ross Welford
Jacket art copyright © 2016 by Jim Tierney

All rights reserved. Published in the United States by Schwartz & Wade Books, an imprint of Random House Children's Books, a division of Penguin Random House LLC, New York. Originally published in paperback by HarperCollins Children's Books, London, in 2016.

Schwartz & Wade Books and the colophon are trademarks of Penguin Random House LLC.

Visit us on the Web! randomhousekids.com

Educators and librarians, for a variety of teaching tools, visit us at RHTeachersLibrarians.com

Library of Congress Cataloging-in-Publication Data
Name: Welford, Ross.
Title: Time traveling with a hamster / Ross Welford.
Description: First edition. | New York: Schwartz & Wade Books, [2016] | Summary: Twelve-year-old Al Chaudhury discovers his late dad's time machine and travels back to 1984 with his pet hamster to prevent the go-kart accident that killed his father. | "Originally published in paperback by HarperCollins Children's Books, London, in 2016."
Identifiers: LCCN 2015036913 | ISBN 978-0-399-55149-9 (hardcover) | ISBN 978-0-399-55150-5 (glb) | ISBN 978-0-399-55151-2 (ebk)
Subjects: | CYAC: Time travel—Fiction. | Fathers and sons—Fiction. | Death—Fiction. | Hamsters—Fiction.
Classification: LCC PZ7.1.W4355 Ti 2016 | DDC [Fic]—dc23

The text of this book is set in 12.25-point Whitman.
Book design by Rachael Cole

Printed in the United States of America
2 4 6 8 10 9 7 5 3 1
First U.S. Edition

To Gunnel, Astrid, and Ewan

(and Jess)

PREFACE

My dad died twice. Once when he was thirty-nine, and again four years later when he was twelve. (He's going to die a third time as well, which seems a bit rough on him, but I can't help that.)

The first time had nothing to do with me. The second time definitely did, but I would never even have been there if it hadn't been for his "time machine." I know—that sounds like I'm blaming him, which I'm totally not, but . . . you'll see what I mean.

I suppose if you'd asked me before, I'd have said a time machine might look something like a submarine, or perhaps a rocket ship. Anyway, something with loads of switches and panels and lights, made of iron or something, and big—I mean, *really* big, with thrusters, and boosters, and reactors. . . .

Instead, I'm looking at a laptop and a zinc tub from a garden center.

This is my dad's time machine.

It's about to change the world—literally. Well, mine, at any rate.

CHAPTER ONE

Just across the road from the house where we used to live before Dad died (the first time) is an alleyway that leads to the next street with a patch of grass with some bushes and straggly trees growing on it. I called it "the jungle" when I was little because in my mind that's what it was like, but looking at it now, I can see that it's just a plot of land for a house that hasn't been built yet.

And that's where I am, still in my full-face motorbike helmet, sitting hidden in a bush in the dead of night, waiting to break into my old house.

There's an old fried-chicken box that someone's thrown there, and I can smell something foul and sour that I think might be fox's poo. The house is dark; there are no lights on. I'm looking up at my old bedroom window, the small one over the front door.

By day, Chesterton Road is pretty quiet—a long curve of

small, semidetached houses made of reddish bricks. When they were first built, they must all have looked exactly the same, but now people have added fancy gates, garage extensions, even a massive monkey puzzle tree outside old Mr. Frasier's, so these days they're all a bit different.

Now, at nearly one a.m., there's no one about, and I've seen enough films and TV shows about criminals to know exactly how *not* to behave, and that's suspiciously. If you act normal, no one notices you. If I wandered nervously up and down the street waiting for the right time, then someone might spot me going backward and forward looking at the houses, and call the police.

On the other hand, if I'm just walking down the street, then that's all I'm doing, and it's as good as being invisible.

(Keeping the motorbike helmet on is a gamble, or what Grandpa Byron calls "a calculated risk." If I take it off, someone might notice that I'm nowhere near old enough to be riding a moped; if I keep it on, that looks suspicious—so I'm still of two minds about it. Anyway, it won't be on for long.)

I've worked all this out on the journey here. About a year ago, when we still lived here, the local council turned off every second streetlight in a money-saving experiment, so where I've stopped the moped it is really pretty dark.

As casually as I can, I come out of the bushes, take off the helmet, and put it in the moped's top box. I pull my collar up and, without stopping, walk over the road to number 40. There I turn straight up the short driveway and stop in the shadows, well hidden by both the hedge that divides number 40's front garden from the one next door and the small Škoda that sits in the driveway.

So far, so good—the new owners of our house have not yet got round to fixing the garage doors. In fact, they're even less secure than they were. There's a brick in front of them to keep them shut, and when I crouch down and move it out of the way, the right-hand door swings open, then bumps against the Škoda. For a dreadful moment I think the gap will be too small to let me in, but I just manage to squeeze through—and there I am, in the garage, which smells of dust and old oil. My torch is flashing round the walls to reveal boxes that still haven't been unpacked and, in the middle of the floor, the dark wooden planks covering up the cellar entrance.

Here's another tip if you're thinking of breaking in any-where: don't flash your torch around too much. A flashing light will attract attention, but a still light won't. So I put my torch on the ground and start to lift up the greasy planks.

Under the planks there's a concrete stairway, and once I've gone down it I'm standing in a space about a meter square and to my right is a small metal door that's about half my height with a dusty steel wheel for opening it like you get on ships. The wheel is secured in place by a stout bolt with a combination lock.

I try to give a little whistle of amazement—a "whew!"—but my lips are so dry with nerves and dust that I can't. Instead, I set the combination lock to the numbers Dad instructed in his letter—the day and month of my birth backward—grab the wheel with both hands, and twist it counterclockwise. There's a bit of resistance, but it gives with a soft grating noise, and as it spins around, the door suddenly pops open inward with a tiny sighing noise of escaping air.

I grab my torch and aim it ahead of me as I go through the little doorway, crouching. There are more steps down and a wall on my right, and my hand finds a light switch but I daren't try it in case it's a switch for something else, like an alarm or something, or it lights up the garage upstairs, or . . . I just don't know, but I'm too nervous to flick the switch so I look at everything through the yellowy-white beam of torchlight.

The steps lead to a room about half the size of our living room at home, but with a lower ceiling. A grown-up could just about stand up.

Along one long wall are four bunk beds, all made up— blankets, pillows, everything. There's a wall that juts out into the room, and behind it is a toilet and some kind of machinery with pipes and hoses coming out of it. There are rugs on the white concrete floor and a poster on the wall. It's faded orange and black with a picture of a mum, a dad, and two children inside a circle, and the words "PROTECT AND SURVIVE" in big white letters. I've seen this poster before when some guy came to talk about peace and nuclear war and stuff in assembly once, and he made Dania Biziewski cry because she was scared and he was really embarrassed.

This is what people built years ago when they thought Russia was going to kill us with nuclear bombs.

I turn round and see what's behind me. The torch beam picks out a long desk with a chair in front of it. On the desk is a zinc tub, like you would bathe a dog in or something. In it is an old-style Mac laptop—the white one—and a computer mouse. There's a cord coming out of the back of the computer leading to a black metal box about the size of a paperback book, and coming out of that are two cords that are each about a meter long, with strange sort of handgrips on the end.

Next to the tub is a coffee mug printed with a picture of me as a baby and the words "I love my daddy." The inside of the mug is all furred up with ancient mold.

And beside the mug is a copy of the local newspaper, the *Whitley Bay Advertiser,* folded in half and open at a story headlined "Local Man's Tragic Sudden Death" above a picture of my dad.

I sit down in the swivel chair and run my hands over the underside of the desk. When I can't feel anything, I get on my knees and shine the torch upward, and there it is: an envelope, taped at the back, just as Dad said there would be.

But there's no time machine. At least, not one that looks how I imagine a time machine might look.

That's how I end up staring at the zinc tub and its contents.

Surely, I'm thinking, *surely* that's *not it?*

But it is.

And the craziest thing? It works.

One Week Earlier

CHAPTER TWO

This whole thing—the breaking and entering, plus robbery, arson, stealing a moped, and killing someone (sort of, anyway), not to mention time travel—started on my twelfth birthday.

That day I got a hamster, and a letter from my dead dad.

I suppose if you were being precise—and precision, as Grandpa Byron says, counts—it started when me and Mum moved in with Steve and the Stepsister From Hell, Carly. That was just after Mum and Steve got married in the world's smallest wedding (people there: Mum, Steve, Grandpa Byron, me, TSFH, Aunty Ellie).

If you were being super-precise, it kind of started when Dad died, but that was a long time ago and I don't really want to get into that. Not yet, anyway.

So there we were, on my twelfth birthday, which is May 12, so I was twelve on the twelfth, which only happens once in anyone's life, and some people have to wait until they're thirty-one, by which time I guess it's not so much fun.

Steve is always trying to make me like him, so he spent a lot of money on my present, a replica Newcastle United shirt with my name and age on the back: "Albert 12." Except my name's now Al, not Albert, and I don't really like football. I've sat and watched a few games with him, because it makes Mum happy to see us "bonding," but to be honest I don't really see the point of the whole thing.

"Well, put it on, Al—see if it fits!" says Mum, and she's smiling this too-smiley smile, and I'm smiling too to make up for the fact that I don't like the present, even though I know it's kind of him, and Steve's smiling a sort of puzzled smile, and about the only one smiling properly is Carly, probably because she can tell I don't like the present and that makes her happy.

It's on the big side, so there's no chance I'll grow out of it soon, which is a shame.

Mum's present is much better. It's there on the countertop: a big box, wrapped up in colored paper, with a ribbon and a bow, just like presents look in drawings, and I have *no idea* what it is until I unwrap it and the box inside says "HAMSTERDAM—THE CITY FOR YOUR HAMSTER."

There's a picture on it of tubes and boxes and a cage and everything, and I'm grinning so hard because I have guessed what's in the small box that Mum's holding, and sure enough there's a hamster in there, a cute, small one that's not fully grown yet, and he (or she; I don't know how to tell yet) has got this twitchy nose and light-brown fur and I love him (or her) already.

I'm wondering what to call him when Steve says, "I've got a great name for him!"

"Steve," says Mum, "let the boy choose his own name."

Steve looks a bit disappointed, so I say, "It's OK. What's your idea?"

"Alan Shearer!" Steve sees me blinking, blank-faced, so he repeats, "Alan Shearer. Greatest striker the Toon ever had? Premier League's all-time top scorer?" I still look blank. "Bloke on *Match of the Day*?"

I nod and force a smile, but as I'm doing so, it kind of turns into a real one, because whichever way you look at it, giving a hamster a proper name like "Alan Shearer" has got to be better than calling it "Fluffy" or "Hammy," which was as far as my imagination had got. So Alan Shearer it is.

I notice that Carly has stopped smiling. She comes over to me as I'm unpacking the plastic tubes and bends down close so that only I can hear. "A hamster?" she murmurs. "They're just rats for *babies*."

You know what, though? I don't care.

Then Grandpa Byron arrives to give me a ride to school like he always does since Mum and I moved farther away to live with Steve and Carly.

I open the front door and he's standing there in his long saffron-colored robes, gray hair in a plait, little round sunglasses, and huge biker boots. Under one arm—the bad one—he's holding his motorbike helmet, and under the other—the good one—is a birthday card in an envelope.

"Happy birthday, bonny lad," he says, and I give him a huge hug. I love Grandpa Byron's smell. It's a mixture of the minty oil he puts in his hair and these sweet-smelling cigarettes he sometimes smokes called *beedis,* which he buys in boxes from a man who runs a Lebanese takeaway, even though he's from Bangladesh, and the licorice-flavored toothpaste he uses, which I have tried and is pretty gross, but it smells nice.

As I hug him I take a deep breath. He waves through to the kitchen, which isn't far from the front door. "Morning, Byron!" calls Mum. "Come on in!"

Carly shimmies past me to go up the stairs. "Hi, Byron,"

she says sweetly. "Lovin' the robes, dude!" It's only when she has passed him and is out of his sight that she turns to me, wrinkles up her face, and wafts her hand in front of her nose, as if Grandpa Byron's smell is something bad, which it totally isn't.

He's got a funny way of talking, my grandpa: his Indian accent sounds Geordie and he uses Geordie expressions and old dialect words all mixed up together. He's my dad's dad, but my dad didn't really talk Geordie, not much.

Grandpa comes in and sits at the breakfast bar. "Sorry, mate—I wasn't having a chance to get your present." He wobbles his head in that Indian way, probably just because he knows it makes me laugh, and he's smiling as he does it so I can see his big gold tooth.

"S'OK," I reassure him, and I open the card. Out fall two twenty-pound notes.

"Thanks. Thanks a *lot*!" And I really mean it.

Then Mum says, "I'm glad you're here, Byron. It's time to give Al the letter," and she gets up and goes over to a drawer. She's behaving a bit strangely, like flighty and excited and nervous, when she skips back with this big fat envelope. Steve's watching her, smiling quietly, but it's clear from Grandpa

Byron's face that he hasn't got a clue what this is about. Mum puts on her serious face.

"Now, Al. This is for you, from your dad."

I don't know what to say.

"We found this in your dad's things after he died. He must have written it ages ago."

I'm staring at the envelope in her hands. Grandpa Byron's expression hasn't changed.

"What is it?" I say eventually.

"I don't know. It's personal, addressed to you. But I think you should regard it as highly private"—and here she pauses—"not to be shared with anyone else."

I take the envelope carefully and read the spidery writing on the front. My dad's handwriting, and my full name: Albert Einstein Hawking Chaudhury. Below my name is written "IMPORTANT: Do Not Open This Envelope Until Sixteen Hours After Receiving It. To Be Delivered on His Twelfth Birthday."

I look across to Grandpa Byron. "Did you know about this?" I ask.

He shakes his head, and there's something in the quick side-to-side movement and the tightness of his mouth that is odd. I even think he's turned a bit pale, and he's staring at the envelope.

Steve, meanwhile, is just sitting there with this big daft smile that looks slightly forced, and I get straightaway that he's jealous. He wants so much for me to like him that he's angry that my dad has come back between us, and this makes me like Steve just a little bit less.

"Well, I can't open it till later anyway," I say, pointing at the directions on the envelope. Now obviously I'm boiling inside to see what it says, but there's something about seeing my dad's handwriting that's like getting an instruction directly from him, and I want to be respectful. That, and Grandpa Byron's stony face, has kind of freaked me out.

"Come on, son, you gonna be late," he says, picking up his helmet from the breakfast bar. And that is the last thing he says to me until he drops me at the school gate, saying, "You coming round after school?"

I nod and he scoots off on his bike, not even waving.

All of which makes it a very unusual morning.

CHAPTER THREE

Twelve Things I Know About Grandpa Byron

1. His full name is Byron Rahmat Chaudhury-Roy and his birthday is on New Year's Day, although he never celebrates it. "Why celebrate getting one year closer to death?" he once asked me. "It's just passing time; it's not important." He still gets me birthday presents, though, so he can't be that serious. He's around sixty or so, but he looks much younger, apart from his nearly white hair.

2. He has got the most awesome memory—I mean, like, *unbelievable*. From the age of ten until he came to England, he studied under some Indian guru who taught him all these meditation tricks, and it means

he can remember anything. He's never forgotten anyone's name he's ever met.

3. He was born in a part of India called Punjab, and his mum and dad sent him to England in the 1960s because there was a lot of fighting there. Some people call it "the swinging sixties," but Grandpa Byron said he didn't see much swinging in Wallsend.

4. He lived with an auntie and uncle, but they died yonks ago and I never met them.

5. He married Grandma Julie in 1972. I know that because he told me that a song called "Without You" by Nilsson was number one and I looked it up on the Internet. Grandma Julie died before I was born.

6. Grandma Julie's parents didn't come to their wedding. Grandpa Byron said they were too busy, but that seems odd to me. Perhaps they were racist and didn't like her marrying Grandpa Byron. Everyone was racist in 1972, apparently.

7. He didn't always dress in yellow robes. Actually, he still doesn't always. But when Dad died he went away for a while, for months Mum said, and when he came back he had grown a beard and started wearing the long robes. (The beard didn't last long. He said it itched.)

8. He wrote a book while he was working in a factory in North Shields. He would write it in the evenings on a typewriter, which is like an old-fashioned computer but with no memory—just a keyboard and printer in one, which is pretty cool. No one would publish it in England, so it was published in India.

9. His right arm got wrecked in a fireworks calamity, of all things. He was setting off some for a big display, and part of the metal rig they were resting on had a loose bolt or something, and the whole thing came down and crushed his arm. He can't use it much and it looks a bit weird, kind of twisted to one side. He got some money from the insurance company, and he stopped working at the factory.

10. He put some of his money into the first tandoori restaurant in the area: the Spice of the Sands, on the Culvercot seafront. (It's still there, but it's run by some Bangladeshis now, and serving much nicer food, said Grandpa Byron once, but he was laughing.)

11. He won a trophy from the factory when he was in a talent show with the other workers. Everyone else was singing or telling jokes, and one guy could imitate the voices of all their bosses brilliantly, but Grandpa Byron just did memory tricks, and he won! Someone shuffled a pack of cards and read them all out, and Grandpa Byron remembered them all in order. He told me that was "Level One" stuff, in other words not even remotely difficult.

12. He doesn't own any photographs. He says the best pictures are in his head and that taking photographs is just lazy.

CHAPTER FOUR

So school is OK.

Miss Henry, who's usually quite nice to me anyway, is especially smiley and tells everyone it's my birthday. Freddie Stayward—who last week started a chant of "loser, loser" when I dropped an easy catch (until Mr. Springham yelled at everyone to stop it at once)—even gives me his pudding at lunch. Obviously I check it for spit/hairs/boogies, but once it has received the Chaudhury All Clear, I eat it.

(I knew exactly no one on my first day at St. Eddie's, by the way. We had moved in with Steve and Carly during the summer holidays. Mum did that grown-up thing of making it all seem like a big adventure, and kept telling me how much fun we'd have, but I wasn't sure, and I'm still not, to be honest. I suspect—don't know, mind you, but I suspect—that finances came into it. Dad left us not very financially secure,

Mum once told me. It's about the only time I can think of her saying anything negative about him.)

Anyway, after lunch I'm sitting by the coats in the little alcove where you can't really be seen if you pull your feet up. I discovered this spot on my second day at St. Eddie's back in September when I didn't know anyone, and there's no way I was going to sit on the "buddy bench." Besides, I quite like it there among the coats and the musty smell of muddy wellies and gym shoes.

I've taken a book from the school library about hamsters, and I open it. That's when I hear Jolyon's voice. I draw my feet up, but too late.

"Reading, eh?" Jolyon drawls, pointing at the book. His whole tone is caring, concerned, and so warm that it sends a shiver down my back. My hands give an involuntary little tremble, which I hate because it looks like I'm scared. It makes the book in my hand shake.

Jolyon Dancey talks in this sort of fake, mixed-up posh-and-Geordie accent. He gets a new mountain bike *every* Christmas and his dad (who he hardly ever sees) does a late-night weekend jazz show on Radio Metro, which is about as micro as microcelebrity can get, but which I've heard Jolyon boasting about more than once.

What's worse is that Carly sort of hangs out with him, even though she's in the year above, and she's standing there with him now, chewing gum. It's not like she's his girlfriend or anything, but she's definitely in his circle, or would like to be. She has hitched up her skirt so high that you can't really see it under her school blouse, which is not tucked in. It's like she's standing there in just her shirt and tights.

He's a complete pain, and almost a class bully, except that nothing that Jolyon Dancey does could ever get him into trouble for bullying, because he's being *nice*. Not *nice* nice, but *nasty* nice.

"Reading!" he repeats, pointlessly, and he crouches down so that his face is level with mine, getting really close, grinning insincerely like one of those crocodiles on nature documentaries.

"What we got here, matey? A book? Aw, I love hamsters, don't you, Carly?" Carly nods. "Can I see it?"

He puts out his hand, and I find myself handing over the book. Jolyon takes it and stands up, and starts to read the cover.

"*Hamster Fancying for Beginners*, by Dr. A. Borgström." He gives a little snort. "You fancy hamsters, do you, Albert? Really fancy them?" He smirks at Carly.

"It just means, you know, looking after them. . . ."

"Right, I believe you. Can I borrow this? Can I?"

A wave of nausea starts in the bottom of my stomach as he starts to put the book in his blazer pocket, even though it's just a library book. Then Carly says, "Leave it out, Jol. Not today."

Jolyon pauses, confused.

At that moment, Mr. Springham's voice booms from down the corridor: "Walk on the *left!*" His heavy footsteps are getting closer.

Jolyon hands the book back to me and moves away, giving me another grin and a wink. A *wink*. Honestly. And he probably thinks *I'm* a loser.

That's the thing with St. Eddie's: I don't really have any friends. To be honest, it's not St. Eddie's, it's my life generally. It's not that I don't like people, or even that people dislike me. But even when people are being nice to me, they still just seem to sort of look through me. It's a good thing I like my own company; otherwise it could all make me quite sad.

I'll give you an example: hugs. I don't think I have ever hugged or been hugged by a friend. It's no big deal, really—I mean, I get hugs all the time at home from Mum and Grandpa Byron (and sometimes from Steve, which is less good, but still)—but there are boys at school who are forever doing this backslapping hug thing, and it looks kind of fun.

Anyway, like I say, school is OK.

CHAPTER FIVE

Grandpa Byron is meditating when I let myself into his house with my own key. The curtains in his sitting room are drawn, and a stick of incense is smoldering, a smell of sweet leather permeating the house.

He sits on the sofa, cross-legged, his hands resting on his knees and his back dead straight. He raises a forefinger to acknowledge my presence, which I am relieved about, because sometimes he doesn't do that and it's like he can't hear me or anything. I once stayed until he opened his eyes, and it was ages. I had finished my homework, run down the battery on my MP3 player, and read most of his *Daily Telegraph,* and all he said was, "Oh, hi—how long have you been here?"

This time I don't have to wait long. He slowly opens his eyes and unfurls his long brown legs from underneath him.

"You are just in time for chai. Why not put on the telly? Maybe today you will be faster than those dimwits."

There's a crinkling around his eyes when he says this because he doesn't think the contestants on TV quiz shows are really stupid, they're just not as smart as he is. Not many people are.

We sit in front of the TV drinking the super-sweet Indian tea and eating *badam barfi,* which is an Indian fudge that Grandpa Byron has made because it's my birthday.

There is always a TV quiz on around this time of day. Usually we'll watch one of the main channels, but if it's a show Grandpa Byron doesn't like, he'll find an old show on Challenge or one of the other channels instead.

For him to like it, it has to involve questions that require you to know stuff—what he calls "general knowledge." Stuff like capital cities, or obscure foreign presidents, or dates of wars, or chemical compounds, or great works of art, or . . . well, you get the idea.

Today's program is a new one on BBC Two called *Mind Games,* in which six contestants try to kick one another out of the contest by forming alliances with each other and betting points on how certain they are of the answer. The thing about it—and the thing that Grandpa Byron likes—is that the questions are really hard, for me, at any rate.

The presenter is a bloke who usually reads the news,

except here he's dressed in a black turtleneck and jeans, which look a bit weird on him. He's talking really fast.

"All right, Darren, you've teamed up with Celia; let's see how you get on—together can you eliminate Adnan from the competition and get yourselves closer to the big prize? Three questions on popular music coming up; you have thirty seconds starting from . . . now. What was the last UK number one hit for the Beatles before they—"

"'The Ballad of John and Yoko,' number one for three weeks in 1969," says Grandpa Byron before the guy on telly has even finished.

"Which record album, released in 1982, became the biggest-selling album of all t—"

"*Thriller,*" barks Grandpa Byron, "by Michael Jackson!"

"And finally, which artist paired up with Alicia Keys to record the hit single 'Empire State of Mind' in 2010?"

I know this one. "Eminem!" I shout. Grandpa Byron shakes his head and smiles. "Jay Z. And it was 2009, not 2010."

Of course he gets them all right.

He always gets them all right—or nearly always, anyway.

"How do you do it?" I ask for what must be the hundredth time. "How do you know so much?"

And he gives the answer he always gives. "Don't confuse knowledge with memory, Al. I've got a good memory because I have trained it, but that is not the same as knowledge, and neither memory nor knowledge is the equal of wisdom."

He gives me a grin and takes a large swig of chai.

There's this thing with Grandpa Byron: when he's done watching a TV program, he turns the television off. At my house, we normally just leave the room, or flick around to see what else is on—either way, the telly stays on. But not Grandpa Byron. It's like when he's reading the paper: he folds it up carefully when he's finished an article.

So when *Mind Games* finishes, off goes the telly and we sit in silence for a bit. Grandpa Byron's got this half smile. Perhaps he's pleased that he got all the questions right, or that for the first time I got one or two of them within the thirty seconds.

"One of these fine days you will be memorizing better than me," he says. He's looking at me through half-closed eyes. "You see, with the power of your mind you can do almost anything, Al. That plus, of course, *The Memory Palaces of the Sri Kalpana*."

This is the book Grandpa Byron wrote ages ago that's

now so rare that he owns the only copy, which I have never seen. He has mentioned it to me before, but only in passing, whereas now he's looking right into my eyes and smiling.

He kind of bounces to his feet effortlessly (without that *oof* sound that most old people make when they get up from a sofa). He takes a book down from the shelf and hands it to me. It's a thinnish paperback with a plain yellow cover, the same color as Grandpa Byron's robes. The only writing on the cover is the title, *The Memory Palaces of the Sri Kalpana,* and underneath it says "by Byron R. Chaudhury-Roy."

"I was going to wait before giving you this," he says, "but, well . . . now seems like the right time. Now you are twelve."

"Really? I mean, thanks a lot. . . ."

He holds up his finger to quieten me. His eyes go a bit blank until he blinks hard. "We'll study it together. Meanwhile, feel free to take it with you."

I grin and shrug. "Cool!"

There is something going on here, though, and I can't put my finger on it. It was the way Grandpa Byron said *"Now you are twelve"* that made me think that giving me this book was somehow connected with him going all weird when he saw that letter from my dad. I don't have to wonder long.

"That letter from your father . . . ," he begins, without looking at me. He is being altogether too casual, like he's practiced this. I just nod and wait while he sits down opposite me and looks at me intently.

"Your father and I, we had some disagreements. Over the work he was doing."

"Over his *work*?"

"Not his job. But some research he was undertaking in his spare time. He told me about it and . . . well, I didn't really approve."

"What was it?" (Remember, at this stage I have *no idea* about my dad and time travel.)

Instead of answering directly, Grandpa Byron reaches over and takes the book from my hands.

"Life, Al, is such a wonderful gift that we should open our minds to every possible moment and cherish the memory of those moments. Because people change. Places change. Everything changes, but our memories do not. Accept life the way it is, Al. That's the way to be happy."

I think I narrow my eyes skeptically, because Grandpa Byron takes a deep breath, closes his eyes, and continues. "In my head, Al, in my mind, are some most wonderful places.

Some are like palaces, huge and ornate; others are much more humble. And all of them, room after room, are crammed to brimming with memories. Some of these imaginary rooms are like offices, with drawers and filing cabinets—that's where I keep all the facts, like football scores, and dates, and horse-racing winners, and presidents. But the most precious rooms, in the grandest palace of all, they contain the memories I love the most: the day your father was being born, for example; the day me and your grandmother got married; or just five years ago when you and I had that picnic in the rain in Druridge Bay and you were losing your Crocs. There's a memory for every day of my life, back to when I was about your age. I can revisit these rooms whenever I like, take out the memories, relive them, spit and polish them up, then put them back for another time. I am going there any time I like."

"Is that what you do when you meditate?"

"Aye. Usually, anyhow. Keeping my memory palaces clean and tidy. They can get a bit cluttered, you know, just like real rooms. Memories can go astray, or get a bit faded, and I am liking to keep everything shipshape!"

"And what's that got to do with Dad's letter?"

Grandpa Byron opens his eyes and looks at me as if he'd

forgotten about it. Eventually he says, "I'm not sure. It might not have *anything* to do with it. But read my book anyway. Well, if you want to, that is."

Well, of course I *want* to. But what I want more is to understand why he is telling me all this now.

CHAPTER SIX

When I get back Alan Shearer is asleep, and Mum tells me not to wake him. My book says that hamsters are "crepuscular creatures," which I think means "sleepy," so I just sit for a bit and watch him sleep. I try accidentally bumping the bit of Hamsterdam where he's sleeping to see if it wakes him, but it doesn't.

The letter from my dad is still in my schoolbag. I am itching to get it out, but at the same time I don't dare to, in case I am disappointed.

Steve comes back from work. "Hey, champ," he says, "glad you like the shirt!" I had put it on to please him. Well, to please Mum, really, because I knew she'd be happy if I liked the thing that Steve had got me.

He goes straight to the TV. Newcastle United Under-21s are playing in some European game with a team whose name I have forgotten.

"Come on, son—they're about to kick off!" He pats the sofa next to him.

"You know what, I think I'll just, um . . . I've got homework to do." I hold up the memory stick on my key ring that I keep my homework on and back out of the sitting room. It isn't fast enough to avoid a glimpse of Steve's crestfallen face.

"But it's Dortmund! The Germans!" he calls after me, a bit sadly, I think.

That's the thing with Steve. It's so obvious that he wants me to be the son he hasn't got, but even if I *was* his son, there's no guarantee I'd like football, is there? I mean, take Daniel Somerset in my old class. His dad does brilliant magic tricks and once made a colored hankie appear in my pocket at a party. Daniel thought the whole idea of magic tricks was totally lame, but his dad didn't seem to care, and he even went off for weekends with other amateur magicians and didn't drag Daniel along with him every time.

So I'm up in my room, lying on my bed trying to read Grandpa Byron's book, and The Letter is now propped up against my clock. By midnight the sixteen hours will be up.

I can't concentrate on the book. It's not like it's boring or anything. It's just that Grandpa Byron wrote it years and years ago, so the language is a bit difficult, and there are no memory tricks or anything. I haven't quite grasped it.

So I put the book down carefully, marking the page I've got to with a bookmark. Normally I would fold a corner over, but as this is the last remaining book by Grandpa Byron, I don't think he'd like that.

I turn to stare again at The Letter. I stare for ages, then reach out and pick it up as I lie with my head on the pillow. Dad's instructions say not to open it until sixteen hours after I receive it. But surely a few hours won't make a difference?

"Al!" Mum calls up from the kitchen. "Dinner!"

I sigh and put the letter on my bedside table, then go downstairs.

Because it's my birthday, Mum has made lasagne. She's been trying to ring Carly to come back for supper, but she's got her mobile switched off again. Steve's phone is on the counter and it pings with a text.

"She's with that Jolyon Dancey again," says Mum, reading the screen. I can't tell whether she's pleased or not. "Is that her boyfriend?" she asks me.

"How would I know?" Where Carly and Jolyon are concerned, I figure it's wise to steer a very cautious path.

"I just think it would be nice if she had come home for her stepbrother's birthday supper."

I say nothing, using a mouthful of lasagne as cover. Mum has timed the serving up for halftime, and Steve joins us.

"Nil–nil," he says.

I grunt and raise my eyebrows in pretend interest.

Come bedtime, I still haven't opened The Letter, but I am wide awake when I hear Carly's key in the door at ten-thirty, and then there are raised voices—hers and Steve's—from downstairs.

By eleven o'clock I'm dizzy with tiredness, and I can't wait any longer. I reach for the envelope from my bedside table, and, one hour sooner than I should, I ease my little finger under the glued-down flap.

CHAPTER SEVEN

Dear Al,

With luck, you won't ever be reading this.

And that, I reckon, is the oddest start to a letter I will ever read. No "How are you?" or anything like that. Anyway . . .

But let us assume you are. I have given this letter to your mum to hand to you when you are older. Did you wait the sixteen hours?

I sort of shake my head in reply to the question. Like he can see me.

That was just a test of your resolve. If you did, then well done—you may find what I am about to ask a little easier. If you didn't ... well, I'd still like you to do it.

If you are reading this, then what I fear will happen has happened, and that means I am not around to help you into adulthood. This, then, will be the only gift I can give to you, my most precious son.

First, let me reassure you: I am not scared of dying, although it makes me sad to think of the times we will miss together.

I won't see you going up to secondary school, or graduating from university, or marrying and becoming a father yourself.

These are the big things. Yet it is the small things, the tiny little things, that make me sadder. I love your smile, and our shared jokes, and the way you liked my lousy stories. I love the smell of your hair when I hug you and the way you are so glad to be awake in the morning.

Yet ... all these things may not be gone forever. For if you follow my instructions, and if you are as brave and smart as I think you are, then you will be able to prevent my death.

Right now as I'm writing this, you're just eight, and far too young to understand the implications of what I am about to tell you. You have had to wait, and now the time is right.

You are about to learn, Al, how to travel in time.

At this point I stop and reread what I've just read. *"Prevent my death"? "Travel in time"?* What in God's name is my dad talking about?

The ability to travel in time has fascinated humans ever since we came up with the idea of time itself.

Just imagine, Al, if we could go forward in time to see what happens in the future. Or go back and correct our mistakes.

The Greeks, the Egyptians, the Chinese—all the ancient civilizations tried.

The ancient Sumerians, who lived in what is now Iraq between maybe four and six thousand years ago, left behind texts and archaeological evidence that suggest they discovered the secret. Trouble is, it was so long ago that the answer—if it was real and not just mythology—has been lost to us.

I have recently had a huge breakthrough using the power of modern computing, which was unavailable to the ancients.

Al: are you ready to travel in time?

No, Al: this is not science fiction, and you will not be battling strange monsters in faraway galaxies. Instead it is mathematics: pure, but very, very far from simple.

For I have discovered the formula that allows for the physical movement—"travel" we might call it—between parallel dimensions, allowing us to seem to be "traveling in time."

Notice that I say "seem."

You see, as Albert Einstein first described it, time is "relative." I'm sure you've heard of Einstein's theory of general relativity? There was another one too: his theory of special relativity.

One day, perhaps, you will understand them, for believe me—they are fabulously complex. We all happily acknowledge Albert Einstein as a "genius"— but very few of us have any idea at all of just how *amazing his discoveries were. Our brains and our thoughts are so firmly rooted in our lives on Earth that most of us are simply unable—unequipped mentally—to imagine the true meaning of Einstein's theories.*

I pause in my reading and look at the Newcastle United team poster that Steve put on my wall, as if it might help me, but the players just stare back at me, blankly.

Of course I've heard of Albert Einstein; after all, I was named after him. Wild hair, bushy mustache—a completely mad scientist and a nickname at school for anyone a bit clever. And yes, I've heard of the theory of relativity, but I thought there was only one, and I have no idea what any of it means.

It's like a goldfish in an aquarium. He might understand everything there is to know about his environment: every rock, every stone, every bubble. He may even understand that when the rattling vibration comes from above (the lid of the aquarium being lifted off), then that means food is coming. But he doesn't know what people are, what cars are, what a fruit smoothie is, what a cup-winning goal looks like, or what any of it means, and that's because he simply <u>cannot.</u>

A goldfish's brain can't even imagine these things. And most human brains cannot even imagine the vast possibilities that Einstein's theories suggest.

Don't worry, Al: I'm not going to try to explain relativity to you. Even Einstein had trouble putting it into words. The best he came up with was this:

"Put your hand on a hot stove for a minute and it seems like an hour. Sit with a pretty girl for an hour and it seems like a minute. THAT'S relativity."

Was Einstein being serious? Well, perhaps. Sort of. His point was this, I think: that the passage of time is something we see and feel, and because we see and feel it, we describe it. But just because we can describe something does not make it real. You, no doubt, could give a vivid description of an imaginary animal, but that doesn't make it real.

"Traveling in time" is a poor description of what you are about to do, Al, but we are constricted by the words we have in our language. "Relatively *shifting between space-time dimensions" is perhaps more accurate, or "nongravitational multiversal static matter repositioning" or ...*

See what I mean? "Time travel" will have to do. Do you remember that time we went to Seahouses and the night was so starry, and I told you about seeing things that had happened many years ago? That was only a few weeks ago as I write this, but I hope you can remember.

I put Dad's letter down for a moment and think, closing my eyes. We're in a field, me and Dad, looking at the stars. It makes me smile.

Now, read carefully. This is what you must do.
In the garage of our house, there's a hole cov-ered over with boards. It leads to a small cellar—there are steps down to it.

This was our *old* house, then. Obviously Dad had no idea we'd be moving. I read on, but I'm getting worried that I won't be able to do what he wants.

It's a small, narrow cellar, and at one end is a heavy metal door with a wheel to open and close it, like they have in submarines. There's a code on the lock. It's 5021—your birthday backward. No one else knows this. Open the door and go in. You'll find Letter Number Two taped under the desk.

Trust me like you have never trusted anyone before in your life.

Things will become clearer.

Make absolutely sure no one sees you.

Your loving dad

P.S. You must act within a week of reading this.

I read the letter again, and then again. The fourth time, something strange happens, and it's as if I'm not reading with my eyes but with my ears, and instead of seeing the words, I can hear my dad's voice, soft and a little raspy, his slight Geordie accent, his habit of sometimes going up at the end of sentences, like he's asking a question?

I imagine our old house, the garage with cellar steps.

And I just lie, staring at the ceiling, in a sort of trance, and I'm with my dad in our old house. I'm not eight, I'm me, now, I'm twelve; I can smell him and hear him, and he's asking me again, *"Al, are you ready to travel in time?"* and I can feel his hand on my cheek.

For the first time in four years, I fall asleep in my dad's arms.

CHAPTER EIGHT

It was the Easter holidays when I was eight, and Mum and Dad and I were in a tiny rented cottage just outside of Seahouses, which is on the Northumberland coast near Scotland.

Dad was a brilliant engineer, but I don't think he earned all that much money, because we never went abroad for holidays and we had an ancient car.

So the three of us were walking back along the road that leads out of Seahouses to where our cottage was, and it was late, like ten o'clock, and really, really dark. We'd had dinner in the Seahouses Magna Tandoori, and Dad had spoken some Bengali to the waiter, who hadn't understood him, because Dad's Bengali is pretty rubbish actually. Anyway, we were all chattering away, me and Mum and Dad, and then Dad stopped and gasped and said, "Look, guys!"

He was staring up at what must have been the starriest

sky I had ever seen. There were no streetlights, and Seahouses was a mile behind us and round a curve in the road. The sky wasn't even black; it was a sort of dark navy, and there were so many stars that some of them merged into each other and formed smudges across the sky.

It was a chilly night, and Mum said she wanted to hurry back to the cottage, so it was just me and Dad. "Come on," he said, "I'll show you something." He hopped over a gate into a field and turned back to help me follow him over. We walked together over the black-green grass, the only light coming from the stars, and then we lay down on our backs, gazing upward. I felt Dad's hand reach over and grip mine.

"Do you want to see something that happened nine years ago?" he asked.

"Um . . . yeah?"

"It's not a YouTube clip or anything, it's real life."

"OK."

"Can you see that star there, the brightest one?" He was pointing not straight up, but more toward the horizon where a bright, bluish star was flickering. "That's Sirius," he said, "nicknamed the Dog Star. It's a huge sun, bigger than our sun, and it's eighty-one trillion kilometers away."

Now, I don't know about you, but when someone starts

talking about numbers like trillions, I kind of glaze over. I can't even imagine what eighty-one trillion kilometers is like. As if reading my mind, Dad went on, "That's eighty-one thousand billion."

I wasn't any wiser.

"Or in other words—nearly a million times greater than the distance between Earth and our sun."

OK—that's a little bit easier to imagine. Just a bit. I gave Dad's hand a squeeze to let him know I was sort of following him.

"So, Al: the light from Sirius has taken nearly nine years to travel to earth. Nine years from leaving Sirius to hitting your eyeballs. In other words, you are looking at something that happened nine years ago."

I gave this time to sink in. I think I understood, but I was only eight. I understand it better now.

Dad leaped to his feet and stood, hands on hips, head thrown back.

"So how many are there?" I asked. "Stars, I mean."

There was a long pause, and I wasn't sure Dad had heard me.

"Dad?"

"Yeah, yeah . . . I'm just thinking how to answer, because

no one really knows for certain. You see up here, the ones we can see without a telescope? That's probably only a few thousand. But you see that whitish blur there?" He pointed to one of the smudges. "That's the Milky Way. . . ."

"Named after the chocolate bar?"

"Well, the other way round, but yeah. Our star, our sun, is part of the Milky Way. We sort of live on the outskirts of it; that's why we can see the center. And the whole Milky Way has about one hundred billion stars in it. Probably.

"They're nearly all farther away than Sirius—and some of them have already exploded"—he turned to me, his dark eyes shining in the starlight—"but the light from the explosion hasn't even reached us yet! We're still seeing what happened hundreds of years ago!"

He helped me up. By now we were both shivering.

"To look at the night sky, Al—that's traveling in time!"

We walked back to the gate, and Dad was still talking about the stars and the galaxies, and how there're billions more galaxies like the Milky Way, but I wasn't listening anymore. Not because I was bored, but because I was remembering what he said: that looking up at a night sky is traveling in time. I gazed upward all the way back to our cottage, looking into the past.

CHAPTER NINE

I have, according to the letter from my dad, one week to act on his instructions.

That's a whole week to consider, very carefully, exactly why it's a truly epically bad idea.

So the next day I'm deep in thought all the way to school. I'm walking because Grandpa Byron's off on some meditation retreat in Wales. I'm going over and over in my head the reasons why I can't do what my dad wants me to do. In order, they are:

1. How do I get to my old house—ten miles down the coast—without being noticed?

2. How do I break into my old garage?

3. What if I get caught?

I decide I will think them through one by one, starting with the easiest one.

Number three is no biggie. I keep telling myself: what's the worst that could happen? Yes, I'd get one heck of a telling off, but twelve-year-olds don't get sent to jail, and I could always pretend that I was suffering some sort of mental breakdown and that I wasn't responsible for my actions, that I went crazy with delayed grief for my dad—that sort of thing. Back in primary school Hector Houghman stabbed Conrad Wiley in the thigh with a compass, and he wasn't punished *at all* because his mum came to school and said he had ADHD and that it was the school's fault for not "adapting to his needs," so I should be OK.

I've reached the school gates, and I feel better now that I can tick one reason off on my list, but the other two are battling for attention. Thankfully it's PE first period and it's cricket, which is just brilliant for thinking, especially if you're always given a distant fielding position.

So I'm as far away from the proper bat-and-ball action as I can be without looking like I'm actually doing nothing, in a position called deep mid-on, or deep mid-off (I've no idea), and I'm on to reason number two—breaking into my old garage.

Unlike every other house on the street, our garage had old-fashioned double wooden doors rather than automatic metal doors, and the lock never used to work properly. You can get your fingers under the two doors and sort of joggle them till they ease apart. I did it once when I was locked out and Mum was late back and it was raining.

Anyway, there I am thinking I can almost tick that one off and feeling quite pleased, when I hear yelling.

"Al! Al, man! Chaudhury! Catch it!" A cricket ball is sailing toward me from out of the sky and a tiny wave of despair comes over me. I am truly hopeless at catching (and throwing, and batting for that matter; cricket's not really my game). Without any confidence I cup my hands in the vague direction the ball is heading and . . .

Plop! The ball lands *exactly* in my grasp. And doesn't fall out again. There's a wild cheer and over at the wicket Freddie Stayward is glaring at me as he tucks the bat under his arm and starts to walk. I decide that it's a good omen, and even my throw back to the bowler is not as bad as usual.

It's reason number one that's really bothering me, though, and the question lingers with me all through double maths, lunch, geography, French, and history. How do I get to my old house in Culvercot?

Years ago there used to be a train between Blyth and Culvercot; then it was replaced by a bus service, and then *that* stopped as well, so now you have to take two buses and change at Seaton Sluice, and it takes forever. Besides, if I'm going to break in somewhere, it'll have to be at night, so there goes that idea.

I'd cycle, except my bike was stolen last year when I left it unlocked outside the house.

This is all, of course, ignoring the biggest objection of all: what if it goes wrong? The "time travel" bit, that is. I mean, I trust my dad, but still . . . he's basically asking me to go to our old house, which is ten miles away; commit a bit of breaking and entering; and then use an actual time machine to travel through time.

Great birthday present, Dad, I think.

But I have to, don't I? If there's a chance—even a small one—of preventing his death, of having him back again.

And I have to admit it: there's a part of me (quite deep down, I think, because it's not always there) that's so excited it makes me feel a bit sick.

CHAPTER TEN

That afternoon, Mum and I are eating soup in the kitchen.
(It's one of her "experiments," coconut and Stilton, which
doesn't really work, to be honest.) Steve's working late, and
Carly said this morning that she's in the school choir, which
I know to be a big fat lie; and besides, I saw her heading off
in the other direction with Jolyon when I came out of school,
but I haven't said anything. I know far better than that.

The soup is hot and we wait for it to cool a little (which
suits me fine).

"Mum . . ." I'm trying to find the right words. "Did Dad
have any hobbies? I mean, things that he did apart from
work?" I'm trying to find out if Mum knew about his Top
Secret Underground Laboratory.

Mum thinks for a while and lifts the soup spoon to her
mouth. She drinks it without slurping even a little, then
answers, "Ee, well, not really." (This "ee" that Mum says is

part of her Geordie accent, and it usually makes me smile, but right now I'm too interested in what's coming next.) She looks a little puzzled, as if she had never really thought about it before.

"Your father was a very clever man, and he thought about things a great deal, but . . ."

"Was he, like, into science fiction or, or . . . stuff like that?"

"Science fiction? Your dad?" Mum gives a slight snort. "No. Definitely not! Not his thing at all. Why?"

"Ah . . . no reason." Mum's looking at me intensely, so I invent something quickly. "I was just thinking of the stories Dad used to tell me, and I wondered what he liked to read."

Mum smiles. "Detective stories. Real-life crime. Mysteries. Anything with a puzzle. That was your dad. Always trying to work things out."

We eat our soup in silence for a bit. After a few spoonfuls, it's not as bad as it sounds. Then I get a brilliant idea.

"Did Dad ever fix cars?"

"When we first got married, we had an old Ford Fiesta that he'd work on. Why?"

"In the garage at Chesterton Road?"

"No. We didn't live there then. Why?"

"It's just that there was that hole in the floor for mechanics to stand in, and I thought he may have used it."

"The pit? Ee, no. I don't think he ever used that, apart from when we first moved in and we checked out the fallout shelter."

I furrow my brow. "The *what*?"

"The people we bought the house from were terrified there was going to be a nuclear war. MacFaddyen, they were called. Rough, they were, and . . ." She makes a twirling motion with her finger next to her head. "Anyway, they converted the cellar into a shelter under the garage to protect them from a nuclear bomb. It was tiny and creepy. They thought it increased the value of the house, but it didn't. We only went in it the once, when they showed us round."

"You never told me this before."

Mum shrugs. "You never asked. You never asked about the loft either, but that was there as well. I suppose I didn't like the thought that you might want to play there, so I just never mentioned it. To be honest, Al, neither your dad nor I gave it a minute's thought."

Mum's taking a deep breath and looking at me with her head tipped to one side. She's about to change the subject and I think I know where it's headed.

"The boys in your class . . ."

I was right.

"Is there anyone you'd like to invite back for tea one day, or just to play?"

Now, Mum has asked me this, or a clever variation on it so that I don't think she's obsessed, roughly once a month since I started at St. Eddie's. The answer's always the same.

"Not really, Mum. Most of them are busy with other stuff. You know—homework and that."

Mum nods and looks away. She's not going to pursue it today. Finally she says, "That letter from your dad. Was it . . . OK?"

It's a funny choice of word, and I smile. "Yes, it was OK. It was . . . private. Growing up advice, and"—I add this next bit to try to deflect her attention—"guy stuff. Man to man, you know? Growing up, drinking, drugs, girls."

Mum smiles warmly and a bit sadly, but says no more.

Which suits me because I'm just sitting there thinking: *Fallout shelter. That's where the time machine is.*

CHAPTER ELEVEN

Ten Things I Know About My Dad

1. His name was Pythagoras Chaudhury. I know, right? Who'd call their kid Pythagoras? Well, Byron Chaudhury-Roy, for one. Grandpa Byron had got his name because *his* father loved English classical poets. He once told me, "It could be worse, Al. I could have been called Elizabeth Barrett Browning." I laughed, even though I didn't know who Elizabeth Barrett Browning was. Anyway, Dad called himself Pye, and sometimes for a joke wrote his name like the Greek letter pi. You know: π. His sister's called Hypatia, and she lives in Canada, but I've only ever met her the once. Well, twice, actually, if you include when she was five, which we'll get to later. Dad said

that Hypatia was the "mother of modern maths." The original Hypatia, that is, not his sister. She's an estate agent.

2. He loved me very much. This is what Mum always tells me, so it must be true.

3. His favorite meal was fish and chips with chili pickle. He said to Mum that, like them, it was the perfect Anglo-Indian marriage. Except he was only half-Indian, because Grandma Julie was Welsh.

4. He was very, very clever. He once built a dishwasher in the garage from old parts that he got off a friend. Mum said it never worked very well, but she never said that to him.

5. He and Mum met when Dad was a student at university becoming a doctor. Not a real doctor, but an engineering doctor. That's what they call you when you pass an exam called a PhD, so his name was really Dr. Chaudhury, though he never called himself that in case people thought he was a real doctor and

wanted him to cure them. Mum was working at the university bookshop.

6. He wasn't very handsome. I know that sounds mean, but he wasn't. He wasn't ugly or anything, not like Tara Simmons's dad, he was just . . . all right. I've seen photos and video and stuff, and he was sort of skinny, with loads of black hair ("a bird's nest," Mum says) and a slightly pointy nose. It's his smile you notice, though. Mum says it was his smile that she fell in love with first. There's a picture that we had up on the mantelpiece until shortly after Mum started going out with Steve, and Dad was grinning at the camera and you could see what she meant. When he smiled he became almost good-looking, except for a crooked bottom tooth. I think he looks nice. I wish Mum hadn't taken the picture down. She probably thinks I haven't noticed.

7. My dad didn't really have any hobbies, like football or fishing. He just liked doing stuff with computers. At work he wrote software programs that helped other programmers write *their* software programs.

8. He died four years ago, when I was eight. I've tried to forget most of it, but I do remember the ambulance and going to stay with Aunty Ellie. Everyone said I was being "brave," but I just didn't feel like crying until a few days later, and by then it was too late to start.

9. He could sing songs in Punjabi. There was one he taught to Mum as well that they'd sing to me at bedtime, but she never sang it after he died. I asked her about it not so long ago and she said she had forgotten it, but I think she might have been fibbing.

That's only nine, but I can't think of anything else. Is that really bad of me?

I'm sometimes scared that I'm forgetting what my dad was like.

CHAPTER TWELVE

Look: put yourself in my shoes.

It's been nearly a week now and the truth is, I'm not even sure whether to believe what The Letter says. Would you?

And I'm thinking about this—what we believe and everything—when something occurs to me that sort of tips the balance in my indecision. (Indecision, by the way, that is now so bad and so distracting that last night I hardly slept at all and my teacher, Miss Henry, kept me back after school for one of those "Is everything all right with you?" chats.)

You see, my mum believes in ghosts, even though she told me there's no such thing.

I've started to think about it now because of the letter from my dad, and *because* I've been thinking about it, I've remembered this stuff from a book I tried to read called *2001: A Space Odyssey*, which everyone thinks is just a film, but it's actually a book as well, and the writer predicted loads of stuff long before it ever happened, like the satellites that let us use mobile phones, and men visiting the moon.

Anyway, in *2001* the writer said that "behind every man now alive stand thirty ghosts." Now, by "man" he meant "person," because that's how people wrote back then, and the ghosts thing just meant that for every person then alive, thirty people had died in history.

He wrote that in 1968 when the world's population was about half of what it is now. If he was writing it now, it would be "behind every person now alive stand fifteen ghosts."

That means that more than one hundred billion people have died on Earth since humans began, which is funny because that's the number of stars in the Milky Way, according to my dad.

I don't think Arthur C. Clarke, who wrote the book, believed in ghosts—I mean, actual proper ghosts like you get in stories: the kind that haunt places. Dad didn't either—he told me so. Actually, what he said was that he thought it was *"stupendously unlikely."* That's what he used to say about things that he thought weren't real, but that no one could prove.

Stupendously unlikely. It's a cool phrase.

Like, you can't prove that ghosts *don't* exist, can you? All you can say is that it's stupendously unlikely.

Mum wasn't so cautious, though. I had a bad dream once when I was little, and I thought there was a ghost living in the loft and she told me—definitely and certainly—that there was no such thing as ghosts; that it was all just our imagination.

So I grew up not believing in ghosts. Stuff like *Scooby-Doo* was good fun, and I got really scared one Christmas by a ghost in a play, but I knew it wasn't real.

But after Dad died, Mum changed.

It wasn't long after he had died, maybe a month, and I overheard Mum talking to Aunty Ellie. We were still living on Chesterton Road in Culvercot then. I couldn't sleep so I had got up to get a glass of water, and I heard them talking in the front room and stayed to listen on the stairs.

"Come on, Sarah," Aunty Ellie was saying, sort of soothing.

"No, I did, Ellie, I did, plain as day. He was standing right there. The funeral director was sitting where you're sitting, and he came through the door, and sort of looked at me, and looked at Dennis Harrison, and his mouth went *no!* and he went out the door as quiet as anything."

"What did you do?"

"Well, I was in a daze. I just stared, and Dennis Harrison

saw me gaping at the door, and he asked me, *'What's the matter?'* and I said, *'I've just seen Pye!'* and he just nodded. *'A lot of people say that,'* he said."

"And that was it?"

"That was it. He didn't look like a ghost or anything."

"What was he wearing?"

"Like, did he have a sheet on him? No, Ellie; he was wearing his normal stuff. His jeans, his blue cotton checked shirt, you know? The one he liked."

"Listen, honey, it's a very stressful time; I think—"

"Ellie, don't tell me I was imagining it. It was *real,* he was *there.* Right there!"

"I'm sure he was."

"And don't patronize me either."

They stopped talking for a minute; then I heard, "Al? Is that you?"

But by the time Mum came out to check, I was back in bed.

I still don't believe in ghosts. But what if Mum hadn't seen a "ghost"?

What if she had *really* seen Dad, only that Dad was a "ghost" from the past? In other words, what if Dad had traveled from a time before he was dead to a time after he was dead, and accidentally turned up while his own funeral was being planned?

I know. Stupendously unlikely. But it all pushes me closer to the decision I know I have to make, even though I *still* don't know how I'm going to get from Blyth to Culvercot at night.

I'm going to do it. I'm going to follow my dad's instructions, and travel in time.

I'm not sure it's a good idea.

I'm still not.

CHAPTER THIRTEEN

Grandpa Byron was ten minutes early this morning, so I'm at school before everyone else, and he's not in a hurry, so we're just leaning on the low school wall. He lights a *beedi*. He's wearing jeans today, and with his big boots and leather jacket and gray plait, he looks like some really cool old Hells Angel from an American film, except for his moped: a tiny 50cc scooter, and mauve. Its top speed is 30 mph, less when there are two people on it.

He once let me ride it, just up the back alley. He showed me where it switched on, and how to twist the handle to make it go. He ran alongside me to the end of the alley. It was pretty awesome.

I can smell the *beedi* and it's nice, sort of fruity. He sees me sniffing and smiling.

"Mango," he says. "I'm usually smoking vanilla-scented,

but Baz had run out." Baz is the guy who owns the shop that sells them.

"Have you always smoked them?" I ask, and he thinks about his answer before replying.

"Never much. Your Grandma Julie didn't like the smell."

"I like the smell."

"I know, but when you are loving someone, you make compromises. Then when she died . . ." His voice trails off and he takes another puff.

I had heard about Grandma Julie, but she died years ago from "birth complications" after Aunty Hypatia was born. I don't know what that means, actually, but it's what Grandpa Byron said. I've seen a photo of Grandma Julie that Dad had, though: she looked really nice and I'm sure I'd have liked her. When she died, Grandpa Byron and Hypatia and Dad lived in the same house in Culvercot for years. (It was only later that he moved up the coast to Blyth, quite close to where Mum and I ended up living.)

And then he asks me the question I know is coming.

"Have you started reading the book yet?" He's trying to sound dead casual, as if he doesn't care one way or the other, but I know he does.

I haven't, not really. "Yeah!" I say a bit too enthusiastically, but I don't follow up with anything else, and my "yeah" kind of hangs in the air between us. Grandpa Byron glances over at me and waits.

"It's . . . great, it's just . . . not that easy to read sometimes?"

He smiles. Phew.

"Some things take a little bit of effort, Al, man. You want to know how I memorize all that stuff? Well, that takes effort an' all. But it's easier than you think. How far have you got?"

"A few pages."

"Keep goin', man. It'll be worth it."

Grandpa Byron has walked away from the wall to dispose of the *beedi* in a litter bin when Jolyon Dancey comes round the corner.

"Hey, look who it is! Come on, man—high five!"

I hold up my hand and he slaps it so hard that I wince, and then Jolyon notices Grandpa Byron walking back toward me and edges away without saying anything more.

"Who was that?" There's something wary in Grandpa Byron's tone, as if he's seen something he's not keen on.

"That's, um, Jolyon Dancey. Kid in my year."

Grandpa Byron smiles a tight little smile, shakes his head

slowly, and gets astride his moped (which just sort of involves sitting down). He winks at me, and as I see him *putt-putt*ing up the road, something inside me changes.

It's partly a hot flush of shame that rises from my still-stinging hand to my eyes and makes them prick with tears. The whole thing is hateful because I know I'm being mocked. And Grandpa Byron knew it too, as soon as he saw Jolyon Dancey edging away, and his face showed that he knew; and I hate myself for putting up with it, and I hate myself for not having the courage to stop it, and I hate myself for not carrying out my dad's instructions and for my indecision and dithering.

And it's partly because I now know how I'll get from Blyth to Culvercot.

CHAPTER FOURTEEN

It's tonight.

Tonight I have to creep downstairs (and not get caught) and then travel ten miles down the coast to our old house in Culvercot.

There are a number of reasons why this will be practically impossible:

1. There are only three bedrooms in Steve's house. Mum and Steve's room is right across the landing from mine, and Carly's is a little farther down. So sneaking out of my room without being heard will be hard.

2. Mum's a really light sleeper. If I get up in the night to use the toilet or get a drink of water, she'll always call out softly, "You OK, love?" (Carly, on the other hand, is usually a really heavy sleeper.)

3. I've then got to get out the front door. The lock makes a noisy clunk when it's opened, and there's a big bolt at the bottom, which also makes a noise. The back door might be easier, but that's stiff and you have to bang it shut.

In other words, going out the front door or the back door is out. That leaves my bedroom window, and the only way I can get out that way is with a ladder and we don't have one. So what's it to be?

Once I've managed this impossible task, another awaits me: I'm going to steal Grandpa Byron's moped.

This at least will be easier than getting out of the house, though. I've already located the spare key to the moped. "Located" sounds like it was hard, but in fact it just hangs with the other keys on the hook in his kitchen. I took it this afternoon, during the ad break in *Mind Games,* and it's now safely in my pocket.

There are some other things I need to do:

1. Clothing. Grandpa Byron says it gets cold on a moped, so I'll be fully dressed and wearing my winter coat. The spare helmet is in the box on the back

of the moped, which doesn't lock. It's got a dark visor over the front, so no one will be able to tell it's a kid riding a moped.

2. Route. That's easy: I know the way.

3. Schedule. Mum and Steve are nearly always in bed by ten-thirty. They watch the news on TV, then come upstairs, brush their teeth, lights out by eleven. Steve's a real early bird and his alarm goes off at six, so I've got plenty of time to do what I need to do. The problem is the "Mum's a really light sleeper" thing.

4. Carly goes to bed at the same time, but watches videos and does Internet stuff with her headphones on. No worries there.

5. Equipment: torch, new batteries.

It's only when I think about what I'm doing all this for that my heart starts to pound and I get a little sick feeling in my stomach. So instead I return to the problem at hand: how to get out of the house.

It's ten-thirty, and I can hear the end music from the TV news coming up through the floor.

I've decided that there is no option. It'll have to be the front door, and I'll have to do it really, really slowly and quietly.

I tried to behave as normally as I could this evening, but Mum knows something's up. Once she asked, "Is there something the matter, love?" and I just said, "No—I'm just a bit tired," which normally works when I don't want to talk about something. It was a good reason to go to bed early and I threw in some yawns for good measure. She still looked at me funny, though.

Instead of getting undressed for bed when I came upstairs, I took off my school uniform and put on jeans and a thick sweater. I'm lying on the bed listening to Mum's and Steve's going-to-bed noises when I hear the handle on my bedroom door—Mum's coming in, and I'm fully dressed.

I just have time to flick the duvet over myself as Mum comes alongside my bed. I'm holding the duvet up to my chin as Mum sits down on the edge of my bed and starts to stroke my hair like she did when I was very little. Normally I like that: I can smell the hand cream she uses and when she leans over I can check if the little gray streak of hair in the middle of her head is advancing any further through the brown. But tonight I'm screaming silently, "Go away! Go away!" My eyes are shut tight and I'm trying so hard to look like I'm asleep.

It seems like she's there for ages, but eventually she bends over, kisses my forehead, and gets up. She spends a little while standing by my bed—looking at me, I guess—and then walks out.

I tell you—she knows something's up.

So it's eleven-thirty now, and all's quiet. I don't think I've moved since Mum left the room, and there's a rush of cool air as I lift off the duvet and tiptoe to my bedroom door. I can hear Steve snoring—not comedy-loud, just normal—but Mum never snores so I'll just have to hope she's asleep. If Carly's up, there's usually a light from under her door, but tonight it's dark.

It's only three steps to the top of the stairs, but it takes me about thirty seconds to make them, since I'm pausing after each one to make sure no one has woken up.

The stairs are even slower. The third and fifth stairs from the top are creaky, so I carefully step over them . . . and then I'm downstairs.

Slowly, slowly, I ease the bolt at the bottom of the front door. Slowly, slowly I turn the lock. I grab a scarf from the rack and hold it over the lock just as it's about to go *clunk,* and the noise is muffled. I'm out.

Ten minutes later, I'm outside Grandpa Byron's house, down his side alley, and there it is: silver and mauve, splashed with mud, and I'm having a little trouble breathing because I'm so nervous. I push the moped off its stand and start wheeling it up the path. My helmet's on now, and I figure I'll push the moped down the street before starting it in case it wakes up Grandpa Byron with its distinctive, raspy engine note. "Guttural," he calls it, and he is right, if guttural means sounding like an old lady clearing her throat.

At the corner of Percy Road, I put the key in, hold the brake, and turn it like Grandpa Byron showed me that time. The engine comes to life and I look around nervously, but the street's empty. There are a few lights on in the windows and I can smell the sour exhaust fumes. Because everything else is so quiet, the engine sounds deafening, so I figure the best thing to do is get going. I sit astride the moped, release the brake handle, and twist the throttle with my right wrist, and we're off, through misty air tinged yellow by streetlights.

CHAPTER FIFTEEN

Inside the motorbike helmet the noise of the engine is muffled and the wind whooshes past. I can hear myself breathing rapidly as the needle on the speedometer creeps past 20 mph, then 25, before I have to slow down for a roundabout. There's a car coming from the right. "Give way to traffic from the right," I say out loud to myself, and I stop and watch the car go past. The driver doesn't even look at me.

Off we go again, over the roundabout, down toward the coastal road. I find the indicator under my thumb and signal right. Even at midnight, the coastal road is busy. I'm just looking straight ahead, and every time a car overtakes me I tense up, so by the time the buildings thin out and I'm past the Elf garage, I'm aching all over and I can feel drops of sweat running down my back despite the cool wind.

A couple of miles later the orange road lights finish, and there's no more traffic; it's just me and the moped. Its headlight gives off a pool of white light ahead of me, and anything else I can see is just what the moon lights up. It's funny: I've been in the car loads of times at night, but only as a passenger, when you can look out and all around; but you can't really do that when you're driving—you have to look ahead pretty much all the time, especially when the twin headlights of another car are coming toward you, then zooming past, dazzling you a bit until your eyes adjust again.

On my left is the sea and it glints a little silver from the moon, and then the road goes between some hills so I can't see the sea anymore, but then the hills end, or the road bends round, and there's the sea again, and I like that—it feels comforting somehow, black and silver. At one point the road goes quite near the beach, but much higher, and I can see the white line of the foam where the sea hits the sand. I can't hear it, but I can smell it—the salty, seaweedy smell of the beach.

I want to know what time it is, but I daren't take my hand off the handlebar to look at my watch. It feels like ages, and my bum is aching now as well, and the speedometer needle has been just above thirty for miles, when I see the big white dome of Whitley Bay's Spanish City, which Dad said used to be a dance hall, and then an amusement arcade, and now I don't know what it is. Culvercot is after Whitley Bay, but they kind of merge into each other.

Ten minutes later, I'm driving into Culvercot, and the feeling I get is very strange indeed. I think it's happiness, and relief, and scaredness, and also a bit of sadness seeing all the places I used to know, like the café where I had my sixth birthday; and I even drive past Oscar Rudd's house, who was my best friend in primary school till he moved to Sweden in Year Four. He promised he'd email loads, but he never really did.

And then I'm on my old street, Chesterton Road, and ahead of me is my old house, number 40. I stop the moped a little down the street and turn the engine off, and I let the roaring in my ears settle down and the feeling return to my arms and wrists. Now all I've got to do is break into the house, and I've already told you about that bit.

Less than five minutes later, I'm staring at my dad's time machine—a zinc garden tub and a laptop—in the cellar fallout shelter and thinking, *Surely* that's *not it?*

Like I said, I was expecting something a bit more . . . well, technical. A bit more? A *lot* more.

And now I'm standing here, holding Letter Number Two, which as you know was taped under the desk in the fallout shelter, and the only light is coming from my torch beam, and for probably a whole minute I'm too terrified to move.

I kept myself calm enough till now to do all the stuff required to get here. I think I even prepared myself for testing a time machine, but now that there isn't one—or at any rate, anything that *looks* like one—the massive risk of what I've just done begins to overwhelm me. I'm suddenly very aware of the silence and the dark, and I can hear myself breathing short, raspy gulps of air, and at one point I even imagine I can hear my heart beating in my chest.

There's only one thought in my mind: *I want to go home.*

CHAPTER SIXTEEN

Once I've got my legs moving and calmed my breathing down a bit, I come out of the cellar quickly and close the heavy steel door behind me, spinning the wheels of the combination lock.

I'm still terrified of being caught, but my movements are smooth and quiet. I replace the planks over the concrete stairway and slip out of the garage, remembering to put the brick back in front of the double doors, then walk briskly among the shadows back to the moped. I get on it quickly, buzzing to the edge of town and back along the coast road, my head spinning with what I've just done.

The moon has moved across the sky and is higher and brighter than before. I am feeling really hot inside the helmet. On the outskirts of Blyth, level with the long stretch of beach, which is silvery gray in the moonlight, I stop the moped and take off the helmet for a moment, feeling a cool breeze through my sweaty hair.

Then I see the headlights of a car coming along the road. I turn my head to look, remembering too late that I shouldn't be showing my young face, and there's another light above the headlights on the car's roof. The police car passes me as I put the helmet back on and start the bike again.

To be safe, I turn left at the roundabout, straight up a residential street that runs off the coast road, and it's just as well I do, because in my rearview mirror I see the red brake lights of the police car come on and I see it turning round to come back. To follow me.

Desperately, I open the throttle of the moped as far as it can go, and the little engine whines in protest. I know I can't go faster than a police patrol car, and as I look behind me, the car turns into the road I'm on and I hear the growl of its engine as the driver puts his foot on the accelerator.

In seconds the car is nearer, and his blue flashing lights are on—no siren yet, though. The road ends in houses arranged around the wide turning circle of a cul-de-sac. I'm trapped, and I'm going to have to brake soon anyway if I'm not to crash into one of the low front garden walls.

Then I see it—a narrow footpath between the two end houses.

I mount the curb with a rattling thud, which nearly knocks me off. I hurtle toward the alleyway as the police car screeches to a halt behind me, and I hear the doors open and the beat of feet starting to run.

There is a metal post in the middle of the entrance to the alleyway and it's going to be a tight squeeze, but I just manage it, scraping the side of the moped's back end against the wall as I get past, and I know I've made it. I dare to look back and the two officers are running back to their car to try to get me on the next road.

I emerge from the footpath and I'm not even that sure where I'm going, so I turn right on the road in what I hope is the direction of Grandpa Byron's street, although by now I'm panicking and my breath is coming in short bursts.

I turn left just as I hear the police siren, and the car turns onto the main road in pursuit. They must have seen me. To my relief, I recognize the street: one more right turn and there is Baz's corner shop, and still the siren is getting closer. I have the throttle open fully as I get near Grandpa Byron's house, and the engine is buzzing loudly in the quiet night, and I completely forget about waking him up, so scared am I that the police car will catch up.

I turn into Grandpa Byron's driveway and kill the engine and lights immediately, and push the bike up the side of the house.

Then the siren goes quiet.

This is almost the worst bit. I'm sitting on the ground, trembling and panting. Me and the moped are pretty much hidden from the road when the police car creeps past at walking pace. I can see the officers' heads turning from side to side and I shrink back farther, hoping the wall will somehow swallow me up.

But then it passes and I breathe out. All the same, it's a good twenty minutes before I can stand up and hurry back through the shadows to my house, creep up the stairs, and flop into bed.

And now I feel like I want to cry, but I stop myself, and instead take out of my pocket the letter that was taped under the desk.

CHAPTER SEVENTEEN

Dear Al,

By now you have had a chance to digest my last letter, and there are two alternative outcomes:

1. You think your dad's crazy and you have told Mum, or the police, or a teacher, or a friend. That's a shame, and it means I misjudged you. But that's my fault, and I don't blame you.

2. You have done as I asked. I hope it's this one.

Did you do it all within a week as I asked? My guess is that you did, and that shows real courage. That's what the time limit was about, a kind of test, because it would be easy to wait and wait and never do anything. I promise you, Al—there will be no more tests. What's coming next is far too serious for that.

You're probably terrified. That's OK. I think I would be too. Be scared: it'll keep you alert, and if you're alert you won't make a mistake, and if you make no mistakes then all will be fine.

People have always dreamed, Al, of traveling in time—either into the future or the past. Sometimes both. (Do you remember the play we went to see when you were younger—_A Christmas Carol_ by Charles Dickens? Scrooge sees Christmases in the past and the future. I think it scared you a bit!)

Recently, we have imagined grand machines that would do the job for us—often, vast spaceships that would zoom through the centuries faster than the speed of light.

And herein, Al, lies the problem.

For nothing can travel faster than light. No matter how much energy you have, from whatever source—existing or yet to be discovered—physically moving faster than a beam of light cannot happen.

If it could, then it would mean that all the laws of physics we know, and have tested for centuries, are wrong.

And we know they are not.

It would mean that Einstein's theories are wrong, and so far good ol' Albert has had the last laugh on pretty much everyone who has tried to outsmart him. Sure, there are gaps in our knowledge, but every time we make a new discovery and fill in one of the gaps, it shows us that Einstein was right.

The Higgs boson? I'll bet that's discovered soon. Plenty of people are looking for it, because Einsteinian theory requires it.

The theory of cosmic inflation? That'll be proven soon too, I reckon. It's another thing that Einstein predicted.

(Now, I don't really know what a Higgs boson is, but I know it has been found. And cosmic inflation was in the news too, so that's probably what that is. Yay, Einstein!)

"The speed of light," Einstein said, "is the Universal Speed Limit."

Einstein suspected that the way we think of time as moving in a line—from one minute to the next, one year following another—may not be the <u>only</u> way to look at it. That in fact everything might be happening simultaneously and that our sense of time is only relative—that is, in our heads. Remember his line about putting your hand on a hot stove?

What we <u>perceive</u> as the progression of events— one thing following another—could merely be the growth of an infinite number of dimensions all happening at the same time, and the key to moving between them might be found not in a source of super-energy that could propel us faster than the speed of light, but in a mathematical formula.

I know, it's hard to get our heads round. We are goldfish, remember!

I put the letter down and sigh. I'm not sure I've understood a single word, and the frustrating thing is that I know my dad's trying to explain it really simply.

Do you remember learning multiplication in primary school, and instead of saying, "*What's five times four?*" the teacher would say something like, "*There are five dogs, and they each have four legs—how many legs are there alto-gether?"* so you wouldn't get freaked out by the maths-ness of it all? Well, I can tell that's what my dad's doing, but I still don't get it.

I rub my eyes and read on.

Perhaps that's as much as you need to under-stand. You'll get the rest when you turn on the lap-top on the desk.

That, in case you hadn't guessed, is the time machine.

It wasn't always there, Al. I was not getting up in the night and sneaking away to a secret under-ground laboratory. Most of the work I did was in front of a computer screen, in my room at home, while our family life was going on around us.

Calculations, coding, more calculations ...

Only when I knew I had the right formula did I open up the bunker and install the required appa-ratus, when you and Mum were out visiting Aunty Ellie.

Which means that everything is ready for you to travel back to when I was a boy, and save my life. That might sound odd but it will make sense soon.

Now it's down to you, Al. Go to the time machine laptop and switch it on. Further instructions will appear.

See you in 1984!

Your loving dad X

I've read the letter three or four times before I notice a sliver of pale light sneaking through a gap in my curtains as the sky outside lightens.

I yawn, but I can't sleep, and my head is spinning and I can hear my dad's voice and if I close my eyes it's OK; I don't feel sad. I can even pretend he's here with me, and as I let my mind drift I feel his weight on the bed next to me, and he's really here, even though he's really not, and I can smell him, and I smile. . . .

It was close to Christmas, and Mum and Dad's friends Peter and Annika and some others as well had come to our house for dinner. I had been allowed to stay up late, and Peter had given me a two-pound coin before I went up to bed, but I hadn't really fallen asleep, not properly, so when my dad came in to check on me I opened my eyes.

"Hi," he said softly, with that little jerky nod of his head that he had, and he smiled his crooked smile.

I smiled back. "Hi," I said sleepily. I loved it when Dad came in and sat on my bed, and I knew exactly how to play it. If I was too wide awake, he'd be a bit cross with me for not getting to sleep, and he would tell me to put my light on and read for a bit until I was sleepy. But if I was quiet enough and acted drowsy, he'd come and sit on the bed, and sometimes stroke my hair, and sometimes chat with me, especially if he had been drinking wine.

I moved my legs to one side of the duvet to make room for him to sit down. From downstairs came Annika's loud shriek of laughter, and I smiled at Dad, who smiled back.

"Tell me a story," I said.

Dad had loads of stories. He would add little details and do funny voices, so they were a bit different each time, which meant you could hear them more than once without getting bored. Whenever I asked him, Dad would usually say, *No, it's too late,* and then I would beg, and he would say, *But you've heard them all,* and I would say that it didn't matter (because it really didn't), and he'd say, *What sort of story then?* and I'd say, *One from when you were young,* and he'd think really hard. Sometimes I would prompt him, and that's what I did.

There were two stories that were my favorites. The first one was the story of when he and Mum met.

They were about twenty years old, and apparently he rescued her from drowning in a lake, or the sea, and he went in fully clothed, or was in his swimming trunks. (That's what I mean about them being a bit different each time.) Once when he told it, he said she was never drowning anyway, but just called out to him pretending to be in trouble because she fancied him. The only thing that never changed was that Grandpa Byron was with him—they were having some beach party or something with a bunch of other Indians, and they had gone to the water's edge and heard Mum shouting for help and Dad had gone in to rescue her.

The other story, though, was the one I asked for this time.

"Tell me about how your teeth got crooked," I said.

"What, again?"

"Yes." I settled back onto my pillow and pulled the duvet up to my chin. I loved this one.

"Well, I must have been a bit older then you are now, maybe eleven or twelve, and Grandpa Byron had built me a go-kart, which back then we called a bogey. . . ."

I snorted with laughter. "A bogey! Why'd you call it that? It means snot."

"I dunno. We just did. I think it just means something on wheels."

"And you used pram wheels?"

"Yeah, in those days you could still find old-fashioned pram wheels, so that's what we used. Your grandpa made a wooden base, like a seat, and he brought all the extra bits like bearings and screws and fixings from work."

"He stole them?"

"No, not your grandpa Byron. I think they just sort of fell into his pocket as he walked around, you know?"

I laughed. I loved the idea of things falling into someone's pocket, like if they walked past a shelf these things would just roll off by themselves.

"Anyway, the only brakes on this thing were a wooden lever that you had to pull up against the back wheel to slow it down; that was all. And I painted it with the only paint I could find, which was left over from painting the garage doors, so it was this weird olive green."

"Olive green?" This was a new detail.

"Yeah. I called it the Lean Mean Green Machine. I wrote its name in white poster paint down the middle board."

"You never told me this."

"I'm telling you now. And me and your grandpa had already tested out the Green Machine, and it was pretty lean and mean, I can tell you!"

"Did your friends like it?"

Dad hesitated. "I think perhaps . . . I can't remember them ever . . . I guess they must have been busy with other things." There was then a longish gap, so I nudged him on.

"So this one day I was out with the Green Machine—"

"The Lean Mean Green Machine," I corrected him.

"Yes indeed, the Lean Mean Green Machine, and it was only me, and I was on the long slope that goes down to the promenade above the seawall. You know the one—perfect for bogeys!"

I nodded. I liked the promenade. That's what we called it anyway. It was really just a pathway on top of the wall that dropped down to the beach. There was a metal railing to stop you from falling off, and twice a year the tide got so high that it came right up against the wall and sometimes the waves would crash below and splash you.

"So I'm in the bogey, I'm on my own and heading down the slope, and there's this thing from the telly I'm shouting at the top of my voice, *Fan-dabby-doziiii!* And then—"

"You hit a brick in the middle of the road!"

"That's right: a huge brick, or a cinder block, or something, I can't really remember, and the front wheel comes clean off, and I go *wheeee* through the air and land right on my face in the road—*cruuuunch!*"

"Was there loads of blood?"

"Blood? I looked like I'd just gone ten rounds with Mike Tyson, and—"

"What? Who's he?"

"Doesn't matter. Blood all over the place, down my front. One tooth missing, two others knocked out of line, my face all scraped from the road, and a wire spike from an abandoned supermarket trolley has gone right up my nose."

I remembered this bit and I winced. It really sounded horrible.

Dad continued, "I'm crying my eyes out, not with pain, but because the Green Machine is broken. And some guy who's driving along the road at the bottom of the slope stops his car—I can remember it was a blue Austin Allegro—and he yanks the spike out of my nose, puts me in his car, and takes me home, while I'm dripping blood all over the inside of his car."

"Didn't you go to hospital?"

"No. Perhaps I should have done. Maybe they'd have sorted my teeth out. But your grandpa, he just said, 'Oh my Lordy! You've been in the wars!'" (Dad did Grandpa Byron's head wobble for good effect.) "He cleaned me up and put me in front of the telly, and I was back at school the next day."

"You were brave," I said.

Dad smiled. "Not sure I was brave. It stopped the other kids picking on me for a bit, though."

"Did that happen a lot?" I asked, but Dad had stood up. The chatter from downstairs was still going on, and Annika was still laughing her laugh. Dad bent over and kissed my head. I could smell the wine on his breath and I hugged his neck hard. I tried to imagine anyone being mean to my dad, and I couldn't really, so I just hugged him again until he gently pulled away and went downstairs.

CHAPTER NINETEEN

Mum's looking at me carefully as I stare glumly at my cereal, not eating it. She's holding her tea mug in both hands. It's just her and me. Steve is off at some conference called *New Directions in IT for Municipal Libraries*, according to the flyer on the fridge, and Carly leaves early anyway, largely—I suspect—to avoid having breakfast with me and Mum.

I don't feel well, it has to be said, but it's entirely down to having been up virtually all night. I don't think I fell asleep till about five.

"Are you well enough for school, Al?" she asks.

This one has to be played carefully. I need to work out how to get back to the time machine, which means I don't want to go to school. But if I'm too eager to stay home, she'll think I'm faking. If I sound too ill, like with a croaky voice or something, she'll think I'm faking. In short, almost anything I do will make her think I'm faking, *but ...*

I have one advantage. A year ago, I wasn't faking and she packed me off to school anyway and I threw up in assembly and she had to come and collect me. That's like having one in the bank, and I have saved it up to spend wisely. I opt instead for The Shrug.

Now, what The Shrug says is this: *"I'm very poorly. In fact, so poorly, I can't even be bothered to have an opinion on whether or not I'm too poorly for school, especially since last time I was too poorly for school you sent me anyway and I was sick down Katie Pelling's back."*

It's a risky tactic, but it's working.

"I think you look awful, love. I'll get the thermometer."

Best of all, I don't even have to spend the one I have in the bank, because *I'm not asking to stay home from school.* I have a feeling that I may need that one soon.

Mum puts the thermometer in my mouth. "Keep that there; I'll be back in a tick," she says, and she leaves the kitchen. Her mug of tea is on the table in front of me, and the minute her back is turned I dip the thermometer into it. I can see the red line climbing, and I figure I'd better not overdo it or she'll call an ambulance. By the time Mum's back, the thermometer's in my mouth again. She looks at it and shakes her head.

"Poor love," she says. "I knew you looked ill."

For the next twenty minutes, Mum fusses me back into bed, making sure I have a glass of water, a bucket to be sick in, a sandwich if I get hungry, books to read.

"I can't take the day off," she says, "but I'll try and leave early. You get some rest, and call me if you feel any worse. You'll be OK?"

I nod and smile wanly and wait for her to leave. But she stops at the door and wrinkles her nose. "What's that smell?"

I can smell it too. Fox poo. Faint, but distinct, and somewhere on the clothes that are still heaped by my bed.

I sniff, then say, "Sorry. That was me. Bad tummy."

Mum sniffs again, then puts her head to one side and gives me her most sincere "poor love" look before leaving the room.

The second the front door slams shut, I'm out of bed and on my laptop, searching the Internet for "Einstein," "theory of relativity," and "time travel."

Two hours later I'm asleep, my head resting on one arm, the other hand still clutching the mouse. And I'm no closer to understanding it, although:

1. I saw a cool cartoon on YouTube in which a talking cat traveling at the speed of light had his spaceship struck by two simultaneous lightning bolts.

2. I read a long article by that bloke who does the planets on TV titled—promisingly—"Relativity for a smart twelve-year-old." Smarter than me, obviously, and without meaning to boast, I know I'm pretty smart. At maths, anyway.

3. I learned that quantum physics means that one thing can exist in two places at the same time, but I still didn't know why. Or how.

4. I discovered Albert Einstein didn't learn to talk till he was four, and then he said out loud at the supper table, "This soup is too hot!"

5. I scraped off the fox poo that was on my jeans, put them through a quick wash and tumble dry, and put them back in my drawer.

I sleep for ages, dreaming that I'm in a spaceship, being chased by a police spaceship; dreaming about Einstein, about Jolyon Dancey, about everything and nothing all jumbled up; and then, eventually, I sleep a deep, dreamless sleep.

CHAPTER TWENTY

Ten Things I Know About My Mum

1. My mum can cook five things brilliantly. Spaghetti bolognese; sausage and mash and onion gravy; macaroni and cheese (except when she puts weird cheese in it); fish pie (except when she puts weird fish in it— you know I'm talking about you, anchovies); and, for special occasions, lasagne. Everything else is a bit experimental. Curries and stuff she used to leave to Dad, but Steve's not keen on spicy food, so now I just have curries at Grandpa Byron's.

2. She has never been on a diet. She's not fat or anything; she just says that she stops eating when she's full. Steve says this is unusual. Even Carly's on a

diet. (Not to be mean, but I don't think it's a very effective one.)

3. She can read *really* fast. I once timed her (secretly, so she wasn't trying too hard) when she was reading a book, and she turned the page about once a minute, which is twice as fast as normal people read. It's handy, I suppose, because she works in a library.

4. Sometimes, though, she reads *really* slowly, mainly when she's reading poetry. Then she'll stare at a page for ages and ages, and her lips will move, which is funny to watch because it looks like she can't read very well.

5. Her favorite poet is T. S. Eliot. I have never read anything by him, but I did see *Cats* with the school when it came to the Theatre Royal in Newcastle, and I think he wrote that.

6. Mum's parents moved to Ireland to look after her granny years ago and never moved back. We don't see them much. Mum speaks to them on the phone,

and whenever I speak to them they have to ask me how old I am now. Mum goes over about once a year. Aunty Ellie visits them more.

7. Mum can't swim. She never learned, which is crazy. If Mum and Dad ever took me to the pool when I was little, Dad would come in and Mum would sit in the café with the big window drinking coffee and reading (really fast). She says that ever since she nearly drowned that time that Dad rescued her, she's been too scared to get into the water.

8. Mum sometimes gets this dreamy look when she looks at me and calls me "Wonder Boy," which is nice (but a bit embarrassing). She and Dad tried for ages for a baby until I came along. The doctors had told her she was unlikely to have children *at all*, so they were *really* happy when I turned up. (Yay, me!)

9. Her favorite actor is some guy called Richard Gere who is seriously old—white hair, glasses, everything. She said he's "lush" and that she has always liked older men, and that's when I ran from the room with

my hands over my ears because that's just embarrassing. (Mum was a bit older than Dad, but Steve is older than her and *not* like Richard Gere. Not even a tiny bit.)

10. I saved the best one till last. My mum's got webbed feet! We both do actually. OK, that's a complete exaggeration. She has a thing called "syndactyly," which means that each of her little toes is joined with skin to the toe next to it. It's hereditary. Her mum has it; that's why I do too (although I don't really show anyone because it looks a bit alien, and besides, when do you go around showing people your toes?). It's pretty rare, but not dangerous or anything.

CHAPTER TWENTY-ONE

When I get up, Grandpa Byron's sitting at the kitchen table in his yellowy-orange robes and fiddling with his mobile.

"Bloody kids. Not respecting property, not respecting anything. Bloody great scratch down one side, and, y'beggar, the faring stinking of fox sh—" He sees me come in the room. "Fox's . . . doings. My goodness gracious, stinking to high heaven, to be sure."

When Grandpa Byron gets agitated, his speech patterns in English go a bit strange, and he's apt to use phrases that are hopelessly outdated, or very regional.

"You've called the police, haven't you, Byron?" says Mum.

"Most certainly. They saw the flipping rascal last night and chased him, but he got away."

"Your grandpa's moped was taken last night by joyriders," explains Mum.

"Oh no," I say, and then a bit more forcefully, "Oh *no!*" I hope I'm not overacting. Grandpa Byron, though, is far away.

"The thing I'm not really understanding," he says, "is why return the bike to my house? Up the side alley, back where it belongs. Don't joyriders normally just, well, leave it somewhere?"

"Isn't it locked, Byron?"

"Well, there is another curiosity. The lock was not broken. I can only suppose I forgot to lock it. Now, come on, Al: *Mind Games* is about to start." He moves toward the sitting room when I have a brain wave.

"Can we watch it at yours?"

He looks at me a bit funny. "Why in heaven's name?"

"It's just . . . it's better there. We—we can drink chai!"

That works. He gives a big smile. "Come on, then, hurry up. We might miss the start, but that's just the simple questions. No one cares about that!"

"Hang on—just forgotten something!" I run upstairs and take the spare moped key off the yellow plastic key ring, and replace it with one from my desk drawer that belonged to my old bike D-lock. They don't really match very well, but at a casual glance it should stop him realizing that the spare key is gone, and that way I might be able to borrow the moped again.

When we get to Grandpa Byron's house, I feel really bad about the damage when I see it: it's a huge scrape down one side, ruining the paintwork and cracking the plastic leg guard.

Worse, he wheels the moped up the side alley and takes a big, fat padded chain, brand new, from its top box, and chains it through the wheels to a drainpipe.

He sees me watching and winks. "No chances am I taking!"

I've still got to get the fake spare key back on its hook though, and so with Grandpa Byron installed in front of the TV, I'm safe to sneak it back on the rack of hooks in the kitchen while I'm making the chai. Except when I look round he's standing in the kitchen doorway and I don't know how long he's been there.

Did he see me? There's no way I can know. He's still in the kitchen doorway and I squeeze past him, and I think I see his eyes flick toward the rack of key hooks, but I can't be certain. I'm probably just imagining it.

That afternoon, for the first time in ages, he misses loads

of questions. I've never seen that happen before. He's rattled, I can tell, and then he asks me a question I've been dreading.

"How you gettin' on with me book?"

I screw up my face in embarrassment. "I've been really busy, Grandpa Byron, what with—"

"It's OK. It wasn't really written for young lads. Perhaps it's better if I just tell you?"

And that's what he does. Thank goodness, actually, because it saved my life, eventually. Well, one of them. In a way.

CHAPTER TWENTY-TWO

This is what Grandpa Byron tells me:

The Sri Kalpana was—is—a very little-known book of ancient Hindu scripture and dates back to maybe 1500 BC, which makes it one of the earliest of all written things. That's over 3,500 years old.

In it are the secrets that Indian gurus kept to themselves for centuries—among them, the methods used to memorize vast amounts of songs, poetry, family trees, and historical tales. Grandpa Byron pours more chai and relaxes a bit when he sees I am listening.

"Back then," he continues, "that was pretty much all there was to remember. Hardly anyone could write or read, mind you, and there were no football scores. But stories of battles, and who was related to who—these were dead important, and if you couldn't read or write then someone had to remember it all, and if you wanted to remember so much stuff, you'd need special techniques, and if you knew *them* then you'd be really important."

"Techniques like what?"

"Well, rhymes help, and rhythm. Do you know the kings and queens of England in order?"

I look at him, puzzled. "No! There's loads!"

But then Grandpa Byron begins to sing, to the tune of "Blaydon Races."

(You might not know how "Blaydon Races" goes, but I think everyone in the northeast does. It's kind of the Geordie national anthem, the one with, "Oh me lads, you should have seen us gannin . . ." No? Oh well, it's a sort of bouncy tune, a dum-de-dum-de-dum tune. Look it up if you want.)

Anyway, Grandpa Byron sings it:

"Willie, Willie, Harry, Steve,
Harry, Dick, John, Harry three,
One, two, three Eds, Richard two,
Harrys four, five, six, then who?"

I interrupt him then by saying, "But there's no King Harry, or Dick!"

"Harry's a nickname for Henry, Dick's short for

Richard—so you've got William the Conqueror; William the Second; Henry the First; King Stephen; Henry the Second; Richard the First; King John; Henry the Third; Edward the First, Second, and Third; Richard the Second; Henry the Fourth, Fifth, and Sixth; and so it goes on all the way to the present day."

He sings it again, all the way through, and by the third time I'm joining in. Grandpa Byron starts giggling.

"See! Hee hee! It's easy!"

I give him a skeptical look. "Please tell me that's not all there is to it. Rhyming stuff."

"Ah. No. But it's the start. Rhyme and rhythm make things easier to remember. The ancient Greeks called it mnemonics, and made it world famous, but it was we Indians who invented it all!"

"Hang on—world famous?"

He nods. "Memory systems were taught in schools and universities across Europe. But somehow it was abandoned. Now, no one bothers remembering anything"—Grandpa Byron gets up from the floor where he's been sitting—"Google will do it all for you. Now—I think there's some fudge left from your birthday," he says, and he goes into the kitchen. "Next time, I'll tell you about memory palaces."

"And how come Dad didn't do any of this? Didn't you teach him?"

Grandpa Byron's eyes move left and right as he chooses his words. "I tried to. But I think I left it a bit late with your dad. He preferred computers to his own imagination." He looks at me, a bit sadly, I think. "A lot of people do these days."

On the way home, I sing the kings and queens song to myself, all the way to the present day. I can't forget it now, even if I tried. It has stuck in my head like chewing gum to my shoe.

Willie, Willie, Harry, Steve,
Harry, Dick, John, Harry three,
One, two, three Eds, Richard two,
Harrys four, five, six, then who?
Edwards four, five, Dick the bad,
Harrys twain (that means two)
    and Ed the lad (Edward VI was only nine!),
Mary, Bessie, James the vain,
Charlie, Charlie, James again,
William and Mary, Anna Gloria,
Geordie, Geordie, Geordie, Geordie, William, and
    Victoria

(Geordie is a nickname for people called George, although the only George I know at school—George Pelling, brother of Katie, she of the sick-down-the-back fame—was just called George. It's probably an old-fashioned thing.)

Edward seven's next, and then,
George the fifth in 1910,
Ed the eighth, then George, Liz second,
Charlie, Wills, and George, it's reckoned!

I like it, knowing the order of the kings and queens like this. Not that it'll ever come in useful for anything, apart from maybe the odd test at school.

CHAPTER TWENTY-THREE

And so I'm lying on my bed, reading, and working out how I'm going to get back over to the old house now that Grandpa Byron's chained up his moped, when Carly walks in.

Let me tell you about the Stepsister From Hell, because she's about to feature a bit more significantly in this story.

To say I hate her would be unfair, but I think she hates me. I think she hates Mum, as well, and Grandpa Byron. And as far as I can tell, she hates her dad too, but because he gives her money she isn't so open about it. With him she just tuts a lot, rolls her eyes, and curls her lip behind his back.

Mum reckons she just hates the world because it took her mum away, and she's angry and resentful, and that instead of disliking her I should feel sorry for her, and that I should remember she almost certainly thinks we are invading her space. I try to remember that, I really do. But sometimes she makes it quite hard.

Take the going-to-school thing. She's a year ahead of me at St. Eddie's, but apart from once in my first week—once!—she has not traveled with me to school. (And that one time, as soon as she got on the bus she sat away from me with Noa Menko and the girl with the harelip.)

So now I usually get taken in by Grandpa Byron.

I think Carly is actually, probably, quite pretty, at least when she doesn't do her emo stuff. She's got shiny black hair that she makes even blacker with artificial color, and then she puts loads of stuff on her eyes, but when I once said she looked emo, she sneered at me and said she was a goth, not an emo, but I don't think she's either really, not that I'm an expert. I think she just likes wearing black, because she reckons it makes her look thinner.

When she walks into my room, I am stunned. She has never—and I really think it is *never*—come into my bedroom, and in she walks without knocking, of course.

"Hi," I say.

She doesn't reply, but sort of half nods at me with half-closed eyes, like she's been practicing in the mirror how to look mysterious and threatening.

To give her her due, it's working.

She wanders over to my desk and picks up a clay model

of Yoda that I made years ago but I still really like. She turns it over in her hands, then puts it back.

She pulls out the desk chair and turns it round. She starts to try and sit down on it backward, facing the back, like they do in movies, but she's got a skirt on that makes the move difficult, and besides, it would expose her knickers, so she opts instead for sitting sideways, and then she looks at me with her head to one side.

I know I'm not going to like this. I mean, people don't behave this way if they're about to say, "Guess what, I've bought you a present," or, "Congratulations, you've won first prize!"

"Al?" she says.

"Yes?"

"Where did you go last night?"

CHAPTER TWENTY-FOUR

Ages ago, in the time of sadness after Dad had died but before we'd kind of got a bit used to him not being around, Mum went through this weird phase when she kept saying, out loud, "Pye—is that you? Are you there?"

The first time it happened was when we were watching TV. It was November-ish and windy outside, and I heard the front gate rattle and a tin can clatter along the road outside, and that's when she did it. She sat up straight and looked toward the living room door, which was open.

"Pye?" she said. "Who's there? Is that you, Pye?"

Now this freaked me out. I stared at Mum. "What's up, Mum? Why do you say that?"

She had got up and gone to the front door, but soon came back.

"I'm sorry, darling," she said. "It was . . . it was just the wind."

I gave her a look that meant to say, *"Well, duh."*

She didn't mention it again, but she had this faraway look for the rest of the evening. She wasn't really watching the TV, but I didn't say anything.

She did it again, a week or so later. Same thing—she sat up, this time at the kitchen table. "Pye? It's you, isn't it? Are you there?"

"Mum," I said, quite gently I think, "there's nobody there. Are you OK?"

"I'm fine, darling," she said. "Just very tired." She rubbed her forehead with her hand and sighed.

That night I came downstairs because I couldn't sleep again, and I saw her sitting at the table in the dark with her eyes closed and a candle in front of her, very, very still, and I crept back upstairs.

A couple of days later, I was round at Grandpa Byron's and I asked him, "Do you believe in ghosts, Grandpa Byron?"

"What sort of ghosts?"

"Well, you know—spooky ghosts, ghosts of dead people, you know . . . *ghosts*. Spirits."

He thought for a long time. At that time he had started to grow a beard and he looked a bit wild. Eventually he said, "I believe wholeheartedly in the human spirit. In fact, in the spirit of all living things. And I think that spirit inhabits us while we are alive, and departs from us when our physical bodies die, and rejoins the timeless universal spirit, until such a time that it will be part of life once more, possibly in human form, possibly not."

I thought about this, I really did. But I didn't get it. "Is that what Hindus believe, then?"

He gave a little bark of laughter. "No, son. Not exactly."

"Buddhists?"

He shook his head. "Don't think so."

So I asked him again. "Do you believe in ghosts, then?"

"Oh, aye," he said. "Indubitably." And then he added, "But ghosts as you're thinking of them? No."

"So you do and you don't?"

He wobbled his head and smiled. "How accurately you put it, Al. Spot on!"

I had been thinking about this recently, which I guess is how what happened next came about.

And how I dragged Carly into all of this.

CHAPTER TWENTY-FIVE

So Carly is standing in front of me, one hand on her hip, at the end of my bed, waiting for an answer, and all I can do is stare and sort of puff my cheeks out and go *phoo* as I exhale, trying to look thoughtful. This goes on for several seconds.

"Well? Where did you go? I heard you. I heard you on the stairs, and I heard the front door, and I saw you going down the street. You're rubbish at being secret."

My eyes flick from her to the door, to the window, and back to her face. I can feel myself going red.

"Look, Al, I'll make this simple for you. Either you tell me where you went last night, or I tell your mum that her darling widdle baba is prowling the streets in the dead of night, OK?"

I'm still dumbstruck. But I'm forming an idea.

"And, just to be clear, I'm not even guaranteeing that when you *do* tell me I *won't* tell your mum. Just that, well, it's your only chance. All right?"

"It's my dad," I say.

"Your *dad*?"

And that's how it starts: the lie that ends up changing both our lives.

The story seems to just form itself in my mouth without going through my brain.

I nod at her to close the door, mainly to give myself more thinking time.

"I . . . I'm trying to contact his spirit."

"His spirit? You mean, like a séance-type thing?"

"Uh . . . yeah?" I've got no idea what she means, but it doesn't matter, because—brilliantly—she goes on to fill in the details herself.

"Oh. My. God. That is, like, so *totally* freaky-cool. So, like, you're going to some graveyard? To your dad's grave, yeah? To commune with his spirit?"

"Well, he was cremated, actually, so technically there's no grave, but a graveyard is the, um, best place. I think. Yeah."

"Oh, like, totally the best. God, Al, you have *got* to let me come. I'd be like *so* good at it. I've read loads of books about stuff like this."

I'll bet you have, I think.

"Y'know, Carly . . . it's the sort of thing that's best done in private. I think I should—"

"Oh please, oh please, oh please, Al. . . ." And I realize with some satisfaction that for the first time ever since knowing Carly, I have the upper hand. She wants something from me. She is *begging* me. "Let me come or I'll tell your mum," she says, but she's bluffing. Because if Mum or Steve found out, they would prevent both of us going. And Carly knows that. And she knows I know. And she knows that I *know* that she knows, and so I still have the upper hand.

"I'll let you know when the time is right," I say mysteriously. "I think I'm close to a breakthrough to the spirit world."

"Cool. That's, like, just, *awesome!*" She shakes her head slowly in what looks a little bit like admiration for me.

It's a new feeling.

CHAPTER TWENTY-SIX

They say that once you have broken the law once, then doing it a second time is much, much easier, and I can now say the same is true for undertaking crazy schemes involving midnight moped rides and garage break-ins. Now that I know how I'm going to get back there, I'm itching to continue what I started. Terrified as well, obviously, but super-keen not to lose the momentum, the courage that got me started. Now that Carly's involved, though, things have just got tricky. Tricky squared, in fact.

Assuming what my dad wrote in his letter is true, then I have the chance to prevent him from dying and everything will be back to how it was. Otherwise, I'll forever be trapped in this goldfish bowl, with Mum, Burping Steve, and the Stepsister From Hell.

Speaking of Carly, she intercepts me as I come back from Grandpa Byron's after school the next day and starts walking along the road with me, like it's the most normal thing in the world for her. I know what's coming.

"Well? How about it?"

"How about what?" I feel I have to say. I do not want her to start taking this for granted, thinking that we are co-conspirators in this ridiculous séance thing, or to forget that she has blackmailed me into allowing her to participate in it, even though it's completely made up.

"You know," she says wearily.

"Look, it's not the right time." This time, I have thought about it and am better prepared. "There needs to be a full moon."

"I see." She's buying it. Brilliant.

"But I have to do some . . . preparation first. Alone."

She looks at me out of the sides of her eyes, suspiciously. "Don't try to shut me out of this, Al, because . . ."

"I'm not! I just need to do something alone." I pause for effect, and then say something that I think is very clever. "I really need you for this, Carly. The spell requires, um . . ."

"What?"

"You are a virgin, aren't you, Carly?"

"A *what*?"

"You know, someone who hasn't . . ."

"I *know* what a virgin is, Al. And, as it happens, yes, if it's any of your business, of course I am. Jesus." She chews her gum furiously.

"Well, I just had to double-check, you know. A full moon and the presence of a virgin are two of the things I need."

She marches along, arms folded in front of her, practically steaming with indignation.

"Anything else?" she says sniffily.

"Yes, as a matter of fact. Some moonlit earth from the location where the deceased, er . . . deceased." Can you tell I'm trying to make it sound sort of magicky? It's the kind of thing they have in the books Carly reads. That, and spelling *magic* with a *k*.

"So, like, how are you going to do that?"

"I'm going back to Culvercot tonight. By taxi." Now this is risky, but I figure I have sucked Carly in far enough that she isn't going to tell anyone now.

All she says is, "Wow! Frea-ky!"

CHAPTER TWENTY-SEVEN

So it's half past midnight and I'm in a taxi going to Culver-
cot. In my hand is a carrier bag containing Alan Shearer, the
hamster. Well, he's in a little stiff cardboard box that Steve's
smartphone came in, with holes punched in the ends with a
pencil so that he can breathe.

He's going to go in the time machine first. My hamster,
as it were, will be my guinea pig.

Grandpa Byron's moped is still chained to the drainpipe,
and he has not yet got round to hanging a spare key to the
padlock on the kitchen hook, as I discovered after school
when I came up with the new plan. Besides, I was feeling
pretty nervous about risking a second moped ride. What if
the same cops were on duty?

In my money box there was eight pounds in change I'd
been saving—plus the forty I got from Grandpa Byron for
my birthday.

My mobile is supposed to be strictly for emergencies only. This, I figured, counted as an emergency, so I went on-line and booked a taxi from a company in Ashington, which is the next small town up the coast, as I didn't want to use the local company. I arranged a pickup at the corner of our street, and I felt my stomach flutter when I saw the yellow light approaching and I stepped out from the shadows to flag it down. The driver's window opened and he looked me up and down.

"You book a taxi, son?"

"Yeah," I said as casually as I could and reached for the rear-door handle.

"Hang on, hang on," he said, and I heard the *thunk* of the central locking system. "You're a bit young to be tekkin' cabs in the middle of the night, aren't ya?"

I was ready for this. Carly and I had gone over just about every query and hitch we could think of.

"I'm fifteen," I lied. "And besides, my money's as good as anyone else's. And there's a tip." I held up a twenty-pound note. The quoted fare had only been fifteen pounds. Greed got the better of him.

"Go on, then. Get in quick," he said. The door unlocked.

The next bit we'd planned too. I dial Carly's mobile

number from inside the taxi and she picks it up straightaway. I hold my phone so that the driver can hear Carly's voice.

"Hi, Mum, it's me, Freddie. . . . Yeah, I'm in the taxi now. . . . No, don't, I'll let myself in by the garage. . . . Yeah . . . uh-huh . . . only an hour? . . . Well, if you say so, Mum . . . I'll ask if he can take me back."

And this is where I speak to the driver, who has been watching me in the rearview mirror. "Can you take me back in an hour? I'm going to my dad's but my mum wants me home soon."

Now, I'm figuring that two easy twenty-pound fares an hour apart is worth more to him than pootling around trying to pick up little fares in Culvercot past midnight, and that he'll wait. It's a gamble, though, and I haven't really worked out what to do if he says no.

"I'll wait for 'alf an hour but nae more, mind," he says.

"He says half an hour, Mum," I say to Carly, and then to the driver, "She says OK."

He gives me another long look in the mirror, but says nothing. And even if he had, I was prepared with a story about my mum and dad being separated and my dad living with Aunty Ellie and this being the only time I could visit him, or . . . something. To be honest, Carly and I didn't quite put the finishing touches on this story, which we were hoping—correctly, as it turned out—we wouldn't have to use.

Twenty minutes later, we're outside 40 Chesterton Road. I hand over the money as we turn into the street, as I want to be out quickly. I think about asking him to drop me at the end of the street, but it seems suspicious, and besides, a taxi driver with a passenger my age is going to make sure the kid gets safely indoors.

So here I am: the taxi is in the middle of the road, with its engine idling as I nip up the driveway toward the garage doors. The taxi door shuts with a louder noise than I had hoped, and just as I'm squeezing through the gap in the garage doors, it happens: the light goes on in the front bedroom and my stomach lurches.

By poking my head round the gap in the doors, I can see the taxi, and the curtains parting in the bay window above.

It gets worse. The taxi driver gives a wave to whoever is peering through the curtains, points at the garage, and gives a thumbs-up. It's easy to guess what he means: *I've delivered your son safely, and he's comin' in now.*

The taxi pulls away to the parking spot down the road where he said he'd meet me in half an hour. The light's still on upstairs, and the curtain flicks open in the side bay window as the lady looks to where the taxi driver was pointing. As the shaft of light hits the garage door, I pull my head back. Has she seen me? Will she notice that the garage door is ajar?

So I'm waiting until I get the courage to move again when I hear a key in the lock of the door that connects the garage to the house. The door bursts open, the garage light goes on, and whoever opened it sees . . . nothing. For by this stage, I've snuck back *out* of the garage, and I'm crouching down between the Škoda and the hedge. If the person decides to look outside, I'm done for.

A woman's voice comes from inside the house.

"You've got to sort that garage door out, Graham!"

"Yeah, yeah, yeah," Graham says, and pulls the door shut again.

I hear the key in the connecting door and a minute later the light upstairs goes out. I decide to wait at least ten minutes before going in again, so now I'm going to have to work doubly quick.

It's amazing what you can do under pressure, when you don't have time to waste.

I'm quick and I'm quiet getting into the old cellar—under the old planks, through the circular metal submarine door, down the stairs; and I'm sitting at the desk, looking at the wall and taking deep breaths, trying to stop my heart from racing, but I can't—it's just going *thumpa-thumpa-thumpa* in my chest. I've still got Alan Shearer in the box inside the bag, and I take him out and let him have a little run around on the desk: he seems fine.

So there's the zinc tub with the old Mac laptop in it. There's a cable coming out of the back of the laptop leading to a black metal box about the size of a paperback book, and coming out of that are two cords with the strange handgrips—more like huge metal bolts, really—on the end.

There is a metal clasp on the side of the black box, and I flip it open and lift the lid. Inside is a circuit board like I once had in a home electronics kit and two tiny gold-colored rectangles. A long cable is attached to the circuit board, and at the end of the cable is a bare wire with a glob of Blu Tack attached to it.

It all looks as though a six-year-old made it.

My hands are trembling as I plug in the laptop to a wall socket and there's a slight hum and a delay of a minute or two as it runs through its start-up programs, and then the screen comes to life, and the desktop picture appears of Doctor Who and his TARDIS, only not the guy who's the Doctor at the moment but the one from a few years ago whose name I can't remember because I've never really been into *Doctor Who.*

And there's one folder on the screen's desktop, just the one: a little blue square labeled "Al." With my hand on the touch pad, I click on the folder. There are two subfolders inside: one labeled "map," and another labeled "Al." I click on the "map" one first: it's like a simplified version of Google Earth with a grid laid over it and a box for entering map coordinates. There's a look about it that says, *"Don't mess."*

So I quickly close it before I can hit anything accidentally, and open up the one marked "Al" instead. There is a single document inside it, and a dialog box appears, asking me for a password with the question:

Name a well-known homemade go-kart

I smile and type in "The Lean Mean Green Machine," and the document opens.

CHAPTER TWENTY-EIGHT

*Hello, Al, and welcome to your Time Machine.
I know it doesn't look like much, but what were
you expecting—a spaceship?*

(Well—yeah, sort of.)

*Now that you've come this far, I expect you have
a few questions.*

That's one way of putting it.

*Have I tried it? Answer: Yes, and that is why
you are here now.*

*I am writing this on May 14, 2010. You had
your eighth birthday two days ago, and we went
bowling—you, me, your mum, and Campbell from
your class. Is he still your friend?*

(No. I was never all that keen on Campbell Macross, to be honest, but he formed part of Mum's ongoing "Al Needs Friends" campaign. He'd been bowling loads, and insisted that we didn't use the rails at the sides of the lanes. Consequently, all my bowls ended up in the gutter and he won every game and I had to pretend that I didn't mind. Anyway . . .)

Yesterday, I experimented with my time device for the first time. The first thing I did was place a clock in the zinc tub, attached to the wires. I set the program on the laptop for one hour in the future and pressed "Enter."

Everything—the zinc tub, the laptop, the clock—melted away before my eyes like a magic trick.

And then I waited an hour.

Exactly on time, it reappeared.

I filmed it on my phone. Have a look.

There's a break in the text and a little embedded Quick-Time icon. I click on it.

And there's Dad. He's sitting in the same chair I'm in now, and his phone is propped up on the desk filming him. It starts the same way all these selfie films start, with the person being filmed moving away from the device as they've just pressed the record button.

I gasp and then stare at the box on-screen. "Hi, Al," he says. He gives a little wave and smiles his crooked smile. "Check this out." His hand moves forward and picks up the phone, and the picture swings around toward the zinc tub, losing focus for a second or two, then sharpening on the clock in the bottom of the tub.

"Look at the time," says Dad. It's an analog clock, and the hands point to quarter past ten. "Now watch." His hand comes into view and presses "Enter" on the laptop. I can't really see what happens on the screen because it's flickering the way computer screens do on video, but then the picture zooms out as my dad stands up and moves a little bit farther away from the desk, and then it happens—the tub and everything in it just melts away in about a second. It really is like watching a special effect.

Dad turns the camera round to face him and his head fills the little screen. He's grinning like mad. "Crazy, eh? Now I'm going to wait an hour."

The picture cuts suddenly to Dad in the desk chair again.

"OK, it's been fifty-nine minutes and forty-five seconds,"

he says. "Watch what happens now," and he focuses again on the desk. Out of view his voice counts down: "Ten, nine, eight, seven, six, five, four, three, two, one . . ." And just as the tub and its contents had dematerialized, so they reappear on the desk. Dad goes forward with the camera to show the clock face, which still reads quarter past ten.

That's the end of the QuickTime clip, and I immediately replay it. After the third time, I close it down and discover that I'm breathing really fast, either from the shock of seeing my dad and hearing him talk to me, or—apparently—seeing time travel in action (well, I can't be sure).

I read on.

Obviously, I wanted to do it again, so I repeated the whole process, except this time . . . it didn't work.

I tried again and again to send that clock one hour into the future, and again and again I failed. Just nothing happened.

After about the third or fourth go, I changed the coordinates on the laptop to TWO hours into the future. And then I waited, just as before. This time it worked. I then repeated the experiment a few more times, each time with the same result: I couldn't send the clock twice to the same "time."

My conclusion is quite logical when you think about it, but it has pretty profound implications for what I am about to ask you to do.

An object (or a person) may occupy the same dimension of space-time ONLY ONCE.

Of course this makes perfect sense. Otherwise, there may be two, three, or any number of identical people or objects occupying the same space and time. There would be universal, cosmological chaos.

Think about it: you could (theoretically) time travel (say) Big Ben to its existing location one year ago. But where is it going to go? The space occupied by Big Ben is already occupied by Big Ben!

The laws of space-time—even though we may not yet fully understand them—seem to be beauti-fully arranged to prevent such chaos.

But it means you may only travel to any par-ticular location in time and space ONCE.

But would it work with a human? There was only one way to find out, Al. I put the zinc tub on the floor and stepped into it. I set the program for an hour ahead and pressed "Enter."

Now I'm writing this like it was the most normal thing in the world. It wasn't. I was conducting a massive and dangerous experiment and I was very, very scared indeed. But this was the culmination of six years' secret work. I had to know.

And what happened when I pressed "Enter"? Nothing.

I checked the numbers on the program and tried again. Still nothing. Warily, I reset the program for two hours ahead instead of one. Nothing again. A day ahead? Nope.

Checking and rechecking, I was about to give up when I tried one more time, this time programming the time coordinates for two hundred hours into the future—eight days more or less.

And it worked.

CHAPTER TWENTY-NINE

I was paying no attention to the real time—the time on my watch. My dad's words had me spellbound and I read on, transfixed.

It doesn't hurt, Al. You don't feel anything, really, though your vision blurs a little.

In fact, I wasn't even certain that it had happened at all until I stepped out of the tub and checked the date on my phone: eight days had passed.

I wanted to see more—I wanted more proof. So I came out of the cellar and headed into the house.

I really had no idea what to expect, but in my most vivid imaginings I did not anticipate that I had died.

It was early evening when I came from the garage into the kitchen. I heard voices in the living room—your mum's, and a man's voice I didn't recognize. Something made me hold back on my urge to rush through and tell your mum, "Hi—I'm from the past!"

I was also very scared of bumping into myself. My future self. I wasn't aware at that stage that such a thing was not possible—but I'll get to that.

The <u>Whitley Bay Advertiser</u> was on the kitchen table, and I wanted to double-check the date. That's when I saw it. In that moment, everything changed.

The headline on the open page: "Local Man's Tragic Sudden Death: 'Walking time bomb,' says coroner."

The newspaper was open at the page where there was a picture of my dad, one I hadn't seen before. He looked nice. He had a tie on.

Local Man's Tragic Sudden Death
"Walking time bomb," says coroner

A tiny piece of metal lodged in the head of a Culvercot man caused his sudden death, a Tyneside inquest found this week.

Dr. Pythagoras Chaudhury, 39, died at home last week of a subarachnoid hemorrhage, triggered when the metal shard—a few millimeters long—was dislodged.

The Tyneside coroner, Mrs. Heather Neil, said, "This could have happened at any time. Dr. Chaudhury was a walking time bomb."

The computer engineer, the only son of Mr. & Mrs. B. R. Chaudhury-Roy, is survived by his wife, Sarah, and young son, Albert.

The funeral will take place next Thursday at St. George's Church, Culvercot.

That hit me pretty hard, I can tell you, Al. Not many people get to read their own death notice.

I was in a bit of a daze when I wandered through to where the voices were. Your mum was talking to Dennis Harrison, the funeral director. I backed out of the room, and I don't think she saw me.

"No, Dad, she did," I said out loud to no one, and the sound of my voice made me jump.

I kind of panicked. I grabbed the newspaper from the kitchen table, hurried back to the cellar, and reprogrammed the laptop to return me to where—and when—I had begun—that is, eight days before.

And then I sat, in the seat you're in now, in a stunned stupor. I wanted to know more about my death, and—obviously—if it was preventable.

You'll remember that occasionally I suffered excruciating headaches? I just thought they were normal—everyone has headaches now and then, right? I had no way of comparing mine with anyone else's, no way of knowing that mine were a symptom of something much worse. I would take painkillers, and I once consulted my doctor after a particularly bad one that had lasted a couple of days and left me weak and exhausted. But he just prescribed some extra-strength painkillers, which I put in the bathroom cabinet because the pain had gone by then.

That piece of metal in my brain has been moving since it first got there—on August 1, 1984, the day I came off the Lean Mean Green Machine and smashed my face up. Do you remember the story I told about the spike that went up my nose, which someone pulled out? A small piece was left

TIME TRAVELING WITH A HAMSTER

in, and that's the piece that will kill me in a few days' time.

This is where you come in, Al.

I need you to use my device—follow the instructions incredibly carefully—and prevent me from having that accident.

Remove the brick from the path—the one that caused the accident.

Remove the mangled metal trolley from the side of the path.

And Al—come back safely. Remember to keep the laptop with you at all times. Whatever is with you in the zinc tub will travel with you to the space-time dimension that is your destination.

Without it you are, to put it bluntly, out of luck.

I'll bet you have some questions. Let me try to anticipate them.

Why me, why now? As I discovered when I tried to travel an hour into the future, you cannot be in the same place as yourself. This we will call "Dad's Law of Doppelgangers." A doppelganger is a double of yourself. They have existed in stories forever, but for a reason I have yet to discover—but which we might, when we continue my research—the laws of the universe prevent you from encountering your own self. So you cannot go forward, or backward, in time to meet yourself.

For this reason, neither of the two other people I might trust with this could do it—your Grandpa Byron or your mum.

Your mum is a wonderful person, Al—but I don't think she has the courage to help you do this. A mother's instincts are to protect her child. She would stop you. I can't blame her for this, and nor should you. Just don't tell her, OK?

And your grandpa? What can I say, except that—love him as I do—he doesn't trust my work in this area. I tried to talk to him about it once, and he shut me right down. "These are not suitable subjects for study, Pye," he told me. "You are venturing beyond human limits."

Except I don't think there are human limits, Al. Who determines that?

Great question, Dad, I'm thinking. Only not the one that's in my head right now.

And that is: why involve me in all this? Why not just go to the future and *stay there*? You could, I don't know, reappear at your own funeral as your long-lost identical twin or something? I'm thinking this as I read on, and it's like Dad can read my mind.

Do you have *to do this? Well ... I'm hoping not. As I write this, I'm hoping that my first or second plan will work. If neither does, you will be reading this.*

So what's Plan A?

Tomorrow I will present myself at the doctor's, complaining of severe headaches, demanding tests, X-rays, scans, anything I can to stay in hospital so that if—I should say when—the hemorrhage happens, I will be better placed to survive it. If I don't survive it, well—you will get this letter on your twelfth birthday. Risky? You bet.

There is a Plan B as well. (As the great mathematician James Yorke once said, "The most successful people are those who are good at Plan B.")

Plan B is to travel into the future, to a time after I have died and ... carry on living. There is

*(as I discovered) clearly no physical law that pre-
vents me from being in the same space-time dimension as my own corpse.*

*I can only presume that this is to do with notions
of consciousness, or what your Grandpa would call
"eternal spirit," and is among the reasons that I am
so desperate to continue my research.*

*But exactly how this will work I have no idea. I
need a little time to consider this. Do I just reappear
a few days after my funeral ...*

I find myself nodding as I read this. "As your identical
twin!" I say. (I've probably seen this in a movie or read it
somewhere. It's quite dramatic, especially if he grows a mustache or something.)

*... or do I try to time my return to coincide
with my death, without being seen, and somehow
dispose of my corpse secretly, then carry on as if I
had not died?*

My mouth is hanging open at this point.

I know: it sounds unlikely, or impossible, or ridiculous ... or all three. Think about it, Al: can you really see me secretly getting rid of my own corpse?

No, nor can I.

And all the while I will still have this death sentence hanging over me, this piece of metal in my brain, which I will have to deal with—whatever happens.

And so—to you, Al. My Plan C.

There are dangers, for sure. But I trust you, Al. You are now twelve, an age when I believe you will be able to carry out this amazing task, if it is required.

And when it is done, you and I will carry on this work, which will change the world in ways we cannot even imagine, answering questions that have been asked since the beginning of mankind's journey on Earth.

I really don't want you to do this, Al. But if you are reading this, then I promise you there is no other way.

CHAPTER THIRTY

Well, it went wrong, didn't it?

Either his Plan A or his Plan B didn't work out. I don't even know which one he chose. Thinking of my dad, Plan A doesn't sound much like him: faking headaches, making a fuss, demanding this and that. I don't think he'd be very good at that.

I think he probably went for Plan B, but never got that far. I guess that piece of metal in his brain was always going to kill him, one way or another.

And now I'm here (Plan C), with a dry throat and a pumping heart and a dead dad begging for my help.

Now, remember what I have told you, and follow these instructions to the letter.

See the cable with the Blu Tack on the end? Stick the Blu Tack onto the zinc tub. Make sure it's secure and that the wire has contact under the Blu Tack—metal to metal. The other end must connect to the black metal box.

Now copy the code that's written on the top of the black box into the dialog box, but do not press "Enter."

Sure enough, written on top of the black box, in Chinagraph pencil, is a string of letters and digits, like this: WMAGGGGGWVE7G5E8GL2CWG.

Carefully, slowly, with one finger, I copy them into the box on the laptop.

Done that? Now add the precise time and date you wish to travel to, plus your exact coordinates on Earth. 102030071984 will take you back to two days before my accident. Your coordinates here are 2346-8654-7776-9090-8639-1112. Those digits depict the exact cubic meter of Earth's surface that you now occupy. You do not need to go anywhere else.

The program will translate that into the code necessary to generate the mathematical formula required. That in turn will cause the gold and tungsten rods in the black box to create the sub-atomic plasmic vibration that will shift your space-time dimension.

Now take off your shoes, tie the laces together, and hang them round your neck. You need a good connection between your feet and the zinc tub. Sit in it like you are taking a bath.

This is getting stranger, but for some reason I feel no fear as I bend down and undo my trainer laces; fasten my shoes together; and hang them, as the letter said, round my neck.

Grip one of the metal handles in each hand.
Now press "Enter." And wait.

       Bon voyage! Your loving dad.

Well, what would you do?

CHAPTER THIRTY-ONE

I doubt very much you'd do this without testing it first either.

I lift everything—tub, computer, box—off the desk and onto the floor for extra stability. Then I pick up Alan Shearer carefully, encircling his midriff with my finger and thumb like the book says you should, and I lower him into the zinc tub where he scampers around, a bit confused; poor thing. Soon, though, he just sits still, cleaning his whiskers.

I tap super-carefully on the laptop's keyboard: first all the letters written on the black box, then 102030071984, then all the rest of the digits.

That's ten-twenty on July 30, 1984, at precisely this spot.

Then I press "Enter."

A row of figures scrolls up super-fast on the laptop screen, and something strange appears above the zinc tub. The best way to describe it is that it's like a huge, just-visible bubble.

I saw a clown once at a school science day make these enormous soapy bubbles with a loop of string, and it was a bit like that, but less . . . definite. I reach out nervously to touch it, and it doesn't pop. It just sort of shimmers and wobbles slightly.

I am so caught up in looking at this that a few seconds tick by before the stupidity of what I have done dawns on me:

THE TIME MACHINE TRAVELS AS WELL.

In Dad's QuickTime video, the zinc tub disappeared along with the clock.

I'll be sending a hamster in a metal tub through unknown dimensions of space-time with heaven only knows what consequences, and no way of following unless I can somehow build a replica time machine, and at this stage I think that's doubtful.

These thoughts take about two seconds, max, and by the time I've stopped thinking them, I have leaped through the bubble and into the tub, unplugging the laptop from the wall socket and gripping it so hard it might crack as I sit staring at the screen while the numbers continue to scroll up and then . . . just . . . stop.

And nothing happens.

Well, not *nothing,* exactly. But I have to be really careful in describing this, because there is no flash, no explosion, no whooshing noise or wind or electric shock or searing white light or anything. There's only a strange and brief blurring in front of my eyes, as if a huge invisible lens has passed in front of me. I'm still staring at the computer screen, but at the edges of my vision things are out of place, and I slowly take my eyes off the screen and look round.

I'm still in the bunker, but it seems different.

1. Dad's letters have gone from the desk.

2. So has the moldy cup, and I check with my hands where it was, running my palm over the desktop.

3. A minute ago, that would have sent up a small cloud of dust, but now it's clean.

But some things have appeared that weren't there before.

1. On the desk is a half-eaten packet of biscuits.

2. On the floor is a small heap of comic books— *Spider-Man* and that sort of thing. They may have

been there before, but I think I'd have noticed and they're not the sort of thing my dad would have had.

3. On the wall is a dartboard with some tatty darts in it. Again, I think I'd have noticed this before.

Along the wall are the bunk beds, made up as before. There is a box next to one marked DOLE PINEAPPLE—had that been there before? I couldn't be certain.

There's a scratching noise coming from by my feet, and there is Alan Shearer. I scoop him up in my hands.

"Hello, mate! You made it!" He twitches his nose at me and I shove him in the big front pocket of my coat, which I'm pretty certain is not recommended by Dr. A. Borgström in *Hamster Fancying for Beginners,* but it's not going to be for long. Behind me the steps lead up to the door as before, but instead of being old with blistered paint and rust marks, the door is fresh and smooth.

"So that's time travel, then," I say to Alan Shearer out loud. I check myself over—everything seems all right. I put my right foot out and touch the floor beyond the zinc tub like I'm testing the water in a swimming pool. Seems all right, and I'm about to make for the door when I turn back and look carefully at the laptop. This, I realize, will be crucial to getting me back, and I'm nervous in case it's damaged. Its screen is still on, which reassures me, and I turn for the steps and open the steel door.

Crouching, I come out where the stairs are, and the planks are replaced over the hole. I ease a couple of them to one side and climb up the steps into the garage.

Into a different world. Well, the same world, but a different time. You'll get used to it. I did.

CHAPTER THIRTY-TWO

It takes a second or two for me to notice that it's day instead of night.

The sun streams through the bobbled glass of the garage doors, illuminating racks of tools, shelves with plant pots, a lawn mower, and flecks of dust. It smells of cooking, and I can hear a radio playing quite nearby. I'm still in a sort of half crouch as I'm so nervous, and I slowly straighten up and turn around to see that the connecting door to the house is half open and there's the sound of footsteps on a hard floor. Then there is a voice—a woman's voice—and she's in the kitchen only a couple of meters away from me. It's a wonder I can hear anything, so loud is the beating of my heart in my chest.

"How man, Stokoe," she says harshly, "put that doon. You shouldn't be playing with that, you little bleeder!" Her Geordie accent is pretty strong, and I'm just guessing at *Stokoe,* which is what it sounded like, but it isn't a name I've ever heard before.

I'm still in the middle of the garage—it's like I'm stuck with glue—and this kid, who must be about two years old, toddles across the kitchen past the open door, looks straight at me, and points.

"Ba! Ga!" he says, and smiles.

"What is it now, man, Stokoe?" I see the back of the woman as she scoops the baby up, and then she opens the door to the garage fully. "Ba! Ga!" says Stokoe again, and his mum says, "Shut *up*, will ya? There's nowt there," and of course there isn't, for I am now crouched behind an old gas cooker thinking that this is twice in ten minutes that I have nearly been caught breaking into this garage.

I hear her footsteps move away from the door and out of the kitchen, but I stay still for a few minutes, listening as Madness finishes singing "Our House"—I love that song; we did it in a school play once. There's a jingle on the radio that goes "BBC Radio One!" in happy, singy voices, and a man's voice that I think I recognize from a show Mum listens to, except she listens to Radio Two. The man on the radio says, "It's twenty-two Radio One minutes past ten," and I'm wondering how a Radio One minute is different from any other minute, when I figure I'm safe to get out of the garage.

There's no Škoda in the driveway, and no hedge either; just a wooden fence. I nip down the driveway and I'm out on Chesterton Road, and I feel sort of safe out in the open, not having to hide. I cross the road and notice the first thing that's different about 1984. The "jungle," the patch of undeveloped land opposite my house, has been cleared of bushes. It's just bare earth and a few weeds. (I suppose it's more accurate to say that the bushes haven't grown yet, rather than they have been cleared.) In the intervening decades between this time and my time, the neglected patch has been overtaken by the weeds and scrubby bushes, but now it's still just a clearing. There's still an alleyway running down the side and a low wall. I can sit on it and see in both directions up Chesterton Road, and not really be noticed. I take a few deep breaths and look across at my old house and try to notice everything that's different.

The woodwork's painted a different color. When I lived there, the front door and the garage doors were dark red and the window frames were all white. All the woodwork now is a sort of mustard yellow, and it's flaky and needs repainting.

The rest of the street's newer-looking, that's for sure. In

front of where I'm sitting there's usually a big tree, a syca-more that in the autumn sheds seed pods that spin to the ground like little helicopters. Right now it's a spindly-looking thing, still supported by a stake and a canvas strap. The mon-key puzzle tree at old Mr. Frasier's isn't there at all.

Another thing that's not here is cars. Well, there are a few, but they're mainly in people's driveways and there are only five that I can count parked on the street. When I lived here, both sides of the road were pretty much lined with cars. And the ones here look old. That is, new-looking, but old in style, sort of smaller and squarer, except for one *really* old one next to me that I know is a 1950s Austin Cambridge be-cause I have a tiny model one in my bedroom that's exactly the same as one that used to belong to Dad.

Three people have walked past on the other side of the road while I've been sitting here, and I've been check-ing out their clothes. I was expecting crazy, multicolored eighties-style fashions, like Mum and Dad wore once to a costume party, but these people are dressed pretty normally. (At least that's what it looks like to me, but I'm not exactly a fashion expert.) Now there's someone coming up the alley-way behind me, and there's something I need to check, so I stand up and turn to see a middle-aged man holding a pipe between his clenched teeth, which strikes me as pretty funny.

"Excuse me," I say. He stops and takes the pipe out of his mouth, exhaling a plume of smoke. He looks down at me.

"Aye?"

"I wonder if you would mind telling me today's date?" I ask, in my politest talking-to-the-head-teacher manner. The man gives a little smile on one side of his mouth.

"Today's date? Why, laddie, it's the thirtieth of July. Monday, July the thirtieth. And aren't you a wee bit warm in your coat?" He points with the stem of his pipe to my thick coat, which I had put on last night. His voice, a rich Scottish accent, is oddly familiar.

"Ah! Aha—no, I'm fine, er . . . thanks. No, I meant the year. What year is it?"

At this he takes a draw on his pipe and actually smiles with his whole mouth. "The year? Aw, now ye're havin' me on. Have some of your friends dared ye to ask me a daft question?" And he looks up and down the street for the guilty parties.

"No—honestly! I—I've forgotten," I say lamely.

He shakes his head and makes to walk off, putting the pipe back between his teeth. He has taken a few steps on his way, when he turns his head and calls back over his shoulder, "It's 1984, lad, 1984."

I watch him walk up the street and turn into old Mr. Frasier's house, where one day he will plant a monkey puzzle tree.

That's it then. It works.

My dad's time machine works!

That's when I look at my watch, and . . .

I'm not really one to panic, but—with no regard for being discovered—I sprint back over the road and into the garage. It's already ten minutes past the taxi driver's deadline. If I'm stuck in Culvercot in the middle of the night with no means of getting home, then I'm truly out of luck. That's if I even get back to my own time, which I keep telling myself *I will I will I will* because Dad's time machine *works*.

Little Stokoe and his mum are nowhere to be seen, and I slip under the wooden planks and through the steel door in no time.

And now I'm standing in the zinc tub about to press "Enter" again when I have an idea. Fishing my keys from my pocket, I find my key-ring memory stick and plug it into the side of the laptop, then click and drag the folder marked "Al" onto the stick's icon. The "Copying Files" dialog box pops up, and in a few moments, all eight gigabytes of the program will be copied onto my stick.

The progress bar creeps along. Four minutes to go. I'm clenching my fists so hard with tension that it hurts, so I shove them in my pockets, where I find a plastic sandwich bag. I'm supposed to fill it with earth for Carly's spell. Now obviously any old earth is going to do—she won't know—but I feel compelled to do this properly. It's the "precision counts" thing again, and it's better than watching the progress bar, so once again I creep out of the cellar, into the garage, and out into the front driveway where I can scoop up a handful of soil.

A minute later, I'm back in the bunker sitting in the zinc tub, and I press "Enter."

Thank God—the taxi driver's still there, head back, snoring loudly. A few minutes later I'm in the backseat, and I put the sandwich bag in my coat pocket alongside . . . I feel around in my pocket for Alan Shearer. With a lurch in my stomach, I don't find him.

Think, think. I definitely had him when I was talking to Mr. Frasier because I remember him wriggling. And I put my hand in my pocket to protect him as I climbed in through the steel door after collecting soil.

So he *must* be in the underground bunker.

I sit for a few minutes more in a panicked silence. Finally, I say to the driver, "We have to go back."

He looks at me in the rearview mirror.

"You're jokin' aren't you, son?"

"I, er . . . I've forgotten something."

He pulls the car onto the side of the road and stops, with the engine idling. Turning round in his seat, he says, "It's gonna cost you. It's another tenner."

"But I haven't got any more."

"What about yer mam? She'll have it, won't she?"

"No. She, er . . ." I'm thinking hard, but nothing comes out. "She hasn't."

I know: lame, lame, lame.

He starts driving again. "Sorry, son. I don't drive for nowt. Whatever it is you've forgotten, you'll have to get another time."

Alan Shearer's going to have to wait to be rescued.

Back home, before I fall into bed, I look it up on the Web: two days. That seems to be the majority opinion on how long a hamster can survive without food or water. (Again, not an action endorsed by Dr. A. Borgström.)

CHAPTER THIRTY-THREE

The Day My Dad Died

I don't mind if you skip this bit. It's really sad. But you probably didn't know my dad personally, so you may be OK with it.

The thing is, most kids these days don't have to deal with people dying very much, at least not in real life. Don't get me wrong—I think that's a good thing, I really do. It's just that when it happens, we're not ready for it.

Look, take Grandpa Byron. When he was a kid, pretty much everyone in a family he knew, including a boy he played with, was murdered one night just because they were Muslims, or Hindus, or something. Not that that was normal or anything—there was some kind of war or "civil unrest" going on at the time—but still . . .

His own grandpa had lived with Grandpa Byron's family, and died on the veranda one afternoon, and Grandpa Byron discovered him, still holding his teacup. This guy, Grandpa Byron's grandpa, had been taken by his own dad to see loads of men being hanged outside a prison in the city they lived in. Can you imagine that?

My mum's mum, who lives in Ireland, was alive during World War Two, when loads of people died; and her mum, my great-grandma, had four brothers and only one of them lived beyond twenty years old. One was killed by the Germans, one died two days after being born, and one was a fisherman who drowned at sea.

I found all this out after Dad died.

I suppose what I'm trying to say is that in the olden days, people died all the time, and I guess kids just got used to it.

That's scary, isn't it? It keeps me awake sometimes, or it did, at any rate, for a while, until I stopped thinking about it so much.

Dad was really weird in the days before he died. Obviously I know now why that was, but at the time I didn't. He went for a long walk, like *really* long, on his own one day. It must have been a weekend. And he kept hugging me really hard. It wasn't like Dad never hugged me; it's just that he did it more, much more, and harder. It got to the stage when I asked him to stop, and that really hurt his feelings and we had a bit of a row about it, which I'm still sad about, because now I know what was going on. Now I know that he had learned he was going to die.

Then on the night it happened, he just went to bed like normal. He and Mum were reading in bed. Mum put out her light and went to sleep, and when she woke up the next morning he was still there, propped up on the pillows, bedside light on, but dead.

The first I knew about it was Mum coming into my room. She was really, really calm. That's how I knew something was seriously up, because Mum only gets that calm, and talks in her deep, calm voice, when there's something very wrong. If something's gone a bit wrong, like she's burned the dinner, or dinged the car again, she'll be all, "oh oh oh!" and flapping around; but if it's something serious, she'll be all calm, like when I was six and she told me that the baby brother she was growing for me had died inside her tummy.

She sat on my bed in the same place that Dad usually sat when he told me stories.

"Al," she said, "wake up. I have something important to tell you."

I was awake straightaway.

"Your dad has been taken very ill in the night. The doctors

will be here any minute. I need you to be very grown-up, and get dressed quickly."

I'm sorry. Do you mind if I don't write the rest of this? It's making me really sad.

You kind of get the idea, though, yeah?

CHAPTER THIRTY-FOUR

The days and weeks that followed were all a bit of a blur, to be honest, and it was all so crazy sad that I've forgotten quite a lot of it on purpose—I mean, properly forgotten it.

There was an inquest, which is a legal inquiry they always do when someone dies unexpectedly—I think it's to make sure that they haven't been murdered or anything. Dad died of a subarachnoid hemorrhage, which is very rare, and sometimes happens if there's a history of it in the family (which there isn't in ours), and sometimes just happens. That's what happened to Dad. They discovered afterward that it had been caused by a piece of metal lodged in his brain that had moved about and then—bam—the lights went out.

His accident, I know now. The one I have to stop.

Then there was the email that Mum sent to Aunty Ellie. I wasn't looking for it or anything; it's just my laptop had been going a bit mental because of some virus it got when I tried to download a game for free from a torrent site, so I borrowed Mum's to look up something for my homework, and there it was, and I just sort of read it.

Hi, E.

Thanks for being so good on the phone last night. You're a star, sis.

Things are just mad here, but like I said, people have been so kind. Byron came round this morning, and God, he looked awful, he seems to be about twenty years older.

Don't know when the funeral will be yet for certain, prob a week on Thursday. Dr. Bannerjee confirmed that it was SAH and as far as he was concerned there were no suspicious circs (obvs) and that the inquest should be straightforward, and they release the body to Harrison's who are doing the funeral.

Got a call from Pye's sister, Hypatia—remember her? All big hair and fake nails. She's flying back from Canada. Not a peep from her for years, and now she's all concerned. I wish she had called him more often.

Listen to me, L—I'm planning a funeral and I'm only 38. I've been OK the last few days; I just can't shake off the guilt that something was troubling P and he couldn't tell me, and the stress of it brought on the aneurysm. I can't put my finger on it, but he wasn't himself. He and Al had some row, which neither of them would talk to me about, and P and I were tetchy for days and I'm super-guilty about that.

Oddest of all, though: he went to see Jack Robson, the solicitor, last week to talk about OUR WILL. We made a will when we had Al and haven't touched it since. JR said he made no alterations, just wanted to check that everything was in order because we'd lost our copy of it (true!) and could he post us a new copy, and that was it.

How weird is that, L? JR reckons it was definitely just a coincidence, and that he's not going to bring it up, least of all at the inquest because that would just confuse and delay matters, but I mean . . . WHAT? Anyone would think that he knew he was going to die, but that's not true; he was healthy and everything.

Maybe I'm just being overanalytical. The solicitor's probably right, but it's still weird, isn't it?

Al's bearing up, but God he's going to find it hard in the next few months and years. That's what I find more upsetting than anything.

Thanks for your offer to take him for a few days. I think he'd like that: getting away from here for a little while. But not too long—I need him here; he's the man here now.

Steve from work has been great too. Did I tell you he lost his wife three years ago? Cancer. Life's a bitch, L.

Sarah

x

CHAPTER THIRTY-FIVE

Ten Things I Know About Steve

1. He's old, like in his fifties. He has white hairs on his chest and a potbelly. I don't know what Mum sees in him, really.

2. He and Mum met at Mum's work. She's a librarian and so's he, but in a different branch, or the head office, or whatever they have in libraries.

3. The first time I met Steve, I knew he'd end up as my stepdad. Mum had mentioned him a few times, and then one weekend he took me and Mum to Chessington World of Adventures. That's what Mum said, anyway: "Steve's taking us to Chessington World of Adventures," but what she really meant was "Steve

and I are taking *you* to Chessington World of Adventures because I really want you to like him." That's when I knew.

4. The first time he stayed over at our house, I couldn't sleep in case I would hear them, you know, doing it. But I don't think they did. Mum's a bit old-fashioned like that. (Not long afterward, I went to stay with Aunty Ellie for the weekend and I'm fairly sure he stayed with Mum then, because when I got back there were two cereal bowls in the dishwasher.)

5. He thinks Carly is the funniest person in the world. "Sassy" he calls her, but I think she's just rude to him. And Mum.

6. He got a bit drunk last New Year's Eve and gave me a big hug and twenty pounds. He called me "a little smasher."

7. Steve's house is smaller than the one Mum and I used to live in with Dad, but Mum said we had to move for "financial reasons" and that even my offer

of getting a Saturday job wasn't enough. So that's why I had to move schools as well. My friends from primary all went to Sir Henry Percy Academy. That said, I didn't have many friends at primary either.

8. Steve loves football. I don't, as I think I've mentioned.

9. Steve is a Good Man. I've put this one in because it's what Mum says all the time. That's only nine things, but it doesn't really matter—oh, I've got one.

10. He burps really loudly. I thought it was funny at first. It's not; it's pretty gross really.

So that's Steve. I kind of wish I liked him more. Perhaps it's just because I miss Dad.

CHAPTER THIRTY-SIX

Steve has waited till Mum is out of the room; then he lets it rip.

Bburrrrp!

"What about that one, then, Al?" he asks.

I try to smile, but I'm miles away. I've got *The Memory Palaces of the Sri Kalpana* open on my lap, but I'm barely even reading it.

"What's up, Al? You've been on another planet for days now."

"You're close, Steve: not another planet, but another dimension of space-time, actually. 1984 to be exact, thanks to a revolutionary algorithm perfected by my late father that mathematically compresses disparate cosmic dimensions to permit physical shifts between them, as postulated in Albert Einstein's theory of special relativity. And my hamster, which you named Alan Shearer after some footballer, is currently starving to death in the dimension we call the 1980s."

OK, I don't say that. What I really say is "Yeah, sorry. I'm just . . . really tired, that's all."

"School holidays soon, son. And then it's . . . Anglesey!"

"Yay!"

I try to sound enthusiastic, I really do. There are kids in my class—the Jennings twins, for example—who have never really been on holiday. Their mum is disabled and their dad works for the company that cleans the school, and they're just really poor, and besides, their mum can't leave the house much. I tell myself that they would love a week in a caravan in Wales, and I tell myself not to be such a spoiled brat, and I tell myself it'll be nice for Mum, but still . . .

It's me, and Steve, and Mum in a caravan for half term. Carly's not coming. She's been invited to Jolyon Dancey's parents' cottage in Norfolk. It's not just her, there's others, because apparently it's huge. Jolyon's dad will be "making an appearance," she says, making him sound like a celebrity.

As for the caravan, we went on a similar thing last year, in Minehead. I hated it. Carly came that time, but she hardly spoke to me. The caravan site had a kids' club, and by the second day the other kids had all made friends with each other, but I hadn't. Whenever a game required you to form pairs, I was the one left out that the leader had to partner with. I stopped going in the end.

Holidays with Mum and Dad weren't like this. I was still on my own, but it didn't feel lonely, probably because Dad and I would hang out together, or play some sort of game that didn't involve a ball.

That's the thing with Steve. If ever he sees me sitting on my own, reading or just daydreaming, he's like, "Come on, on your feet, let's have a game of footie!" and then we're outside and I'm either trying to take penalties at him, or—worse—he puts me in goal and fires shots at me *really* hard, which I have to try and stop. I'm not very good. He keeps shouting things like, "Use your hands! You're the only one on your team who's allowed to, so stop trying to kick it away!" And when I get mud all over me, he's delighted. Unlike Mum, it has to be said.

Anyway, Dad didn't do stuff like that. If he saw me reading, he'd most likely ask me what it was, and it would usually be something he had read himself years ago, or if it wasn't, he'd ask me about the plot and be interested and try to guess the ending.

Today is Sunday, and Grandpa Byron's taking me out. He always asks me where I want to go.

Today there is only one place, and I have Formulated a Plan.

CHAPTER THIRTY-SEVEN

So—Grandpa Byron's book. Tough going, that's for sure, but pretty cool all the same.

I'm going to tell you a bit about this memory palaces thing, but not too much because I don't want to distract you, but I do want you to understand it because it's kind of relevant later on. (This is much, *much* cooler than the kings and queens rhyme, by the way.)

Basically, you have to imagine places—rooms are best— that you're very familiar with, and then make all sorts of crazy images in your head that link the things in the room with the things you want to remember.

For example, if you want to remember three random items—say a chimpanzee, a tractor, and some chewing gum—then first imagine you're standing on your doorstep and walking into your house.

The first mental image you make is of your front door.

You're about to go in when a chimpanzee's arm shoots out of the letter box and grabs you by the throat. It's a huge, hairy, smelly arm, and you're wrestling with it. (That's the point, by the way: you've got to make it a vivid mental image. Something boring doesn't stick in your head.)

Now, assuming you've overcome the imaginary chimp attack, you're through your front door, and what do you come across next? In my house, it's the doormat. Except in my imagination, now the doormat is transformed into a mini-field. The coconut matting has been plowed into lines by a tiny tractor that's driving up and down the mat, and I have to be careful not to step on it. So that's mental image number two.

Next it's the coatrack. We have loads of hooks for coats by the door—but now the hooks have been replaced by huge lumps of used chewing gum. Instead of hanging your coat up, you stick it to the wall with a claggy piece of gum.

I know—it's stupid, but it's also funny and it makes you remember stuff. Now obviously, doing it with three items is pointless. Anyone can remember a list of three things. But what about ten, or twenty, or a hundred?

In *The Memory Palaces of the Sri Kalpana,* Grandpa Byron talks about Indian mystics who—in their heads—had room after room after room, and these rooms would have doors off them leading to other rooms, and gardens, and antechambers, and forests, so that they could store and memorize anything they wanted, all with these crazy imaginary pictures.

I've started trying to do it. I can easily do ten things, maybe twenty.

And here's the thing about Grandpa Byron. All that stuff, all that knowledge that he uses to answer quiz questions? That's him just playing. The real stuff in his main memory palace is his life memories—the recollection of daily events back to when he was a kid. Memorizing things like the *Guinness World Records* he just does for fun.

CHAPTER THIRTY-EIGHT

Culvercot on a quiet spring Sunday is nothing spectacular. The sea's way too cold for swimming or even paddling (though you can in August and September, if you're brave or under five), and there's not much to do since Arnold Palmer Crazy Golf closed down, but there's a café; a fish and chip shop; Spice of the Sands tandoori, of course; and not too many people, although enough to give it a bit of a buzz.

Grandpa Byron and I are on the small cliff top overlooking the main bay. A breeze from the sea is blowing his saffron robes about, and there's a strong, cool sun. On the sand are dog walkers and dogs and a couple of brave families with deck chairs and thick pullovers. Grandpa Byron takes a deep breath of the wind, closes his eyes, and smiles. Time to start my plan.

I try to say, dead casually, "Shall we, y'know, go and have a look at the old house?"

Of course, Grandpa Byron knows that I would want to do that, and isn't fazed at all. You see, if I had been with Mum, she'd have said, "Oh, Al, what do you want to do that for? That's our *old* house. You don't want to be reminding yourself of that. You've got to look forward . . ." and so on. She'd worry that I was "wallowing in the past" and getting all sad for Dad.

Grandpa Byron, on the other hand, just looks at me and winks. "Reckon you know the way?"

We walk up the alleyway from the seafront toward Chesterton Road, past the jungle of scrubland where the foxes lived, and we look at the house from across the road. All the time I'm thinking about how I'm going to get into the cellar to retrieve Alan Shearer without Grandpa Byron knowing. You know how I said I'd Formulated a Plan? Well, to be honest it had some gaps in it.

"Still looks the same," I say.

Grandpa Byron sniffs a bit disapprovingly. "Could do with a lick of paint."

We cross the road for a closer look. "Doesn't it seem a bit nosy?" I say.

Grandpa Byron gives a little laugh. "This is a public street and it's just a house. We're allowed to be looking!"

Just then a lady comes out the front door, and I tug at Grandpa Byron's sleeve. "Come on," I say urgently.

"Well, that really would look suspicious, wouldn't it? As if we're going to break in. Just say hello." And true to his word, he calls a hearty, "Good morning, madam!" to the lady.

She looks at Grandpa Byron in his robes and me in my jeans, and says, "Good morning," a bit warily, if you ask me.

"My grandson used to live in this house. He wanted to see it again!"

She relaxes and smiles. "Oh yes! I remember you—my, haven't you grown! How are you?"

"Fine, thanks." And I smile a polite smile.

She's sort of old middle-aged, this lady, older than Mum but not as old as Grandpa Byron, and she's got short grayish hair and glasses like a teacher. She looks back at the house and pulls a face.

"We haven't done much to it since we bought it," she says. "It's still exactly the same. But all that's going to change."

"Oh yes?"

"Yes, we're putting in a conservatory at the back and that old garage is coming down to make way for an office for my husband."

I feel as if the air has suddenly been forced from my chest.

"The . . . the garage?" I croak.

"Yes. Oh, it's such a mess. I expect you know all about the underground shelter."

"Oh, er . . . yes. I think so." I'm trying to sound unconcerned and casual, but I think I'm coming across as some sort of half-wit. Grandpa Byron's looking at me like I've lost it.

"Well, we had a look down there a few weeks ago. I think your dad, rest his soul, was using it as an office. There were a couple of old computers down there and stuff, but still the old bunk beds, and a toilet. Quite remarkable."

"But . . . but the entrance to it is still blocked up," I say, and then I have to add, lamely, "I suppose?"

The lady looks at me intently, and I compose my face into the blankest of innocent expressions. It seems to work.

"Yes. Well, we'll have to clear it out again when we get started."

Now I really want to know when this is, but I've already spoken too much so I'm keeping my mouth shut, and thank God for Grandpa Byron who says, out of polite interest, "When are you commencing the work?"

"Tomorrow or Tuesday. That's when the men are scheduled to start. But you know what they're like, these builders. Never one hundred percent reliable, eh?" She and Grandpa

Byron both chuckle at their shared familiarity with feckless builders.

"Anyway," she says, brightly. "Got to go. Meeting my husband; nice to see you!" And she gets into the Škoda that's in the driveway and drives off with a little wave.

As I take my hand out of my pocket to wave, a woollen glove falls to the ground, and it gives me an idea.

CHAPTER THIRTY-NINE

Try as I might, I just can't find the appetite for fish and chips because I have to get back to the bunker, without Grandpa Byron, and rescue Alan Shearer—and Grandpa Byron has noticed a change in my behavior, I can just tell.

Still, time to put the plan into action. I pull my remaining glove from my pocket and pretend to look for the other one.

"I've lost my other glove," I say. Then, "I think I know where. I think I dropped it outside our old house."

"Don't worry," says Grandpa Byron. "We'll go past on the way back and pick it up."

But by then I'm halfway to the door.

"Don't worry. It's not far. I'll go and get it." And I'm out the door while Grandpa Byron's saying, "But Al—your fish and chips!"

It really isn't far to our old house from the chip

shop—maybe half a mile, maybe less, but I sprint all the way, and I'm wheezing and light-headed by the time I get there. So long as I can get inside without being detected, get down into the bunker, and grab Alan Shearer, I'll be back in a few minutes—no sweat.

Fine. Yeah, fine. I take a deep breath, look up and down the street, cross the road, and go up the driveway of my old house, and as I slip though the broken garage door, I catch a glimpse of a silver Škoda coming round the corner and up the road.

No chance of moving slowly and silently now. Like I'm demented, I fling off the planks covering the steps. I'm turning the wheel that opens the steel bunker door as I hear the engine of the Škoda coming up the driveway, and the driver's door opening.

I'm closing the steel door behind me when I hear the garage door scrape up and a muffled man's voice mutter, "Bloody Nora!" Then, "Bella! Have you seen this? Have you been in here?"

Inside the bunker, I switch on the light. There's no sign of Alan Shearer, but I haven't got time to look properly because the man's footsteps are coming down the little stairway toward the bunker door.

"Oh my word, Graham!" says the lady I was talking to before. "Someone's been here!"

I know what's coming next, so I grab my side of the metal wheel that opens the steel door and hold it as tight as I can when the man tries to turn it.

"It's stuck," he says, but gives another tug to try it. My arms are aching. "I need something to lever it open."

His footsteps are retreating again, but I know I'll be no match in strength when he comes back with something to force the door, and I can hear him poking around in the garage.

I'm trapped. I scan the bunker, desperately looking for a hiding place. Under the bed? Too obvious. Behind the door? Not enough room.

There is one escape route, though.

Releasing the handle, I dash down the steps to the laptop and turn it on.

"Come on, come on!" I'm muttering at the screen as it goes through its start-up stuff. There's a broom in the corner of the bunker, and I grab it and shove it through the spokes of the wheel handle. It'll buy me an extra few moments.

I can hear the guy coming back across the garage floor now. "This'll shift it," he says to his wife.

I'm in the tub and typing in the password now—the Lean Mean Green Machine—and waiting again for the program to load. When it does, I type in the letters copied from the top of the black box: WMAGGGGGWVE7G5E8GL2CWG.

Then the time and coordinates like before, and I wait.

And nothing happens. I can hear Graham at the door, and he's trying to get in and the time machine's not working, and I'm hitting the "Enter" button again and again, but all that happens is . . . nothing.

I'm going to be caught.

CHAPTER FORTY

Then something unexpected happens and I am overcome with calm. Although I can hear Graham rattling the door and scuffling outside, there is not a single bit of me, not an atom, that is panicking.

My breathing steadies, and I hear my dad's voice as if he's right next to me. I even turn my head slightly in a reflex to where I hear it, but of course it's all my imagination. The only noise is the creaking of the wooden broomstick as it resists Graham's assault.

It's suddenly clear to me exactly what I have done wrong. The words Dad wrote come back to me:

The laws of space-time seem to be beautifully arranged to prevent such chaos.

I cannot go back to the same place and time I was in before: it has already been occupied—*is* already occupied—by me.

With my fingers hitting the keys noisily, I retype the co-ordinates, altering the time to an hour later in the day, and two things happen simultaneously.

1. I hear a crunch as the broomstick bends and snaps, but the remaining pieces are still holding the door shut, just.

2. I see Alan Shearer scampering across the floor of the bunker.

Without thinking, I leap out of the tub, kicking the swivel chair aside, to scoop him up. I shove him in my pocket, grab the laptop and the handgrips, and get back into the zinc tub.

"Did you hear that, Bella? I reckon there's someone down there!"

The pieces of broomstick finally give up and fall to the floor. The wheel is turning when I press "Enter," and the room goes blurry.

CHAPTER FORTY-ONE

In case you were wondering, I don't know much about the "theory" of time travel, or the rules, or what you can and can't do.

I don't think anyone does, really.

I've heard of the "Grandfather Paradox," which says that if you go back in time and murder your grandfather (nice) then you cease to exist, supposedly, because if he's dead he will not have fathered your dad, and he in turn will not have fathered you. And I know about Dad's Law of Doppelgangers, because he told me about it. But I don't know much else apart from what I've learned from watching bits of *Star Trek* and *Doctor Who,* and in those it seems like anything goes, which is handy for the writers, I suppose, but doesn't help me at all.

And besides—who invented these "rules"? As far as I can tell, it's all theory—no one has tested anything, although it seems as though Dad's Law of Doppelgangers is holding up pretty well to real-life experimentation.

So I don't know what to expect. I just know I'm relieved as anything when the haziness in my eyes clears, and I'm still in the bunker, but there's no man trying to get in.

I get out of the tub and sit in the desk chair for a minute, letting Alan Shearer run over my hands. He seems pleased to see me, at least. I pop him in a large, loose-fitting drawer under the bunk bed while I work out what to do next.

What has happened with that man, Graham? He will have entered the bunker and seen that the light was on and the swivel chair turning around, but nobody there at all. How spooky will that have been?

Of course, the sensible thing to do, now that I've got Alan Shearer, would be to head straight back to what I have begun to think of as "real time," and Grandpa Byron, waiting in the chip shop. After all, if I don't come back straightaway, he'll start to get worried and come looking for me.

Trouble is, of course, I can't: Graham is waiting there. It's like I'm trapped in a sort of time cupboard in the garage—as soon as I come out, Graham will see me.

My first thought is to set the return time to the present

to just a minute *before* I reached my old house, coming from the chip shop.

But that is a direct violation of Dad's Law of Doppelgangers. If it was possible, I would bump into myself heading *into* the garage, and as I have just discovered, the time machine won't permit that.

The other option is to set the return time to a little later, say twenty minutes, and hope that by then Graham and Bella have stopped stalking the garage looking for an intruder. Except that wouldn't work either. The pesky doppelganger thing means that I—or a version of me—am already there.

I admit it: I'm stumped. Sometimes, though, when you have to think of an answer but none will come, you just need a little time.

Meanwhile, I can't resist taking another look at 1984.

I come out of the cellar and into the daylight again.

It's still Radio One playing, and the same presenter, and I can hear him say, "It's eleven-twenty-three here on Radio One, and this is Cyndi Lauper with 'Time After Time.' . . . "

In the garage everything is the same, but there's no sign of little Stokoe or his mum.

Outside I feel even more nervous than the last time I was

here, as if someone might recognize me. Silly, I know, but that's how it feels.

And here comes not-all-that-old Mr. Frasier, walking in the other direction this time, away from his home. I decide to try something.

"Excuse me," I say. "What year is it, please?"

He glances down at me, but he barely even stops. "Get awa' wi' ye," he says without removing the pipe from between his teeth. "Y'cheeky wee sod." And he strides on past.

Strange, I'm thinking. But then, I'm dressed differently from the last time; I think I phrased the question differently last time too, Sunday-best polite, and so he reacted differently.

I carry on down the alleyway thinking about the last time. Did it exist? It did for *me* but did it for Mr. Frasier? Was he rude to me because I had already asked him the same question an hour ago? Or am I in a completely different 1984?

And if that lot wasn't enough to make my head spin, as I carry on walking down the alleyway, what happens next puts it in actual danger of just going, like, *BOOOM!*

I meet my dad.

CHAPTER FORTY-TWO

OK, so how I meet my dad is really unpleasant, but I thought
I'd better say exactly how it was.

You know there are loads of things that everyone thinks
are true that aren't? Such as "you can see the Great Wall of
China from space." No, you can't, not even from the Inter-
national Space Station, which is only 248 miles up in space.

All right, here's another one that I looked up on the Internet. "A hat stops you from getting cold because you lose half
of your body heat through your head." Mum is always telling
me this, so I checked, and in children it's actually only about
10 percent.

But you can be pretty sure that this one—that I have just
made up—is true: "Kids who mistreat animals are bad news."
This is about to be proven to me.

It's 1984, July 30, a bright day, but there's a chilly breeze
coming off the sea (Mum calls it a "fret," which I think is a

Geordie word) and a slight haze in the air. I had zipped up my hoodie when I came out of the garage, and I'm heading down the alleyway toward the seafront. The alleyway cuts through another row of houses and comes out on the coastal road, and I cross the road toward the beach.

Straight ahead of me on the sand, as I come down the slipway to the beach, is a group of kids a bit older than me, mostly, though there's one little kid of about six in an anorak with the hood pulled up.

I have turned the corner and seen them, and I would turn back, except the biggest one has seen me and there is something about him that tells me that if I turned and backed away, he would follow.

It's like a sign of weakness. So I decide that the only thing I can do is shove my hands in my pockets, hold my head up, and walk past them, being very, *very* careful not to catch anyone's eye, especially the big kid's, who in any case has turned his attention back to the group, having evidently decided that I am not worth his attention, which is fine by me, thank you very much.

By now I'm about twenty meters from the group, and I can see there's five of them, and they're kind of circled around the big kid, whose back is to me. He's picked up a shoe box from the ground and taken the lid off. They gather round to look in and then all make a collection of noises.

"Eugh, Macca, man! Where'd you get it?"

"It was trespassin.' An' trespassers will be persecuted. With me air rifle!"

"Awww! That's nasty!"

"Uuuuuurh!"

Then, most chilling of all, from a kid with a high-pitched voice, "Aw, Macca, man—it's still alive!"

"Not for long, hur hur! Go on, Chow—go on an' do it," says the big kid, and the others laugh. It's not a good laugh: there's a meanness to it and it's a bit forced. It's hard to describe, but it puts me further on edge.

I'm about five meters away now, and I am *so* not looking in their direction, and all of this is happening to the side of me.

Again the big kid says, "Do it, Chow—do it now, or are you too chicken?" and again the others cackle, and the kid called Chow, who has his back to me, takes something out of his pocket—like a flattish, square tin—and as I pass them the big kid says, "Hold on," and the others glance in my direction.

He's holding up the action until I pass, and at that point, I run toward them, delivering a flying kick in the groin to Big Kid. The others all scatter and I am a hero.

Nope, not really. What I really do is dart past as quickly as I can, and my not-looking-at-them bit has become so extreme that I practically have my head turned to one side because the thing that anyone in my position would dread at the moment is hearing the words, "Oi—what you lookin' at?"

I've already seen enough of the big kid anyway to know that I really don't want anything to do with him. His hair's cut bristle-short, and despite the chilly breeze, he's wearing only a red-and-white-striped football shirt stretched over his stomach, which is almost fat, but not quite. It's his neck that scares me, though: thick and short and pink and aggressive.

I'm at a safe distance, and there's a sort of bend where the beach path goes round a cliff and I'll soon be out of their sight, when I hear the chant start:

"Do it! Do it! Do it!"

I try to imagine what it is they're going to do, and to what, but I can't, or perhaps my imagination just won't go far enough in that direction.

"Hold on, hold on," says Big Kid, who must be the one they are calling Macca. "Have you ever seen a cat bark?"

And that's when my stomach kind of drops because:

A) I know the answer to this question. It's a joke that went around our class. And:

B) I'm going to have to stop them. I know that. I just don't know how.

"No, I'm telling you, I can make a cat go *woof*. Give me that." There's a pause and I can hear some splashing on the ground. The others are like, "Oh, man! C'mon, Macca, don't be mental."

I'm sort of paralyzed.

The joke goes like this.

"How do you make a cat bark? Soak it in petrol and set fire to it: *Woooof!*"

OK, so perhaps it's not the funniest joke in the world, and it's a bit cruel. But when I first heard it, I laughed, because it's so silly. When Hector Houghman told it to me in the playground, he made a little pause before saying "woof," which I suppose is "comic timing," which made it funnier, and besides, no one would really set fire to a cat, would they?

"Right, who's got the matches?" says Macca.

In my jeans pocket, my hand closes around my mobile phone, and I get an idea.

There's the rasp of a match being struck on the box. "Listen," says Macca. "You are about to hear, for the first time in nature, a cat go *woof*."

I step out from behind the jutting-out rock and shout, "Stop! Stop!" just like that, and start running toward the group. I thought it would be Macca holding the match, but it isn't: it's the kid called Chow who chucks it away behind him as soon as I approach. In fact, all of them edge back a little and look down at the sand.

All but one. Macca folds his arms and takes one step forward, nearer to the box so that he's standing right over it. I can see into the box, and sure enough, there's a cat in there, and it's alive (I think) and its fur is wet, and I can see the container that Chow is holding: it's lighter fluid.

They really were going to do this.

Macca cocks his head back and looks at me through his piggy, bulbous eyes. He isn't moving anywhere for anyone.

"Who. The hell. Are you?"

Now I hadn't really thought this through, as you will gather. I'm kind of winging it.

"The cat. It belongs to me, well, to my, er . . . my gran.

Me nan. Me nana. It's me nana's cat. I came out lookin' for it."
In the space of a sentence, my voice has shifted to a slightly
stronger Geordie accent. I need to get Macca on my side, and
this is one way of doing it.

I can see Macca is a bit thrown by this. It's one thing to
fire an air gun and set fire to an anonymous cat. It's different
when the supposed owner of the cat's grandson is standing in
front of you. Even morality can be relative.

Macca's eyes have narrowed to tiny slits. I'm not sure that
Macca's morality is like other people's.

"He was trespassin' in me garden. Me garden's full of
cat crap. Me little brother, Stokoe, got it on his bare feet the
other day." He says all of this as if it justifies the subsequent
torture.

"Look, I'm sorry. How about . . ." I hesitate because I
know this is risky, but I can also see that Macca isn't much
moved by my imaginary grandmother's plight. "How about
we swap?"

I take my phone out of my pocket and hold it up.

The others peer at it curiously. Macca, arms still crossed,
glances at it.

"A pocket calculator? What do I want one of them for?"

"It's not just a pocket calculator. It's got a built-in camera too! Look"—I point it at Macca—"Smile!" Amazingly, he does. Not a proper smile: it doesn't reach his little eyes, but the corners of his mouth turn up. I show them the picture, and they gasp appreciatively.

(I should point out, by the way, that my phone is *rubbish*, with push buttons and everything, and I can't make a phone call with it, because:

1. There are no mobile phone towers, or networks, or anything in 1984.

2. No one else in 1984 has got a mobile, so who would I call?

For a brief moment, though, I wonder if I'd be able to call through space-time to Mum or someone. That would be so cool. But there's no signal, obviously. Anyway, this lot are fascinated.)

I take another picture: this time a selfie of me and the kid, Chow. I show Macca which button to push, and how to make it show the photo. He has it in his hands and is turning it over, impressed.

"A swap, eh? This thing for a half-dead cat?"

I nod.

"What are y'gonna do wi' the cat?"

I shrug. "Dunno. Take it back to me nana's?"

Macca looks at me fiercely. "One word. One word of this gets out and you, my friend, are history." At that moment, I believe him. He pockets my phone and says to the others, "Come on. Leave this loser with his nana's cat."

Then he walks away, and the others follow.

And I'm stuck with a cat I don't know what to do with.

CHAPTER FORTY-THREE

I'm standing there, and without any warning I start sobbing for the poor cat, still alive, curled up in the box; then I hear a noise behind me and I swing round just in time to see a shape dart behind an upturned fishing boat that's been dragged up onto the shingle.

I should, of course, be more cautious, but I reckon that if someone is trying to avoid being seen by me, then they're probably not a threat.

"Hello?" I call, softly. "Who's there?"

No reply. I walk over to the boat and look around the side. Crouched down, facing away from me, is a boy in a blue satiny bomber jacket. This was the kid they were calling Chow. He doesn't turn round. Instead he says, "I didn't mean to. Honest. They made me do it. Macca and them."

I'm looking down at him, and I realize that this kid is the owner of the girl's voice I had heard.

Slowly, he emerges from his crouched position and stands up to face me. His eyes are red and wet, and he's still half cowering away from me, like he expects me to hit him or something.

"Are you the one they were calling Chow?" I ask. He nods: a short bob of the head.

That's when I know.

There were plenty of other clues I could have picked up on: the darker skin color, the high voice; but it was the short nod of his head that was so familiar to me. At this point, it would have been really dramatic if I had fainted on the sand or something. You know—rushed up to him and given him a big hug and said, "Daddy! My Daddy!" like the girl at the end of *The Railway Children,* but that would have been completely weird—apart from the fact that it is simply not how I felt. I read once in the newspaper about a lady who was in a boating accident with her husband, and at the moment she realized he was dead, she was trying not to drown, and she became super-calm and started planning his funeral. I suppose I felt a bit like that, but at the same time the next words I speak are pretty much whispered.

"Are you . . . Pye Chaudhury?" I ask.

"How do you know that?"

CHAPTER FORTY-FOUR

That isn't a question I am about to answer quickly, at least not until I can think of a plausible lie, and there isn't any thinking room in my head right now. It seems like the available space is taken up with the new knowledge that this skinny brown kid in the satin bomber jacket is my own father. The man who kissed me goodnight, who told me stories about when he was growing up (although none of them ever included a half-dead cat), and I'm just standing there looking him up and down stupidly, for I've no idea how long until he says it again.

"How do you know my name?"

With a real effort of will I force myself out of my daze. Instead of answering his question, I create a diversion by saying, "Hang on. Is that them coming back?" I look up the bank at a family walking along the top. It's pretty weak, but it works. Pye ducks down and looks up cautiously.

"No. Not them. So, how—"

"Come on, what are we going to do with this poor cat?" We look at it for a bit. I can see it breathing, because its tortoiseshell fur is moving up and down, but I can also hear it gasping a bit, and there is blood gathering in the bottom of the box.

I have not given away my mobile phone to a psychopath just to watch a cat die in front of me.

"Mr. Frasier," says Pye. "He's a vet." With that, he bends down and picks up the box. "Come on, then."

I had not known that Mr. Frasier used to be a vet. In my time he's old and retired.

As Pye trudges through the dry sand ahead of me, carrying the heavy box, I'm free to stare at him. He makes little noises as he breathes out through his nose, tiny little grunts of air with each exertion. It's not something I remember my dad doing, yet the sound is oddly familiar. Step, *pphhth*, step, *pphhth*, and I'm following, watching and listening, and then I know why it's familiar: it's because I do it myself. Hearing him sounding so much like me, even when he's just *breathing*, starts to freak me out a bit, so I say, "Give me the box," and I catch up with him and take it off him.

"What's your name?"

"Al."

"Al? Al what?"

I have thought about this.

"Singh."

"Oh. OK. Hi."

Singh is a pretty neutral surname. You can't tell anything about a person from the name Singh, not really. It was given as a surname to people ages ago by a Hindu guru who wanted all of his followers to treat each other equally and not be snobby because of their names, so people of all types can be called Singh. Chaudhury, though—that's a bit posh in India. Not always, but sometimes. I just wanted something ordinary.

"Where are your parents from?" he asks. I've thought about that too.

"My mum and dad were born here. My grandparents have gone back to live in Punjab."

"Speak any Punjabi?" It's funny listening to Pye. He pronounces *Punjabi* in a really Indian accent, like "p'njabby."

"Nope. Well, *sat sri akal* is *hello*. That's about it."

"So how did you know my name?"

"Hang on. I want to know why you nearly killed this cat."

I'm scared of what the answer may be, but I have to ask it for my own peace of mind. I do not want to think that my own dad would do that sort of thing willingly, so I'm hoping he's going to give a good answer.

Pye chews his bottom lip in a gesture that I know well from Dad, and mumbles, "I didn't. Macca shot it."

"Are you sick in the head or something? You were about to set it on fire. You had lighter fluid! What d'you want to go and do that for?"

"Like I said, they made me."

"Oh yeah, who made you?"

"My friends."

"Your *friends*?" We are now at the top of the slipway down to the beach, and about to cross the coastal road. "What sort of person hangs out with people who torture animals?" This comes out much harsher than I intended, and Pye glares at me. I know I've touched a nerve, but I also know I've gone too far. His chin is trembling and he looks back at the beach.

"You know what? This is none of your business. It's got nowt to do with you. You can just—just, *piss off*!" And with that, he turns and starts running back down the slipway to the beach.

I put the box down. "Wait! Hang on! Wait!"

But he's still running, and I'm running after him. Only when he reaches the soft sand does he slow down and turn round to look back at me, by which time I'm quite near him and I shout again, but he turns to run. I'm desperate now, cursing my big mouth, but all I can do is try a spurt of speed through the dragging, soft sand until I'm close enough to launch myself at him in what is definitely the only successful rugby tackle I have ever made: arms round his thighs and down we both go with a thud. I'm on top of him now, and he's struggling and wriggling while he's cringing away from me and shouting, "Get off me! Gerroff! I'll get Macca on yuh," and he's shouting so much that he can't even hear me saying, "I'm sorry, I'm sorry, all right? I'm sorry!"

I just keep repeating this, and his arms are pinned to the sand by my hands, and I move my head so it's level to his. I look hard into his brown eyes and say again, "I'm sorry."

He can tell I'm not going to hit him. He stops wriggling, I climb off his chest, and we sit side by side on the sand for a while, panting. Eventually Pye says, "Macca's not so bad. He used to pick on me loads, but he doesn't now, and I prefer it like that, OK?" I can see Pye's eyes are starting to moisten, and I figure there's more going on here than I can see. "I like him. And the others, all right?" I'm not convinced, but I'm thrown off guard when he says, with a harder edge to his voice, "Now tell me how you know my name."

CHAPTER FORTY-FIVE

I take a deep breath. This is going to have to work. "We've just moved here. My mum told me to look out for an Indian kid called Pye Chaudhury. She must know your mum or something. There's not that many of us, so I just guessed."

Even as I say it, it sounds brilliantly believable, especially since I know that Pye's mum—my Grandma Julie—died years ago. It's like a double bluff, and I'm so pleased with the lie that I extend it a bit. "Mums always know each other, don't they?" I laugh, but the laugh hangs in the air, a bit hollow, and immediately I feel rotten for having (1) used the death of Pye's mum to create a better lie, and (2) made Pye think about his dead mum.

He lets it go, though, and says, "Where do you live, then?"

I choose somewhere far enough away to be safe. "Monk-seaton Village. The new estate." No sooner are the words out of my mouth than I realize what I have said.

"New estate? I didn't know there was one."

"Oh, it's er . . . quite well hidden. And very small. You'd hardly know it was there. Where do you live?"

"Sandview Avenue." He gives that little nod. "As you come into town."

We both get up and dust some of the sand off our pants. When I lift up my hand to pat some of the sand off Pye's back, he flinches, then smiles and lets me do it. With his back to me, I notice his shoulders trembling and shaking like he's crying.

"Hey—I said I was sorry," I say as I move round to face him, and that's when I see that he's not crying, but laughing. Just a quiet laugh, with that little exhalation through his nose, but laughing nonetheless.

"What's funny?" I say, starting to laugh myself.

"Dunno," he says, still snuffle-chuckling. "You. Me. Us? Wrestling on the sand?" I start to laugh myself. I think for both of us it's relief—in Pye's case that I'm not going to beat him up, and in mine because I've not screwed up my plan by letting Pye get away. For a moment we just stand there, looking at each other and laughing.

"Come on," I say. "Let's sort that cat out."

We're heading up the alleyway back to Chesterton Road

and Mr. Frasier's house, and Pye is being really strange, and almost hiding behind me and the box as we approach the street.

"What's up with you?" I ask.

"Nothing. It's just . . . um . . . that's Macca's house, and I don't want to see him." He's nodding in the direction of number 40. My old house.

"*That's* his house?"

Pye nods. I remember what Mum said once about the people they bought the house from. Rough. Mad.

"Is his name MacFaddyen?"

Again Pye nods. "Have you heard of them?"

"A bit."

Great, I think, remembering Macca's rant about the cat he'd shot. *Alan Shearer's in a drawer in the bunker under a psychopath's house.*

Mr. Frasier's house is the same as all the others, except on the wall next to his front door is a rectangle of polished brass engraved with DUNCAN P. FRASIER and in smaller letters, VETERINARY SURGEON.

He answers the door himself, and looks at me standing there.

"Ah, hullo, laddie. Ah see ye've brought yer twin brother with ye! Do you want to know the date again?"

Pye looks at me, baffled. By way of answering, I open the lid of the box, and taking one look at the cat, Mr. Frasier ushers us through the empty waiting room (which is his front room, converted) and into the surgery (which is his back room, converted). So far he has hardly said a word. The surgery is clean-smelling and painted in light blue and white, and there are glass-fronted cupboards all around filled with books and packets of medicines and vets' equipment.

He asks us to stand to one side, then gently lifts the cat out of the box and onto a marble-topped bench in the middle of the room. He stoops closer and sniffs the cat.

"Lighter fluid?" he asks, looking over at us with an eyebrow cocked. We both shrug. He runs his hands gently over the cat's sticky, wet fur, parting it to reveal the wounds, and the poor cat barely flinches.

"We found it on the beach. Some big kids were running away," I say.

Mr. Frasier shakes his head wearily as he fills a syringe and injects something into the cat. He smiles at us.

"Well done, lads. I'll tell you the truth: there's no guarantee this cat's going to survive. But I'll do ma best. I have to remove these air gun pellets, and clean the wounds, and stitch her up, give her antibiotics. Do ye's want to watch?"

"Awesome!" That's me.

"Not really." That's Pye. I think he's feeling too guilty about his involvement to take any pleasure from seeing a real-life lifesaving operation.

So we sit in the waiting room.

Pye has gone a bit quiet, so I ask him the universal kids-making-polite-conversation question: "What school do you go to?"

He smiles. "Culvercot Secondary Modern. You'll probably be going to Monkseaton High, if that's where you live. Unless you're at the Royal Grammar?"

I say, "Monkseaton High, I think?" It sounds OK.

"You've got more computers than us. We can use the computers in the technical lab, though—they're ace. They're new this term—there's six of them!"

"Really? Six computers in the whole school?"

"Well, seven if you include the one in Mrs. Spetrow's office. Pretty neat, eh? There's a Commodore, two Sinclair Spectrums—which are great because you get these games that are just ace, and Mr. Melling lets me into the tech lab at lunchtime, and I've been practicing how to link them all up with a motherboard to make a supercomputer. I've managed three so far . . ." He's chatting away quite happily and I'm drifting off, wondering how I'm going to get back to my own world when Pye says, "Oh my God."

There's a glass cabinet opposite us and he is gawping at our reflection like an idiot.

"Look. Look at us. It's incredible."

I see what has astonished him. It is like looking at a picture of identical twins. Pye's skin is very slightly darker than mine, but other than that—barely any difference at all.

He looks at the reflection for a while, and he keeps murmuring "Wow!" under his breath.

Then I hear steps in the hallway, the door opens, and Mr. Frasier's standing in the doorway, but I can't tell from his face whether it's good news or bad. I just have to wait for him to speak.

"She was in a very bad way," he starts, and I'm sure he's going to tell us that the cat has died. "I've done everything I can."

Pye and I are staring at the vet expectantly. Eventually, a tiny half smile appears. "I cannit guarantee it, lads, but I think she's going tae pull through. Come an' see."

Back in the surgery, Mr. Frasier takes us over to a large

cage on the floor where the cat is lying on a clean, folded blanket, totally still. Only the tiniest movement of her chest reveals she is breathing at all. Parts of her fur have been shaved off, and there are dressings on her side and one back leg.

I see Pye swallow hard. "Wh-what will happen to her?" he says.

"Ah, well. I'll make a few inquiries. She had a collar on and I don't think she was a stray, so I daresay I'll be able to trace her owner. Bound to be someone local. I'll make sure they know about your kindness."

He walks with us to the front door, then says, "Ah . . . I don't suppose you have any idea at all who these older boys were, do ye? Only this sort of thing can't be allowed, can it?"

We shake our heads, answering both of Mr. Frasier's questions at once.

I'm aware that I haven't said a word since the vet came into the waiting room.

"Thank you," I say at last as he's shutting the door.

"No, laddie—thank *you*. That's a grand thing you an' yer brother have done!"

We're on the path leading from the front door when I look across at Pye, and his mouth is turned up in a perfect curve of happiness. The whole afternoon has been pretty intense, and for a second I think he's going to cry (I can feel my own chin starting the first tremors of a wobble as well), so I turn to him and start to embrace him in a bro hug, but if the other person's not ready for you to do that—and Pye isn't—then it can go a bit wrong, as it does now. Pye moves back warily and eases himself away from me. I remember Grandpa Byron telling me that men didn't hug much in the olden days anyway, and I'm hardly well practiced myself, as I think I've said.

("Americans, close relatives, and gay people were the only men allowed to hug, until the Male Embracing Act was passed by Parliament in 1995," he told me one day with a straight face. I believed him for a while.)

So Pye and I are both feeling a bit awkward when there's a shout from the distance.

"Oi! Chow!"

At the other end of the street is Macca, and he's coming in our direction.

"I'd better go," I say. The thought of Grandpa Byron sitting in the chip shop where I left him has rushed into my head, and I've got to go, even though I don't want to leave Pye.

"No—don't! I don't want to see him either." But I've made my mind up. Before I turn to go, I fix Pye with a gaze.

"Same time tomorrow? Same place?"

Pye gives a big grin and nods before turning and waiting for Macca, even though he doesn't want to meet him.

CHAPTER FORTY-SIX

As I'm standing outside the vet's, the absolute lunacy of handing over my mobile to Macca has begun to seep into my head, and I comfort myself (very slightly) with the knowledge that there wasn't much battery life left and he won't be able to do much with it. But I will have to get it back, I know that.

I'm also now very keen to get back to my world, my time. The idea of flipping between the two as I wish, of setting destination and return times according to convenience, is something I'm only just becoming familiar with, and I'm very, very far from relaxed about the whole thing. You'd be the same. No one is born with an instinctive understanding of multidimensional time travel. Not yet, at any rate. There's also the risk element. It's the breaking in, sneaking around, lying, hiding, and stealing stuff that's doing my head in, as much as the time travel itself. (Mind you, the time travel would be enough on its own, believe me.)

I wait till Macca and Pye have headed up the road away from the house and there is no one around on Chesterton Road. Then I head back to the bunker under his/my house.

Remember, several hours ago but thirty years in the future, I had only just dodged being found in this same bunker by Graham, who was trying to force the door.

I'd had the brilliant idea of using the time machine to escape imminent danger. Brilliant, cunning . . . and completely stupid. Because I'm now sitting in front of the laptop with *nowhere to go.*

Returning before I had left was a nonstarter because of Dad's Law of Doppelgangers. Remember? I would risk bumping into myself, and that's not possible. And returning *after* I had left wouldn't work either—for the same reason.

That leaves the option I had rejected before as Graham was forcing the metal door: find somewhere to hide in the bunker, and I would have only seconds to do it. In my memory I scan the layout of the little underground room. There's only one possible hiding place, and it's pretty pathetic.

I set the time coordinates for the time I left.

And then I hesitate, going through all the what-ifs I can think of. What if Graham just waits by the door? What if he locked the door from the outside? The main one, of course, is *what if he finds me … what if … what if …?*

Sometimes, despite the what-ifs, you just have to act. I can't be here forever, driving myself nuts with indecision. Instead, reclaiming Alan Shearer from the drawer and stashing him safely in my hoodie pocket, I climb into the tub, grip the laptop tightly, and press "Enter."

Seconds later, I'm back where I left off. I can again hear the pieces of broomstick clattering to the floor, and the wheel that opens the door is turning rustily. One piece of wood remains stuck, jamming the door's mechanism for a vital few seconds as I climb out of the zinc tub and hit the light switch just as the final bit of wood gives way.

"Careful, Graham! There might be a gang of them!" I hear Bella say as he pushes the door open.

There are five stairs leading down into the bunker from the doorway, and all I can do is crouch in the space beneath them.

I know—I told you it was pathetic, right? Worse, the steps are made of grid metal like you see in factories, and if he looks straight down, Graham will see me crunched up in a ball, eyes screwed tight shut as if that could make a differ-ence to whether or not he notices me.

Half opening them, I see a shaft of dim light coming from the doorway and falling on the laptop and zinc tub. The laptop is closed, but between the keyboard and the screen is a thin line of light because it hasn't powered down properly yet. Can he see it? I can't tell. He's crouching by the opened door because at the top of the stairs there's not enough head room to stand up properly, and his feet are directly above me.

"Hello?" he calls. "I know you're in there. You'd better come out or you're in trouble!"

He's scared. I can tell from his voice. Then his feet move and he starts to come down the metal steps.

"Don't go in, Graham. Come back, love."

He stops, and I have an idea. Silently, I take Alan Shearer from my pocket and gently release him onto the floor, where he scampers across the patch of light behind the zinc tub. He's only visible for a moment, but it's enough.

"Oh my God, Bella. There's rats down here."

Yup, I think, *rats for babies,* and I think I even smile a bit, remembering Carly's sly put-down.

Bella's voice has taken on a harsher tone. "Graham. Come away now. You'll catch something if they bite you."

Graham's footsteps move back up the stairs, and I hear him say to Bella, "Come on, love, we'll call the police."

"And the council. We need the pest controllers." I hear the door between the kitchen and the garage click shut, and only then do I realize I have been holding my breath for pretty much the whole time.

Seconds later, I've scooped up Alan Shearer and I'm out of the bunker, down the driveway, grabbing my glove, and sprinting to the chip shop, where Grandpa Byron is waiting for me. I walk in trying to pretend that nothing has happened, and hoping that Grandpa Byron won't notice anything. I mean—what is there to notice? I look fine.

"Oh my jolly goodness—what on earth is the matter?"

All right. So much for that theory. Grandpa Byron's staring at me. He looks at his watch. "You were nearly twenty minutes," he says. "Trouble finding it?"

I blink, then hold up the glove. "Uh-huh. But I got it."

Wow, I'm thinking. *Twenty minutes!*

For me, it's been several hours, but Grandpa Byron has only been here twenty minutes. Except . . . those hours *must* still have happened. Those hours happened to me, so they must have happened to Grandpa Byron.

But *when?*

That's the question I simply cannot answer. How could something happen, yet *not* happen?

All of this is going through my head while Grandpa Byron keeps asking me questions. "Where have you been? I was about to come lookin' for you, man. Are you a'reet? You look terrible. What happened?"

There's a big mirror down one wall of the chip shop, and I look at my reflection. Well, honestly—I don't look *that* bad. A bit disheveled, maybe, and my hands are filthy, and there are a few smudges of dirt and sand on my face from brawling with Pye, and my feet are wet from where a wave caught me and . . . yeah, OK, I look a bit messed up.

"I, er . . . I couldn't find it, and then I was running back, and I tripped up . . ."

"What aboot yer feet? They're soakin', man!"

"Puddle? I, er, stepped in a puddle." If Grandpa Byron realizes the absurdity of this—it's a sunny, dry day with no puddles—he isn't showing it. He stares at me, really carefully, as he slowly eats a chip. Then he makes a face.

"Yuck. They're cold. Come on—let's go."

I'd love love *love* to tell Grandpa Byron that I've just met Dad. But I can't. The frustration keeps me quiet and I can't talk on the back of his scooter anyway. And besides, one thought is crowding everything else out: I must save the time machine from discovery when Bella and Graham's builders get to work. That could be as early as tomorrow.

One way or another, I'm going to be back in Culvercot tonight.

CHAPTER FORTY-SEVEN

Same taxi, same time, and that is the very end of my savings, including the five pounds Grandpa Byron gave me this afternoon just, well, just because he does sometimes.

And this time, Carly is with me.

I know—it wouldn't be my first choice either, but in fact I had *no* choice. I needed twenty pounds for the taxi fare, and I knew Carly would be good for it.

"It's tonight," I said, trying to sound mysterious, when I put my head around her bedroom door, but the effect was lost because she had her headphones on and didn't hear me.

I went in and touched her on the shoulder, making her jump. She swung round.

"For God's sake, Al—" she started.

"It's tonight," I repeated, and her expression changed from one of fury to one of awe.

"There's a full moon, so we have to go back to Culvercot tonight."

"What do I need to bring?"

"Well, I'm twenty pounds short on the taxi fare, but we'll need some other things as well. Some candles, for a start, and a lighter, and"—I was a bit stuck, so I made something up—"a mirror."

"A mirror?"

"Yes. I'll see you downstairs at twelve-thirty."

We avoid each other, mostly, for the rest of that Sunday evening. Mum and Steve go to bed like normal, and at 12:25 I hear Carly's bedroom door open and the sound of her footsteps padding down the stairs.

At 12:30 we're in the taxi, and it's only then that Carly pushes back the hood on her top and I see she's done herself up in full-on goth style: black lipstick, the lot. I say nothing, but the look on my face must have given it away.

"What?" says Carly. "Do you think it's too much?"

"No. Not really. I mean, you wanted to look nice for Dad, yeah?"

She gives me a puzzled frown and I dart my eyes toward the taxi driver. She picks it up.

"Oh yeah. Yeah. Dad. Right," and then she shuts up for

the rest of the journey, plugging her headphones in and listening to music.

When we get there, and I've paid the driver and asked him to wait for half an hour, we start walking toward the patch of bushes in front of the old house.

"What happens now, Al?"

I need to keep her busy and occupied while I go into the bunker and start taking out the equipment that's in there.

"Did you bring the mirror?"

From a pocket she pulls out a small handbag mirror.

"Perfect. Light a candle, and position the mirror so that the candle reflects in it." This is total mumbo jumbo of course, but it sounds like the sort of thing they do in séances. "Meanwhile, I'm going in there to get some of Dad's stuff."

Carly looks alarmed. "Stuff? What sort of stuff?"

"Oh . . . just some computery sort of stuff."

"So what's it doing here still?"

"It was kind of hidden. But I have to get it back, you see, because, well . . . I just do." Poor, I know, but it seems to satisfy Carly, who nods seriously. I then add, "They were prized possessions of his. That's why we need them. They're imbued with his aura." Carly's still nodding slowly, but she has the candle in front of the mirror, and she has lit it. "Picture,

Al—go on! This is going on Facebook!" She hands me her phone and sits cross-legged behind the candle arrangement posing while I have to take a picture. "Great!" she says when I give her back her phone. "I'll send it to you!"

Everything is dark in the driveway, but something's missing. Where the Škoda stood is now an empty space.

They're out! Graham and Bella are out, which is great. It means I'm less likely to get caught. On the other hand, anyone who's out at one a.m. is likely to be back soon and catch me in the act of robbing their garage.

There isn't really time to consider all of this, so I ease open the crack in the garage doors, and my heart sinks. There is the Škoda, parked right over the planks covering the concrete stairs.

There is no way I can get access to the bunker.

Although . . .

After squeezing through the gap in the garage doors, I try the handle of the Škoda's driver's door and it's not locked. I ease the double garage doors open and then stand there, wondering how I'm going to get the car out. I can release the hand brake, put the car in neutral, and push it out of the garage silently, where the slight downward slope of the driveway will carry it into the road. Only I have no control over it at all. It might swerve and crash into the gateposts, or it might not stop when it gets to the road, and carry on and hit something else. In short, someone needs to push and someone needs to be in the car.

Which is how Carly comes to be an accessory to not-really-stealing a car.

I sit in the driver's seat, and she is pushing the front of the car. Slowly, it inches out of the garage. I use the car's brake pedal to control its speed down the driveway, and I stop it and pull on the hand brake. All this time, I'm watching the bedroom windows, terrified that I might see a light go on.

By now, Carly's in a spin of terror and curiosity, even more so when I start lifting the planks off the stairway.

"Al! What are you—"

"Shhh," I say, sharply. "Just help me." To be fair, she does. It's a quicker job with two of us, and in only a couple of minutes, I'm turning the wheel of the bunker door and it pops open with a breath of musty air.

Carly puts her head in the doorway and gives a low whistle. "Frea-ky!"

But there's no time to stand and admire it. "Here," I say, and hand her the laptop and cables. "Take them up the stairs and come back."

While she's gone, I lift up the zinc tub: it's not so much heavy as really unwieldy. Carly's back, panting, and together we get it out of the bunker until it's resting next to the computer on the floor of the garage.

Back go the planks, and we take the tub and its contents to the waiting taxi. All we have to do now is push the car up the driveway and into the garage.

Have you ever tried to push a car uphill? It weighs a ton. Or to be precise, it weighs a tonne. No, really, it does.

Carly's in the driver's seat this time, and as soon as she releases the hand brake, the car starts to roll back, completely ignoring my efforts to push it into the garage. I'm heaving my whole weight against it, and I manage to stop it rolling, but I can't push it forward, however hard I try.

That's when I see the light go on in the upstairs window. It's only a sliver of yellow through a crack in the curtains and I know Carly hasn't seen it. I crouch down behind the car and tap frantically on the back window. As I'm peering through the glass, I groan inwardly—her headphones are on again and she can't hear me. The light is on now in the house's front door window, and *still she hasn't seen it!* I scramble round to the passenger door of the car and begin thumping on the window, when the front door opens and

Graham is silhouetted in the light. I see Carly's head turn in alarm toward the light, and then spin round looking for me.

I hear the *clunk* of the car's central locking system. Graham has locked her in the car with his remote key! Meanwhile, I'm backing out of the driveway, shielded from his sight by the car and the hedge.

"Bella!" calls Graham back into the house. "We've got ourselves a thief!" He walks toward the car, clutching his dressing gown around him, and looks in. "Aw. It's only a young'un as well. What will the police say, I wonder? Was that you earlier today in our cellar, eh?"

I'm watching this unfold from a position of relative safety when Graham takes out his mobile and starts talking to the police.

"Fifteen minutes? That's a long time to respond to an emergency. . . . Well, no. No one is in imminent danger, no. . . . I suppose it gives me a chance to get dressed. . . ."

I have an idea, but I'm not sure if I can pull it off. I can see Bella looking through the upstairs window, but she doesn't see me. And nor does Graham, when I sneak round the back of the car, and when he shuffles in his slippers down the driveway to look out for any approaching police cars, that's when I sneak behind him, and through the open front door.

I grew up in this house, so I know exactly where to go. Immediately to the right of the front door as you go in is a toilet, and that's where I'm hiding when Graham comes back in.

I'm gambling that no one would naturally put their car keys in a dressing gown pocket.

To my relief, I hear the *chink* of his keys on the table by the front door, and then his footsteps going up the carpeted stairs.

"Quarter hour, they say, love," he calls to Bella. "I've locked the little cow in the car. Can't be more'n about fifteen."

And then I'm out, picking up the keys as silently as I can and opening the front door slowly, slowly. I know the trick of closing this door quietly, and lift it a bit by the letter box and it shuts silently.

I can see Carly staring, astonished, as I come out the front door, and I'm about to click the remote key to let her out when I stop. It's going to go *blip* when I open it.

I turn and insert the house key into the front door's lock and lock the door, leaving the keys dangling. Only then do I press the button on the car key. The corner lights on the car flash, and sure enough there's a little *blip* sound, which echoes in the street's silence.

Immediately, Carly's out, and I'm next to her, running

down the driveway. I half turn, keeping my face partly obscured, and see a furious Graham pounding on his bedroom window, followed a few seconds later by the sound of the front door rattling.

His next move will be to go out the back door and through the garage. But by now we've reached the taxi, and I hold my hand out to Carly in a "slow down, act cool" gesture, which she does, and we get in.

It's not until we're out on the coastal road that she holds up her hand and we exchange a silent high five.

CHAPTER FORTY-EIGHT

It's 2:30 a.m. by the time everything's up in my room. Carly and I have hardly said a word, and I can tell by the look on her face that she has several words she wants to say.

Trouble is, I am so tired I can barely sit upright. That isn't going to stop her trying.

"Al," she starts. "I am not stupid."

She's standing by my bedroom desk, looking angry. What can I say? I kind of shrug in an "I didn't say you were" sort of way.

"Are you going to tell me what this is all about? Breaking and entering, trespassing, theft . . ."

"It wasn't theft. It belonged to Dad."

"According to you. Locking that bloke in his house— that's probably illegal too; I mean what are you into here, Al? And don't tell me you're trying to get in touch with your dad, 'cause like I say, I'm not stupid." She gives me the death stare, then adds the clincher. "I could always tell your mum everything."

"You wouldn't dare."

"Wouldn't I? I wouldn't dare tell her how you tricked me into robbing a house? Took advantage of my spirituality . . ."

(As far as I can tell, Carly's "spirituality" involves listening to a lot of emo—sorry, goth—music and watching the Twilight movies, but to be fair my world is turning a lot weirder than any film.)

". . . to—to . . . cynically dupe me, swindle me out of twenty pounds, and then run off and leave me when I get locked in a car by a crazed man?"

"Leave you? I came back to *get* you. I *rescued* you!"

She says it again. "According to you. You're the one who's going to have to explain all this stolen gear in your room. And I'm sure Asif at A–Z Taxis would love to help establish the truth as well."

We stare each other down for a good twenty seconds. There is no question about it, though: she has me.

"Can I tell you in the morning? I'm so tired."

"No. You tell me right now."

I sigh. "You'd better sit down, then."

CHAPTER FORTY-NINE

I've slept in and Grandpa Byron's waiting to take me to school when I come downstairs. Mum and Steve have already left for work, and Carly's nowhere to be seen.

(I don't think she totally buys the time travel stuff, now that I've made my big confession. No surprises there. She is intrigued, though, and that's enough to buy her silence for now. But I'm going to have to produce some evidence pretty soon, or I'm toast. And she's not at all happy about the twenty pounds she's spent.)

Grandpa Byron looks at me, shakes his head, and says, "Oh my flippin' Lordy! What has happened to you?"

I suppose I can't look that great. I have slept for about three hours, and badly at that. I'm shivering and pale, and I still haven't got my school uniform on. Instead my dressing gown hangs loosely around me.

"You look like you've seen a ghost! How do you feel? How's your kyte?"

He means my stomach. It's one of his old Geordie words, I think.

"Pretty rough, actually." There's an opportunity to miss school here, I can tell, so I make my voice croaky, just to be on the safe side, although in truth I feel really sick. Grandpa Byron pulls down my eyelids, and then my bottom lip. He smells my breath and declares that I am "most certainly out of balance." His remedy is what he calls a "hot posset."

Soon the kitchen is filled with the smell of spices: cardamom and cinnamon are the only two I recognize, and he goes out again to fetch some others at the Bangladeshi shop. The resulting concoction—the "hot posset"—is warm, milky, and sweet, and when I sip it, I already feel a little better.

"There, you see! Balance is everything!" He pauses, and I see his eyes flick over to me. "I was telling this to your father just the other day." Grandpa Byron has a sort of faraway look in his eyes when he says this, but then I see him glance at me again to check if I'm listening.

"To Dad? What do you mean?"

"I mean just what I say. Even though your father has passed on from this life, that does not mean he is forgotten."

"Of course not!"

"Well then. Imagine using the power of your mind to transcend time, Al. Thanks to your namesake, Mr. Einstein, the whole world knows that time is relative: it can be different depending on what you are doing."

So he knows, then. Or knows something, at any rate. Stuff like this doesn't come out of the blue.

I say nothing, which I figure is probably the safest thing to do while my mind is racing. I think of Dad's letter when he quoted Einstein's idea of putting your hand on a hot stove and it seeming like ages, and I sip more of the spicy medicine-milk.

"The scholars of the Sri Kalpana knew this many, many years ago, Al."

Ah. The old Sri Kalpana. Grandpa Byron's prized book that I haven't quite got round to finishing. It's on the kitchen table in front of me under a pile of other stuff, poking out. Still I say nothing.

"The mysteries of the universe are multitudinous, Al. And the answers lie within us, not without. Your father, and now you, I think"—and here he pauses, narrowing his eyes a little—"you both seek to transcend these wonders in the physical realm, from which only misery can arise."

I love the way Grandpa Byron talks, but sometimes it gets a little, well, dense. I'm walking through a dark forest of words, and looking for a clearing of sense. He sees that I'm getting confused.

"I know what you have been doing, Al. I am not stupid."

Apparently everyone around me at the moment has this idea that I think they are stupid.

"I never said you were." I'm getting a bit defensive, and Grandpa Byron can tell.

"Don't try being smart with me, bonny lad. I am trying to help you. My book, which I see you have not read, aimed to assist you in this regard."

I put on a pained expression. "I'm sorry. I *have* tried, it's just . . ."

"Difficult to understand? You betcha. But not so difficult to understand as why you would risk everything on this ludicrous adventure of your father's."

I stare at Grandpa Byron, unsure of what to say. I can tell where this is heading, obviously, and I don't like it. I can feel myself being cornered, hemmed in by his calmness and the pretty inescapable fact that he's right: it *is* a ludicrous adventure, or at least very dangerous. I hate it when adults do this, and the only thing I can do is get all self-righteous to try to steer the argument. I stare at him angrily.

"You read my letter, didn't you? The one from Dad to me?"

Instead of answering me directly, he comes to the kitchen table and sits down opposite me.

"One of the hardest things in life, Al, is to accept the things that cause us pain, absorb them, and continue. And no, I did not read your letter. But I imagine it was to do with your father's experiments in, for want of a better expression, time travel?"

"And what if it was?"

"Then you are at liberty to follow your heart. But that is not always the wisest option."

"And what if I had the chance to stop Dad from dying, eh? Wouldn't you want that?" I'm getting a bit upset now, and I have raised my voice, but Grandpa Byron remains unperturbed, which infuriates me further. He just wobbles his head and says, "Death, Al, is not the end. As it says in the Sri Kalpana, 'Live life so completely that when death comes to you like a thief in the night, there will be nothing left for him to steal.'"

"And so I should just do nothing? I have this ability, and I should just do *nothing*? Can you hear yourself? You sit there, spouting this so-called wisdom like you're—you're . . . Yoda or something, and all the while Dad is still dead and you don't want to do anything about it." My cheeks are hot and my throat is wobbling, but I'm not crying. (That'll come later.)

Still, Grandpa Byron just blinks slowly and reaches across the table to pick up his precious book.

"But you cannot undo what has been done, Al. It may appear that you can, but you cannot. It may appear that you can change your world by going back in time and altering it, but you are merely creating another world and living in that instead. Escaping is not changing."

"Well, I want to escape, then."

"Don't do it, Al. It cannot make you happier."

"Why not? Why not?" I can hardly speak, I'm so angry. "Don't you even want to see Dad again?"

"But I can, Al, by—"

"By what? By meditating, is that it? You can *dream* about him? You can *think* about him? God Almighty, I can do that. Anyone can do that! But actually *meet* him? Wouldn't you like to do that? Well, I have. Got that? I *have*. And I'm going to do it again."

"Don't do it, Al. Please, for God's sake. Just. Stop. You're playing with things that . . . that . . ."

"That what? I don't understand? Like *you* understand everything, O holy wise Indian mystic? Give me a break. You and your Sri Kalpana, it's just mumbo jumbo for people who can't handle reality. Take it. Take it away and go away yourself."

Grandpa Byron says nothing more. In fact, that's the last thing I say to him. With an expression of deep hurt on his face, he picks up the old book and silently leaves the house.

I hear his moped coughing and spluttering down the street, but—in case you were wondering—this is not when I start crying. My mind is racing with what I have to do.

CHAPTER FIFTY

Things I Will Do With A Time Machine

I'm beginning to think the possibilities are endless. Just think of the misery that could be stopped, the accidents that could be prevented, if I had the courage to travel back in time and do what was required.

I entertain myself with these scenarios.

1. I could kill Hitler. I can't believe no one's thought of this (come to think of it, they probably have). I could go back to Austria on April 20, 1889, to the Pommer Guesthouse in a village called Braunau am Inn and kill the baby Adolf Hitler, who was born there that day. (I know—anyone would think I'd been research-ing this or something.) Wouldn't that be awesome, although I'm not sure how I would feel about killing a baby, even one I knew was Adolf Hitler and would

grow up to murder millions of people. How could I do it? I'd suddenly materialize in the dining room, say, then go up to the receptionist and ask, "*Wo ist das Hitler Baby?*" Then—assuming I understand the answer and I haven't been pounced on by the terrified locals—what am I supposed to do? Run into the room shouting, "Die, you murderous dictator-to-be," and stab the baby with a steak knife I found downstairs? No. I couldn't do it. And what would the baby's mum say? I'd never get away; I'd be captured and hanged, leaving a time machine zinc tub in the middle of a nineteenth-century Austrian dining room.

2. Stop the First World War. OK, this one is a bit easier. Everyone says the First World War was started by a lone gunman, Gavrilo Princip, who shot the Austrian archduke, Franz Ferdinand, and then everyone else piled in, basically. So I go back to where it happened, outside Schiller's delicatessen in Sarajevo on June 28, 1914. I stand next to Princip in the shop doorway and wait for him to draw his gun, and then nudge his arm so he misses. But what if he hit someone else? Or turned the gun on me?

3. Everyone says that the First World War led to the Second World War, so that would mean no Second World War, and I wouldn't have to kill Hitler. But then Dad used to say that the biggest advances in computer technology came about when we devised ways of firing rockets at Germany (or maybe it was Germany firing rockets at us, I can't remember) and decoding their secret messages. Anyhow, without the Second World War, maybe there'd be no computers, and without computers, Dad wouldn't have built his time machine. So that's all a bit tricky.

4. OK, here's one. I could go back to last week and buy a ticket for the lottery, knowing what the winning numbers are. I could then convert it all to cash and bring it back to now, and be super-rich. You know, that one's quite good. The only difficulty is that I'm not old enough to buy a lottery ticket, *and* I run up against the doppelganger thing. But it's worth bearing in mind.

Meanwhile, though, I have a task—and to do it, I need to fix up the time machine in my bedroom.

CHAPTER FIFTY-ONE

I have never had a row with Grandpa Byron before. Never.

I can't stop thinking about his anguished expression when he was begging me not to continue my travels.

I decide I have to call him and apologize, and I look round for my phone.

The phone I left in 1984.

A chill feeling comes over me. I get it when I think something might have gone very wrong. It's like my neck has gone really cold. What if Macca has lost it? Or given it to someone? After all, if someone arrived now with a gadget from thirty years in the future, I'd be pretty tempted to show it off, however much I had promised not to.

In my room I pull the zinc tub out from under my bed and grab the laptop, and I'm more nervous than when I first did it.

I think it's because I'm trying to rig up the time machine

myself. The first few times it was all set up for me. I just put in the numbers and pressed "Enter." But now that I'm doing it myself, I'm suddenly conscious again of all the things that might go wrong.

I hear the front door open. It's too early for Mum or Steve, so I call down, "Carly?"

"No, it's me," Mum calls back. "Come down, Al; I need to talk to you."

Hm. Don't like the sound of that.

I am now Most Definitely in Deep Trouble.

I'll cut it short for you, because I've already done the row with Grandpa Byron, which I'm still feeling bad about when the next confrontation starts.

For all my efforts to remain undetected last night, Graham at Chesterton Road recognized me, and called Mum at work today.

And if that wasn't bad enough, a friend of Steve's is an out-of-work lecturer who drives taxis for A–Z Taxis in Ashington, and Asif has been telling everyone in the office about these teenagers and their midnight trips to Culvercot, and Steve's friend tells Steve, and Steve calls Mum, and boom!

So I get all of this in about the first five minutes with

Mum, but then I have to wait for Steve to get back, and Carly, and there's the Big House Meeting.

Now in all of this, there's one thing I'm trying to do, and that is protect my dad's secret long enough for me to do what he wanted me to do.

So if you ask me, it's a pretty bold strategy to tell them I'm building a time machine.

CHAPTER FIFTY-TWO

I was counting on it sounding so crazy, so outlandish, that it would be dismissed as the ravings of a nerdy twelve-year-old in the grip of an obsession to prove himself at school, or something like that anyway.

There was absolutely no guarantee that it would work; quite the opposite in fact.

"So. Let me get this straight," says Steve. He's sitting across the table from me and Carly, and Mum is standing behind him, squeezing her hands. I feel a bit sorry for her. I think she thinks I've gone a bit deranged. "You have twice been to Culvercot in the middle of the night—"

"Once," corrects Carly. "*I* only went once. He went twice."

In fact it's three times, but I'm not going to own up to driving Grandpa Byron's moped if I don't have to.

"Yes! Yes! Yes! I have been twice to Culvercot!"

It's tricky playing mental. I have to be careful not to

overdo it. Mum's eyebrows wrinkle in the way they do when she's upset or worried, and I tone it down a bit.

"And you stole, what, a laptop and a garden tub?"

"I didn't steal them. They belonged to Dad! I've just taken back what belongs to us."

"Ee, pet." Mum sits down and reaches across the table to take my hand, shaking her head. "Whatever that stuff was doing down there, it doesn't belong to us *now*. Nothing in that house does, and you can't go breaking into places to get things that don't even belong to you."

"It all goes back tomorrow," says Steve, flatly.

"But it's my time machine!" I wail. "If you get all the co-ordinates right, the computer does the calculations to effect a space-time warp on anything in the immediate sphere of the garden tub. Honestly!"

How brilliant! I'm telling the whole truth, and yet everyone—with the possible exception of Carly, who of course has already heard all of this and, what with being a goth, *may* just half believe it—thinks I'm making it up. But as long as the stuff goes back tomorrow, I'll be fine, because I only need to make one more journey. I'm feeling so confident that my performance has worked that I end up overdoing it a bit by rolling my eyes and saying, "Yeaaaah!"

Too soon.

"Tomorrow?" says Mum. "You're kidding, Steve. It's going back tonight. Right now, in fact," and she stands up. "Come on, Al, you can help me down with that flippin' tub. How the dickens you got it up there in the first place without me hearing, I have no idea. And you're both coming with me to apologize to Graham and Bella. You'll be lucky if they don't press charges."

I go round the table and put my arms around Mum, and she hugs me back.

"I'm sorry, Mum," I say—and I really am. I can tell she's unhappy, but I'm going to make her happy again when I save Dad. Just for good measure, I give her an extra squeeze and say, "I love you, Mum."

As it turns out, I'm really glad I did that, because of what's going to happen next. I give Mum a last squeeze and then run up to my room as fast as I can.

I'm in my room before she's even stepped away from the table, and by the time she's at my bedroom door, I've pulled the bed in front of it, which makes a very effective barricade.

"Al? Al?!" She's pounding on the door, furious and worried, and she's soon joined by Steve, who adds, menacingly, "You're only making it worse, son."

Worse? How could it be worse? I've now jammed my chair between the end of the bed and the wall, and there is no way *at all* anyone can get in. If I can blot out the noise of banging at the door from my head, then I can get on with the task that I feel I've been waiting my whole life to complete.

The main rig-up is easy. The wires go . . . *here,* the cable goes . . . *here,* and that fixes to there, *so!* Plugging it in, switching it on . . .

"Al! Al! Open this bloody door, son!" But I hardly hear him, because I'm watching the program load up again, listening to the hard disk's soft metallic swish, and feeling the laptop getting sweaty in my hands.

The numbers stop scrolling past, and there's just the blank dialog box with the cursor winking at me, waiting for me to input the string of letters from the top of the black box, and the digits that correspond to the exact time and place I need to be.

I'm playing it safe. I know the coordinates for the nuclear bunker by heart. As for the date, I input exactly one day later from when I was last in 1984, which seems *ages* ago but was only last night. And I have to smile to myself, despite the kerfuffle going on outside and despite the sound of Grandpa

Byron's moped sputtering up the path, because that, as Albert Einstein so rightly pointed out, is relativity.

I'm still nervous about the self-rigged time machine.

"Al! Come out; your grandpa's here!" Now that does make me feel bad, because out of anyone on Earth, Grandpa Byron's the only one who understands what I'm doing, and he's going to be so disappointed in me. Still, I continue to ignore Mum, and I pluck Alan Shearer from his cage, putting him in the tub with a large chunk of walnut, which he is content to sit with and try to cram into his face.

Right, me next. I hear something thump against the window outside, but I'm too busy to care. This time I'm better prepared, frantically shoving things into my schoolbag:

1. My phone charger, out of habit.

2. A handful of food for Alan Shearer.

3. A toothbrush from next to the sink in my room.

4. The framed picture of me, Mum, and Dad that was taken on the day he died.

5. A packet of chewing gum.

6. An apple I've been meaning to eat for ages but that has been sitting on my desk for days.

7. A spare sweater. I don't know why; it's just the sort of thing you're supposed to pack. Mum would be pleased. And that's it. No, wait . . .

8. My dad's letters.

And then I'm in the tub, clutching my schoolbag and the laptop and the handgrips, and I press "Enter."

As I do, and as my vision goes a little bit wobbly, I see Grandpa Byron's face in my bedroom window. He has got a ladder from the builders next door and put it up outside, and the last thing I see, before the mist clears, is his smooth, old brown face contorted in fear and sadness, his mouth a big O as he sees his only grandson disappear before his eyes.

I can't bear to see him like this, and I shout out "Grandpa Byron!" and step out of the tub to go to him at the window, but I'm too late. The blur straightens out and my feet touch the ground of the nuclear bunker in 1984.

CHAPTER FIFTY-THREE

Outside the bunker, in the garage, it's all quiet today. No Radio One, no little Stokoe. The garage door is shut but not locked, and the strong sun glares through the bumpy glass of the window squares.

I leave Alan Shearer in the drawer under the bunk bed, and Pye is waiting for me down on the beach at exactly the same spot, probably to the centimeter. "Precision counts," I think and smile to myself, striding toward him. When we're close, we just stand and look at each other.

It's like looking into a mirror. Well, not exactly, because a mirror doesn't show you exactly how your face is; it shows you a mirror image of your face, which is a bit different. And so it is with Pye—ever so slightly different, but still totally weird.

"You came, then," he says.

"Looks like it."

He smiles. "You look like Rocky."

"Rocky who?"

"You know—Rocky Balboa, the boxer? In the film?" He tugs at the hood on my sweatshirt. "Yo, Adrian, y'know whaddam sayin'?" It's a lousy impression, but I laugh anyway. "Where did you get it?"

I shrug. "I dunno. My mum got it off Amazon, I think?"

"Where's that?"

"Amazon? It's a webs—a mail-order company." Smooth.

"A catalog? Yeah, my dad's got one of them. I'll have a look. Hey, the cat's OK! I called in on my way here. Mr. Frasier reckons she's going to make a full recovery."

"Great," I say, but in truth I had totally forgotten about the cat, what with all the other things going on.

We walk along in silence for a bit, and then I say, "My phone. I need to get it back."

Pye looks at me but doesn't say anything. Eventually he says, "Your what?"

"My phone. My mobile. My cell phone. I gave it to Macca yesterday. I need it back?" This is making me nervous because I don't want to mistrust him.

He repeats, "Your *phone*?"

"My"—dammit—"my *calculator,* I mean. And camera. I have to get it back. It's, er . . . it's not mine."

"Well, that might be a problem. But Macca's a friend, after all. Why did you call it your phone?"

I don't answer, because there's a hollow feeling in my stomach, as if I'm suddenly really hungry, except I'm not; it's just hearing Macca described as a "friend" after what happened yesterday is too much.

"A friend, you say? A *friend?* A friend who makes you torture cats? What sort of friend is that, eh? Tell me. He's got my—my *camera* and you have *no idea* how much trouble this creates." I pause for breath and glance across at Pye, who looks like he might actually be blinking back tears.

"Well, let's go to his house, shall we?" he asks, his voice quavering a little.

"OK," I say. Which is basically how everything starts to go wrong.

CHAPTER FIFTY-FOUR

"Do you know this house, then?" says Pye.

"Sort of. A bit." An understatement, of course. "My mum says she'd love to live here, but Dad says it's too big."

"That's Macca's baby brother!"

"Stokoe." I nod at the little boy in the front driveway of 40 Chesterton Road. My old house. Pye's giving me that surprised look again. "I pick these things up," I say, by way of explanation.

We walk up to the house. "Hi," says Pye to Stokoe's mum, who is sitting on the step smoking a cigarette. Her dark-blond hair is tied back, and she's really thin. "Are you, erm . . . Mrs. MacFaddyen?"

She exhales smoke slowly, looks at us through heavy-lidded eyes, and says, "Who's askin'?"

All right, now—even *I* know that saying this to a pair of

twelve-year-olds is crazy. It's the sort of thing gangsters say to each other in movies.

"I'm Pye Chaudhury. I'm a friend of Mac—Paul's. From school."

Mrs. MacFaddyen smiles meanly and looks away. Her teeth are yellow and big. "Pie? As in steak and kidney?"

"Well, no actually, as in Pythag—well, yeah, steak and kidney's fine."

"Paulie's never mentioned a Pie," she says, and when I glance across, Pye looks a bit crestfallen. Just then, Macca appears in the doorway. "This a friend of yours, Paulie?"

"I know him, mam. A'reet, Chow? Who's your boyfriend?"

Pye laughs, but it sounds a bit forced to me. "This is Al."

"Hello," I say.

"Here, aren't you two alike! You brothers? Twins?" asks Macca's mum.

"Father and son," I say, straight-faced, but she isn't even listening.

"Oi, Stokoe, careful with your juice, you little bleeder!" Mrs. MacFaddyen stubs out her cigarette with her foot, stands up, and goes inside. "Watch him," she says to Macca, jerking her head toward Stokoe. "He's in a right mood this morning."

As soon as she has gone, Macca picks up the cigarette end that his mum just left and, fishing a lighter from his pocket, lights it up again.

"So what brings you here?" asks Macca, dragging on the cigarette.

Pye looks at me, then at Macca. "It's er . . . it's that calculator. Al needs it back."

"Yeah," I add, as if that would help.

"Well, it's more than just a calculator, isn't it?" Macca says slowly. He's trying to be dead casual and even blows a smoke ring.

"Well, yes—obviously," I say, "but I need it back."

Macca doesn't move.

"The thing is," I say, "it doesn't belong to me."

"What? You stole it you mean? You naughty boy!" He sucks again at the cigarette end and walks toward us, grinning. This is not going well, I can tell.

"No, I didn't steal it, it's—"

"You just said it wasn't yours."

"Well, yes, but I'm just borrowing it."

"So am I. So am I. Besides, it was a fair swap, wasn't it?"

He blows smoke out of his mouth, and while I can't be sure he's blowing it in my face, it certainly seems like it. He continues: "Meanwhile, thanks for the present you left me."

Pye and I exchange looks. I can't decide which is worse: if he has found the laptop or Alan Shearer.

"What present?" Pye asks.

"The strange present from our little electronical Santy Claus here. I thought it was you at first. You two really are alike, you know. But when I saw you together, I realized that it was *him* coming out of me garage about an hour ago."

I swallow hard because I don't like the direction this is going. Pye is looking at me as if he suddenly doesn't trust me.

"And by the way—Al, is it?—that's an interestin' line in robbin' you've got going there. Unconventional, I mean. Most people *take* things, but you *leave* them! In my bunker, of all places!"

We've been walking up his driveway, and by now we're at the garage doors, which he opens fully. And there it is, on a little table, in a shaft of dusty light, like it's been posed for an ad for laptops. Next to it is the book-sized black box and a tangle of wires.

At least he hasn't found Alan Shearer.

"Wow!" says Pye. "Is that a—a portable computer?"

"I would say it is," says Macca, "though I never knew they could get this small. Is it?" he asks me, and I nod. "How do you turn it on, then?"

Reluctantly, I reach forward and press the on switch at the back. The screen lights up. "It's the very latest model. From America."

"Hey! It's in color!" says Pye, awestruck.

"How man, Stokoe," shouts Macca, "come and see this! It's like the television." This is just the start-up screen, a picture of a globe spinning in space, and I'm thinking, *you're going to love the Internet!*

Stokoe toddles over as fast as he can. "Ba! Telly!"

What happens next is dead simple and is over in two seconds, but it seems to last much, much longer. Relativity strikes again.

I can't blame Stokoe: he's only a toddler. But when I replay it in my head later, I can recall every detail. His sticky chin; his wide, pale eyes; his little potbelly.

His wobbly walk.

He comes up to the low table and, what? Misjudges the distance? Stumbles? Either way, he nudges his cup of juice against the side of the table.

Its entire contents spill out. All over the keyboard.

The laptop doesn't spark or explode or anything. It just stops working. The screen goes blank. We stare at it in silence.

My way home. My way back to Mum and Grandpa Byron. Gone.

CHAPTER FIFTY-FIVE

"Liquid damage," they call it in the computer trade. It's fatal to computers. Most companies don't even cover "LD" in the guarantees. In short, if you get it wet, that's that.

Probably. But I hadn't reckoned on Pye.

"Quick," he says to Macca. "Get me a glass of water," but Macca just stands there like a lump. "Quickly!" And he's off into the kitchen. I'm desperate now, and I really don't know what I'm going to do, but I'm not expecting what comes next. Lifting the black box and wires out of the way, Pye grabs the water and pours it over the laptop.

"Oh great, *that's* going to help," says Macca. I'm too astounded to say anything at all.

"Shut up. We have to rinse out the sticky juice. Where's the battery?" I turn the laptop upside down so it's a tent shape on the table, and the water starts to run out. "Screwdriver. Get me one now! And rubber gloves."

He's unscrewed the battery cover and is pulling on the rubber gloves that Macca has brought from the kitchen; then he takes out the dripping battery. "Risk of static shock. Now cat litter. Bring me the cat's litter tray."

It's by the door to the kitchen, and full of cat turds, but I don't care. Pye and I are working together. Picking them out with my hands, I heap up the gray litter, plunge the battery into the tray, and cover it over.

"It's silica. It's a desiccant. It's our only hope." Macca is looking at us, uncomprehending. "It absorbs water."

"Will it work?" asks Macca.

"No idea. But there's a chance."

"I've got more," says Macca. "Cover the computer with it," and he grabs a handful.

"No! The dust will be too fine. It could damage the PCBs."

Now, I thought I knew a bit about computers, but Pye is way ahead of me, even though he's thirty years behind.

"How do you know this stuff?" I ask, in admiration.

Pye shrugs modestly. "I saw something in *PCWorld*. Do you know it?"

"What? The shop?"

"*Shop?* No, it's a magazine. It's great. I mean, battery-operated computers are pretty new, and this one is way ahead of anything I've seen, but the principle's the same." He has heaped the cat litter onto the battery and covered it completely. "This must be Apple's fightback product. It's really neat. I like the new logo."

"Fightback?"

"Yeah. They've been beaten commercially by IBM. But hey, maybe they'll be a success after all. Who knows?"

Pye's talk, and his movements, have lost all the hesitancy he was displaying before. Suddenly he's more confident and fluent, and the way he has taken charge has had a curious effect on Macca, who is waiting for his command.

Pye has spotted this too. He seizes the opportunity and says, "And Al's calculator. Give it to him."

Macca hesitates.

"Now!"

Macca reaches into his pocket and brings out my mobile. "It, er . . . it doesn't work anymore. Something happened to it."

I take it from him and flip it open. Nothing. It just looks like the battery has run down, but I'm not missing this chance.

"You've wrecked this as well," I say. "What's wrong with you?"

"I—I'm sorry," he stammers. "It's just—"

Pye stops him by holding up his hand. "Enough! Come on, Al. Get the litter tray. I've got your computer. I have an idea. Come on." He starts to leave the garage, holding the still-dripping laptop carefully. Macca starts to follow us, and Pye turns to face him.

"Not you. You've caused enough trouble."

Pye turns away, but I see the look on Macca's face. It's never smart to belittle someone like Macca, I think, hoping Pye's newfound confidence hasn't just overstepped the mark.

CHAPTER FIFTY-SIX

Until recently, I had never broken into anywhere, and now I seem to be making a habit of it.

And I certainly didn't think I would ever break into a *school*. But it's the school holidays, and here we are, me and Pye, in the technical lab of Culvercot Secondary Modern (since renamed Sir Henry Percy Academy and one of the schools that my school plays football against).

It was a short walk from Macca's house, and the high railings that surround the school now—by which I mean in real time—are absent: just a gate and a low wall that we get over easily. Some kids are playing in one of the distant fields, but they pay us no attention.

"I hope you know what you're doing," I say, but Pye just gives his little nod like Dad. "Done it loads of times."

I'm still carrying the litter tray, the black box, the wires, and the battery, and the laptop has stopped dripping, at least.

At the back of the first building, and shielded from the neighboring houses by a clump of trees, is a rusty blue metal door in a large, windowless wall. A thick iron bolt, secured with a massive padlock, keeps it shut.

Pye puts the laptop down on the concrete path and uses his fingers to pull a brick out of its place, low down in the wall near the ground. Reaching into the hole, he takes out a key and holds it up. "I'm the only one who knows about this," he says, grinning. "Well, me and Mr. Hutson, the caretaker. I saw him come out one day and do it." He pops open the padlock and slides back the heavy bolt.

Inside there's a storeroom full of caretaker's stuff: cleaning fluid, metal buckets, tarpaulins, stacks of heavy stage weights to prop up school-play scenery, and tools of every kind, all on shelves in rows. At the end of the storeroom, opposite the door we came in, is another door, which opens onto a school corridor.

I follow Pye with my tray until we arrive at the technical lab—a stuffy, darkish room with tables running along the sides, and a large one in the middle with stools underneath.

Three big old computers sit on the central table, linked with a jumble of multicolored cables.

"My Big Experiment," says Pye, like it's an announcement.

"Linking up all six computers. I've devised my own program to boost the processing power of each microchip so that instead of doubling when you link two computers together, it quadruples, then quadruples again, and again. Once we get to six, the power will be unbelievable!"

I look at the three computers doubtfully.

"Yeah, well, I've only done the first three. The problem is the chips themselves: they're kind of limited, and I have to be—"

"Silicon."

Pye furrows his brow and shakes his head. "What?"

"That's what you need. Silicon chips. Much more stable, able to hold more information. I think someone's working on it. America, probably," I add. But Pye is not really listening. He's tugging at a fridge to pull it away from the wall.

"Here, give me a hand."

We pull the fridge away from the wall just enough so that we can wedge the upside-down V of the laptop between it and the wall. The heat from the back of the fridge is just gentle enough, Pye reckons, to give us the best chance of drying out the laptop. Too fast and the evaporating water could cause further damage, apparently. For good measure, I prop the cat litter tray by the heat source as well. The black box and wires I put down on the table, where Pye peers at them.

"So what's this bit for, then?"

"I think it's, erm . . . an additional, er . . . hard drive?"

"What? Why?"

"Dunno. Just came with it. I don't think you're supposed to open it," I add quickly as Pye's fingers move toward the metal catches.

"Blimey, what a mess. Doesn't look as slick as the rest. That's the problem with Apple. Design." And then he asks the question that I know he's been dying to ask. "So how come all this lot ended up in Macca's bunker?"

"Safekeeping," I say with as much confidence as I can summon. "Like I say, my mum and dad looked at the house a while back. I knew there was this underground, like, den, and I figured no one would find it there." Even to me, it sounds like a stupid story. It *is* a stupid story. But it's the best I can think of. "It's very valuable," I add, but Pye's not buying it.

"So you broke into his garage—"

"I didn't break in, it was open."

"Well, all right then. But even so—"

"I didn't know Macca lived there."

"Obviously not. It's just, I dunno . . . weird." I think he

might have left it there, but then I hear myself saying, "My hamster's there too!" and immediately wish I hadn't.

Pye wrinkles his brow and curls his lip and generally adopts an expression of utter bewilderment and disbelief.

I shrug and say, "That's how I roll."

"That's how you *what*?"

"Doesn't matter. Come on, let's do this Big Experiment."

CHAPTER FIFTY-SEVEN

Listen, I don't mean to be condescending, but I don't sup-pose you've ever linked computers together before, using cables and stuff?

It's not that I don't think you could. You totally could. It's just that most people don't bother. Why would you? I mean, you can link computers up on a home network as easy as pie, but doing it physically, with extra bits and bobs, and a motherboard (two actually), connecting all the other bits—the CPU, the hard drive, and whatnot . . .

Well, all I can say is that I couldn't do it, but Pye makes it look easy.

Not that I'm concentrating much. Nor would you if you were stuck in a past dimension of space-time and your only way back was currently drying out over the back of a fridge or covered in used cat litter. I keep going over to it and lifting it up and looking at it, as if that will make any difference.

"Mr. Melling, the tech teacher? He lets me in here at lunchtime during term, and he lent me all the stuff to make my own computer," Pye is saying as I watch him use a soldering iron to attach a long wire to a printed circuit board. He nods toward the corner of the room. There's a TV screen, a keyboard, and a metal tray with all the insides of a computer revealed.

"It's like a computer's died and that's the postmortem," I say.

Pye laughs. "Yeah, but this one lives! Look." He goes over to it, plugs in a cable, and switches it on. A few seconds later, the screen lights up with the words **"ZZZZZAP!! BY PYE CHAUDHURY"** in blocky letters.

"Wanna game?"

"You invented a *game*?"

"It's not all that good: there's a few glitches, like when you get a new high score, you go back to zero, which I haven't worked out how to fix yet, but"—he gives a shy half smile— "yeah. I wrote the code for it. Took me ages!"

In fact, the idea is pretty good: using the left, right, up, and down keys on the keyboard, you have to move your cursor around to dodge this random creature that looks like a bear with a big mouth, all while picking up boxes with points in them. OK, compared even with simple stuff like *Donkey Kong*, *ZZZZZAP!!* is rubbish, but of course I don't tell Pye that, and in truth it's pretty good fun, although Pye totally beats me because—as he eventually admits—he has a good idea where the bear is coming from next because he hasn't got the random bit working completely.

"Randomness—like, proper randomness—is really hard to program."

Still, he made it himself. The guy is a genius.

After about ten minutes of this, Pye turns back to the main table. As he turns, his elbow catches my backpack, which falls, spilling the contents on the floor.

"Hey—sorry," he says, and he starts picking the stuff up, then stops. He stands up holding the family photo I grabbed from my bedside table.

"This your mum and dad?" he asks, looking at it closely. My mouth goes dry. "They look nice. What are they called?"

I have thought about this, but—so far—reached no conclusion. The thing is, I just can't decide. I've had this debate going on in the back of my head for days. I could:

1. Tell Pye he is my father, that I am from thirty years in the future, and that I'm using a primitive

time machine he designed to save his life. I know. Mind melt or what? What's more, in telling him this, I could be fundamentally altering what happens in the future. If I tell him he designs a time machine, then he may end up making it, I don't know, ten years earlier, or later, or I don't know—it could just change a lot of things.

2. Don't tell him. Well, that's only half knowing some-one isn't it? It's like I'm keeping a big secret from a friend, and I'd really like to hang out more with Pye, and yes, I know it's all a bit strange and I suppose if I do tell him he won't believe me, or if he does, he'll be weirded out. I know I would be.

So for now, I reply, "Albert. Like me. And my mum is Sarah."

He stares at the picture very closely, then smiles. "He looks just like my dad. They could be brothers, in fact."

"Like us."

"Hey—maybe they are! Separated at birth and their par-ents never told them about each other. . . ."

"No," I say quickly, "that can't be true. Besides, they speak with different accents."

"Well, one could have come to Britain before . . . Hang on, how do you know how my dad speaks?"

Whoops.

"Just guessing. Does he have an Indian accent?"

"Yeah. But we're not allowed to speak Punjabi at home. He says, 'Dat is de language of another time, another life, Pythagoras. Ve are British now.'" Pye wobbles his head like Grandpa Byron does, and I'm suddenly filled with regret at how we parted.

I know it would be wrong—it could threaten everything—but I blurt out, "Can I meet your dad? He sounds great!"

"Of course you can. He's working late tonight, but you can come round tomorrow after we've been on my go-kart. I mean, if you want to. And we've still got this to finish," he adds, pointing at the central table with five of the six computers now linked up.

"Your go-kart?" Of course, I know all about this, but I'm doing pretty well at not showing it, I think.

"Yeah. I built it with my dad. It's not a real go-kart, it's just a bogey, but it's completely ace!"

I'm back at the fridge now, looking at my laptop. Outside the sky has begun to darken earlier than usual with a big black cloud looking grim and threatening.

"I'd leave it overnight if I were you. Looks like it's gonna rain. We should be getting back."

Pye puts the key back in the brick hole. We hop over the low wall and he turns to me, hunching his shoulders as the rain begins to fall.

"You go that way, I guess."

"Yeah."

"Um, Al? I've had a really good time today. Thanks for, um . . ." He trails off, and I let him take his time. He chews his lip and looks down, like he's searching for the right words on the ground.

"I don't . . . I don't really have many . . . Look, Macca? He's not much of a friend, you're right, but, well, it was better than nobody." There's a long pause; then he adds, "Till now." And he gives his shy half smile again and walks away quickly. Ten meters later, he turns back. "See you right here tomorrow?"

I decide to risk something. "With the Lean Mean Green Machine?"

A broad grin splits his face. "How the . . . ? Yeah!" And then he adds, "And I still want to meet your hamster!"

I wait till he's gone, then turn and run back to the rusty blue door, letting myself in with the key and shaking the rain off my hair.

Alan Shearer, Alan Shearer, Alan Shearer. How am I going to get him back?

I look around the tech lab. This will be my bed for the night. Half a packet of biscuits and an apple later, it's beginning to get dark and I'm dozing off and then . . .

It's a thunderclap that wakes me, the *boom* making the school windows rattle, and I think, as I often do when the weather's bad at night, how lucky I am to be human and indoors and not an animal outside. Or indeed a hamster in a drawer in an underground bunker.

I take a long breath as I realize something: I'm not going to sleep again until I have rescued Alan Shearer.

I have to go back to Macca's house.

How Thunder Works

My dad used to tell me that thunder is the noise the rain clouds make when they bump together; then they crack and all the rain spills out.

I believed him for ages.

In truth, thunder is lightning. At any rate, it's the noise of lightning. It's just that lightning travels at the speed of light, so you see it pretty much as soon as it flashes.

The sound of the lightning—thunder—travels much, much slower, so you hear it afterward.

When you see lightning, start counting slowly until you hear the thunder. Then divide the number you get by three. That's how many kilometers away the storm is.

If the number gets smaller, then the storm is getting closer.

CHAPTER FIFTY-EIGHT

Ten minutes later I'm back outside Macca's house, soaking wet and contemplating my third break-in of what I think of as the recent past.

I've never had to break into this garage before. And it's properly shut. This is not a case of just edging my fingers in the gap and pulling: that won't be possible for thirty years.

In my hand is a steel crowbar, filched from the school custodian's closet.

When I left the school, I counted thirty seconds between a lightning flash and the thunder. So the storm was ten kilometers away. Now, as I'm standing outside the house, I can only count to five. The storm will be right on top of me soon.

When it comes, the thunder is a growl like a billion angry dogs, followed by a long, deafening crack that hurts my ears. I take my chance and jam the crowbar into the space where the two garage doors join, and push. The door splinters and creaks and bursts open just as the sound of the thunder fades away, and I know that the noise has not been heard over the storm. Seconds later I'm inside the garage, shivering. The planks are stacked up against the wall, and I descend the steps to open the circular door, but I already have a sinking feeling that something won't be right.

Alan Shearer's not in his drawer. The sides are about fifteen centimeters high, and impossible for a hamster to climb. Still, I hunt around the bunker desperately, saying softly, "Alan Shearer! Alan? Come on. . . ."

But he's not there. I slump into the swivel chair and fight back tears, because I know that Macca has him, and I know what might happen to him in Macca's hands.

It's no use. The tears, when they come, are hot and angry, and I cry for my pet; and for myself, stranded in a year where I don't belong; and for my dad, who died too early; and for Pye, whose new friend—me—is not what he seems. And now that I've started, I can't stop, because I'm thinking of Grandpa Byron on the ladder seeing his only grandson disappear in front of him, and my mum who must be so, *so* worried.

And it's no good just setting the return time earlier, as if that makes what has happened somehow unhappen, because it doesn't. I might be able to return and somehow stop Dad meddling with space-time, so I never receive the letter from him, and don't ever time travel or go off on a spree of moped thefts and break-ins. But those things have definitely happened, somewhere in the vast infinity of the universe. They happened to me. And somewhere in that vast infinity there will always be a Grandpa Byron and a mum brokenhearted for a lost Al, a me that one day just disappeared.

What was I thinking? How could I have taken such an insane risk?

The tears and sobs have exhausted me, and I flop down on the bunk bed and sleep and dream of nothing. Nothing at all.

CHAPTER FIFTY-NINE

Sticking my head out from the garage the next morning, I can tell it's really early but that's about it. The storm has passed, but it's still warm and blustery, and the sky is pure white clouds.

Nobody is about on Chesterton Road, except for a small open-sided van humming along slowly and tinkling as if it's carrying glass bottles.

Minutes later and I'm back in the school's tech lab. My heart is pounding and I'm actually finding it a bit hard to breathe because I'm so nervous.

It's August 1. Today is the day that Dad comes off his go-kart, breaks his teeth, and gets a metal splinter up his nose that will give him headaches for years and kill him twenty-seven years later. And I have to stop that happening without radically altering anything else.

So. The Plan For Today is to save my dad's life *and* get

back to my own time, having found Alan Shearer. That'll keep me busy.

My hands are shaking as I slot the laptop battery back into position and screw the cover back on.

I can't bring myself to press the on button, I just can't.

I walk around the room once. Twice.

I'm about to go a third time, but instead I reach out and press the button firmly once, kind of taking myself by surprise.

One second.

Two seconds.

You must have listened to a laptop starting up? It takes a couple of seconds, and then . . .

A soft *ping.*

I feel like crying again, this time with relief. The screen flickers and lights up. And then . . .

just . . .

stops.

No. Please no.

The start-up screen is there, but there's nothing on it. No documents, no folders. There's no whirring sound of the hard disk. The clock is blinking 02:13, which must be the correct time somewhere in the universe. The battery indicator says

65 percent. Yet there's no cursor. I rub the touch pad desperately, begging the cursor to appear. I hit keys randomly.

Nothing.

I slump forward with my head on my arms, and I'm just numb. I hit the keypad again, then restart the laptop, but still—the folder with all the data in it is not there.

I'm just washed over with a sense of total weariness, and I slam the laptop closed.

And then I open it again slowly, chewing my bottom lip. If this works, then I may just have a chance.

Again I stare at the lit-up screen, and I pull my key ring from my pocket. Attached is my memory stick, and I push it into the USB slot at the side of the laptop. The laptop might not read the hard disk properly and can't perform many functions, but there's still a chance it can read a memory stick.

Its little blue light flashes, and an icon blinks to life on the screen. With no cursor, I have no choice but to hit "Enter," and it works—the document opens, revealing page after page of numbers and symbols: Dad's code for the time travel program.

Right. Now I have to work quickly. The laptop's battery life has already gone down to 63 percent, and I have a huge job ahead of me. All the laptop will show me is the information

TIME TRAVELING WITH A HAMSTER

from my memory stick. None of the time travel stuff is loading up, and I have no idea how to make it.

But *this* might work. . . .

Pushing a plug into the wall and flicking a switch, I turn on Pye's six-screen supercomputer, and pull the nearest one round to face me. The screen is old-fashioned: dark with flickery green letters and numbers, but it's my only shot.

Copying from the laptop, and using the laptop's keyboard to navigate up and down the lines of text, I start the task of entering every single character and space into the old computer.

Precision counts, I remember, and I have never been more aware of how right Grandpa Byron was. I cannot afford to make a single, solitary, tiny error.

After a few minutes I work out a method, which is to do five characters at a time. I read them out loud slowly from the laptop:

"Six, five, forward slash, five, two." And then I say them out loud again as I type them into the computer: "Six, five, forward slash, five, two." I then check what I have just input.

It's slow, but it's the only way I can be sure of not making a mistake.

But after half an hour, I have only done a bit more than

half a page of code, and the battery is down to 52 percent. There are seven pages of this stuff. That's 20 percent of existing battery life gone, but only about 10 percent of the code rewritten, all of which means I have to go twice as fast, which I just can't.

But I'm trying. I increase my character input to six, seven, and then eight at a time, shouting out the numbers to myself like a series of phone numbers. To remember them quicker without checking, I shout them, I sing them:

"Four, one, colon, slash! Double six, six, dash!"

"X, X, forty-four, equals, bracket, three, five!"

I take a long drink of water from the lab tap and keep going, hitting the keys harder until my fingers are hurting, yelling the numbers and obsessively watching the decreasing battery.

Thirty percent . . .

Twenty-eight percent . . .

And then it really starts to decrease quickly. Fifteen, fourteen, thirteen percent . . . and I've still got two pages to go.

One page, and I'm hitting the keys like a maniac now, shouting, singing—anything to keep my concentration focused and finish.

And then the screen flickers and dies with half a page of code still to go.

How To Bring A Dead Battery Back To Life

1. Remove it from the laptop or other device.

2. Wrap it carefully in a waterproof casing, such as a ziplock bag. This is important, as moisture will damage the battery.

3. Place in your freezer for two or more hours.

You may get enough life back into it to help you in a sticky situation.

I pass some of the next two hours imagining what sort of sticky situation was imagined by the guy who wrote that entry on wikiHow that I had seen ages ago.

Not being able to print off your homework, maybe? Or potentially missing the last fifteen minutes of a movie?

Not being able to enter the code to transport someone home across space-time probably didn't figure.

But whoever he is, I owe him a big "Thanks, mate!" and countless "likes"—because it worked.

I get twenty more battery minutes, and finish inputting with 4 percent to spare. Now I can use Pye's networked computer to travel back to my time. Hopefully.

Just in case it comes in useful, I connect my mobile with its USB charger, and charge it from the laptop until the laptop has only 1 percent remaining.

I'm exhausted. I slump in front of the homemade supercomputer, breathing hard and watching the green characters flicker.

I jump at the voice behind me.

"How long you been here?"

Pye sits down next to me and looks at the screen. "What the heck's all this?"

"Long story," I say. "Got your go-kart?"

"We'll go and get it," he says.

CHAPTER SIXTY

Before I can object, Pye has left the tech lab and I'm jogging to keep up with him.

"My house isn't far," he says.

"We're going to your house?"

"Yeah. Why? What's wrong?" He must be able to read the expression on my face.

"Um . . . nothing," I say with exaggerated casualness. "No, nothing at all. Excellent. Great." I've overdone it a bit, and Pye's brow creases with puzzlement, but he doesn't say anything.

We're outside the school by now, and Pye's putting the key back in the brick hole. The warm, fresh breeze of earlier has gone, and it feels like another storm is coming. The air is so sticky you can almost taste it, and the sky has turned into a dark gray blanket, making everything feel close.

Pye and I haven't said anything for a few minutes, which

feels strange, so I break the silence by saying, "Is your dad going to be there? Or your mum?" I add quickly, because that would be the normal thing to say.

This, you'll have guessed, is what's worrying me. The prospect of meeting Grandpa Byron is making me sick with anxiety, and I'm also a bit excited. It's exactly the same feeling I had before I went on the Vampire ride at Chessington World of Adventures that time with Mum and Steve: truly terrified, but looking forward to it at the same time. Pye is striding ahead.

"No, my mum's dead. My dad's there, but he was still in bed when I left. He's working late. And my sister."

"Your *sister*?" It's true: I completely forgot about Aunty Hypatia, which is hardly surprising as she is barely mentioned at home and I have met her only that once when she wafted into Dad's funeral preceded by a cloud of heavy perfume.

"Yeah, she's completely annoying, but don't worry: she won't disturb us. She's only five. I'm not really supposed to leave the house if Dad's asleep, but she's watching telly, and to be honest, she'd stay there watching it even if it was only the test screen."

"The what?"

"The test screen. You know—all those colored wavy lines."

"Oh. Yeah." I have exactly *no* idea what Pye is on about, but it doesn't really matter because he's still talking.

"We just got a color telly a few weeks ago. I must have been the last kid in Britain to know that football teams had different-colored shirts."

I stare at Pye in astonishment. He looks at me out of the sides of his eyes, smiles slowly, and points an accusing finger at me. "Kidding! Well, not about the color telly. That is pretty new. Like, I bet you've got one, yeah?"

"Sure." To be honest, I don't think I've ever seen TV programs that aren't in color, apart from the old films that Mum likes but I don't, except for one with Marilyn Monroe and two guys who dressed up as ladies, which was totally hilarious. Anyway, Pye's still chattering on as we turn the corner.

"So what's your favorite program, Al?"

This is tricky. I don't know any TV programs from the eighties, so I mumble, "Dunno, really. I don't watch much TV, to be honest."

"That's like my dad. He only watches quiz shows. *Mastermind* is his favorite. I keep telling him—"

I'm so relieved to hear a title that I know that I interrupt Pye. "Oh, yeah—I like that one!"

He comes back at me with the program's catchphrase: "'I've started, so I'll finish!' I keep telling him he should enter, but he says, 'Nah, man—telly's for watchin', not bein' on,'" and Pye wobbles his head, and the whole impression of Grandpa Byron—the Geordie-Indian accent, the head wobble—is so amazingly accurate that I give a delighted shout of laughter and say, "That's exactly like him! Probably!"

We've stopped outside a small house on Sandview Avenue, a long street of tiny semidetached houses leading down to the beach. Wind chimes are hanging from the little porch, and they *ping* and *pong* in the breeze, which has been getting stronger, bringing a few fat drops of rain.

"C'mon—let's go in before we get soaked."

We go in the back door that's up the side of the house, which opens into the kitchen, and there he is, wearing gold-colored pajama bottoms. His slim, tan back is toward us because he's washing something in the sink, and there's his long plait of hair—not white like I'm used to, but silky black.

I just stand there for a while, my throat so tight that I can't swallow. I glance around the kitchen, and it's just like everything I'm used to with him: there's loads of stuff, things, knickknacks, and whatnots—a souvenir mug, a picture calendar, a tiny glass model of the Buddha—but somehow everything is neat. It doesn't look cluttered, or messy or dirty, it's just . . . him.

There's a door leading to the hallway, and a tiny girl with huge brown eyes looks up at me, then scuttles away toward the sound of a television in the front room.

And then he turns to face us, wiping his hands, and gives a big grin, and I can see his gold tooth, and he's *exactly the same,* only a bit less lined in the face (but only a bit). When I see his smile, it takes all of my effort not to go up to him and give him a huge hug, and smell his smell, but I realize that would be weird, so instead I just smile like an idiot.

"Why, hello, bonny lad! Who's this? Ye've found yer long-lost twin, have ye?" Grandpa Byron is looking at my face really closely, but he hasn't stopped grinning, so I'm feeling more relaxed.

"Daddy-ji—this is Al. He's starting at our school next term."

"Hello, Al, how ye deein'?" He puts out his right hand and I clasp it eagerly. It's the next best thing to a hug, and I pump his hand up and down. As I do, it hits me: this is Grandpa Byron's right hand. The bad one, on the end of his twisted, useless arm. Except it's fine: a strong hand, and a straight, healthy arm.

"Very well, thank you, Mr. Chaudhury, very well." I'm almost laughing, I'm so happy, but that would be weird as well.

"Ah, man—you can call me Byron. Everyone else does. Can I . . . can I have me hand back? That's some grip you've got there, bonny lad." I let him go, reluctantly. He's peering at me again.

"You've got a touch of the tar brush in you, son—where are your folks from?"

"My dad's from Punjab. Originally." I'm nervous about where this is headed, but I'm trying to look relaxed.

"Get away! Me too. *Tuhanu Panjabi aundi he?*"

Now, I know enough to understand that this means "Do you speak Punjabi?"

"Not really," I say. "We speak English at home. My mum's Scottish."

Grandpa Byron smiles and nods. "What's your last name?"

"Singh."

"OK. Well, you're not a Sikh Singh; otherwise you'd have a turban. So what are you?"

This is something I hadn't anticipated. What could he

mean, *"What are you?"* I'm sort of gawping, trying to think what to say, when he helps me out.

"You know—your dad. Is he Rajput, Yadav, Maratha . . ."

I guess that these are some sort of Indian clans, and I pick one at random. "Erm . . . Maratha?" Grandpa Byron looks upward in the expression I recognize as he tries to retrieve something from his memory palace.

"OK . . . OK . . . Maratha Singhs, from . . . Bahawalpur? You'll be descended somehow from Dhani Ram Singh, the great Punjabi poet, who died in 1924, who had ten children, called Rani, Raj . . ."

This is just like listening to Grandpa Byron when he was playing along with the TV quizzes, and I start laughing out loud. But Pye puts a stop to it.

"Dad!"

That's all it takes. Grandpa Byron stops midsentence, and his gaze returns to us. He looks a bit embarrassed. "Sorry," he says with a half smile. Pye is rolling his eyes, but smiling at the same time.

"He's always doing that—showing off his memory!"

"That's all right," I said. "Who won the Wimbledon men's singles in 1967?"

Without hesitating, he says, "John Newcombe from Australia beat Wilhelm Bungert from Germany in straight sets. And at Wimbledon they call it the gentlemen's singles. Pye been tellin' you about my memory, has he?"

Pye hasn't said anything to me about Grandpa Byron's memory, but I nod in reply because I know it will please him. Pye frowns at me, though.

Oops.

But I'm saved from any further quizzing on my fictitious family background and my unlikely knowledge of Grandpa Byron's memory by a piercing scream.

CHAPTER SIXTY-ONE

OK, here's a question for you.

You're delivering newspapers door to door, and you come across a box of strange masks on someone's doorstep. Do you:

a) Completely ignore the box and its contents. It's not yours, after all.

b) Look around. If no one's looking, then perhaps try one on. Quickly.

c) Find the scariest one you can and scare the nearest five-year-old girl so much that she wets herself.

I'm guessing, and hoping, that your answer will be (a) or (b). I'd like to think I'm a (b), but if I'm honest—because I'm honest—it's probably (a).

Definitely not (c).

But then, I'm not Macca.

Grandpa Byron is first to run toward the scream, and Pye and I follow him. In the middle of the sitting room, little Hypatia is standing rigid, staring out the window, a tiny puddle of pee darkening the carpet at her feet. She turns to her dad and buries her face in his legs.

"What is it? What is it, Hypie? Are you OK?" he asks, but she just points behind her out the window. With a jerk of his head, Grandpa Byron indicates to Pye and me to go and check outside.

Opening the front door, we can't see anything; there's just noth—

"RAAAAAAAAGH!" A hideous figure leaps up in front of us from behind a bush, causing us both to yell and jump back.

The mask is truly gross: an ugly head in blue and gold and red and white, with big jagged teeth, a long red tongue, and tiny skulls around the edge. And then the mask is lowered and Macca reveals himself, cackling cruelly.

"Ha! It's the boyfriends! I didn't knaa ye lived here, man, Chow! Eeh, you should've seen your faces. You looked like you were gonna wet yerselves!"

"Well, I think you should be very proud of yourself," says Grandpa Byron, who has appeared, bare chested, in the doorway, still wearing his gold pajama bottoms. "You've managed to achieve that with a five-year-old girl." His voice is completely calm, but there's an icy look in his eyes. "So well done, son. Do you feel big now?"

If this were you or me, or anyone normal in fact, then we'd be really embarrassed and stammer out some sort of apology. But this is Macca, who straightens his back and tilts his head to one side, looking defiantly with his little bulging eyes at Grandpa Byron, who is waiting for him to say something. Behind Grandpa Byron, in the window, little Hypatia's face is pressed against the glass, her big, scared eyes still wet.

"Well?"

Macca says nothing. Grandpa Byron turns to us. "Do you know this joker, Pye? Is he a friend of yours?"

Before Pye can answer, Macca chips in with a friendly note in his voice, "Oh, aye. We're good mates, aren't we, Chow? Pye? We're—"

"I wasn't asking you. Pye?"

Pye's eyes dart from me to his dad to Macca. Macca's eyes narrow as they meet Pye's, and his nostrils flare.

"Is he a friend of yours, Pye?"

Almost inaudibly, Pye mutters, "Yeah."

You know what? I think I'd have done the same. Self-preservation and all that. I think no less of Pye.

"All right then. Give me back the mask, say sorry, and bugger off."

I don't think I have ever heard anyone say sorry and mean it less. Holding Grandpa Byron's gaze with his own hooded eyes, Macca delivers a clipped "sorry" as he hands over the mask, then turns sharply, gathering up his bag of newspapers from the driveway and stalking past us.

As he does so he throws a glance at us, and it's what he does next that sends a chill down my neck.

He winks, and there's a half smirk on his lips.

CHAPTER SIXTY-TWO

So we're standing outside Pye's house, and still the rain's not raining properly: just occasional drops.

Macca's round the corner now, and Grandpa Byron shakes his head as he watches him go before bending down to lift up the box of masks. He sees me looking at them and straightens up.

"They're for Diwali. We're organizing the first northeast coast Diwali celebration in autumn. My friend Baru left them here when he did his milk round first thing. Here." He picks out the mask that Macca had been using. "This is Kali. You know Kali?"

"She who is death," I say, and Grandpa Byron grins.

"Very good! Your father tell you that?" I can't help glancing over at Pye and nodding. He heads indoors.

"Did he also tell you she is the consort of Shiva, the most supreme, the most pure? You see, 'Kal' also means 'time,' and the 'i' means 'cause'—so Kali is 'the cause of time'—the one who allows us to perceive everything, to experience time passing—whereas Shiva, her other half, is timeless. Do you get it?"

I follow Grandpa Byron back into the kitchen—I don't know where Pye has gone—and he picks up the mask again, staring at it a little dreamily.

I'm not sure I do get it actually, not completely, but I nod anyway. It's just good to hear him again. He smiles at me, his gold tooth glinting.

"You're a canny kid you are, son. Too many like you know absolutely nowt about their heritage." He's sipping from a large mug and leaning back against the kitchen counter. "Lose sight of the past and you are blind to the future: that's what I say to Pye."

"Is that chai?" I ask. I have sort of moved across to where Grandpa Byron is standing, and I pretend to sniff at the cup he's holding. Really I'm trying to smell him, but it doesn't work. All I get is the whiff of the sweet milky chai.

"Why, yes, it is—do you want some?" He turns to get another mug and pours from the steaming jug. "That is so jolly splendid you like chai! I am hoping I'll meet your parents soon—what is your father's name?"

I don't get to reply, because at that moment the answer comes back into the kitchen as a very welcome interruption.

"Can I show Al the fireworks, Daddy-ji?" Pye is by the back door with his hand on the handle.

"Go on, then—take these masks with you and put them on the shelf."

Most of the houses on Pye's street have got a tiny shed in the back garden, just about big enough for a lawn mower to mow the tiny lawn. Pye's shed, though, takes up half of the outside space. Inside, just like the kitchen, it's full of stuff, yet tidy. Even the shed windows are clean, and not covered in cobwebs. It smells of fresh wood and old paint.

On the floor, pushed up against the wooden wall, is a huge silvery metal trunk, like a cupboard lying on its side. Straining, Pye lifts up the lid. "Check this out!"

Inside, the trunk is packed to the brim with fireworks, but unlike any fireworks I have seen up close in my life. There are huge cake-shaped drums with countless blue fuses, multicolored canisters the size of a Pringles tube, and rockets that must be nearly two meters long, dozens and dozens of them. I pick one up and hold it up to the light from the window, gasping at its weight.

"Wow! Diwali again?"

"Yep. It's going to be the biggest fireworks display ever seen. You've got to come!"

My attention has wandered already, though. Because propped up in the corner of the shed is the reason I am here, and my stomach gives a little lurch as I remember why.

CHAPTER SIXTY-THREE

It's a beautiful thing, the Lean Mean Green Machine. When Dad—when he was Dad, not Pye—told me about it, I had the idea that it was a tatty, amateur affair, but it's not. It's awesome. The pram wheels are a bit rusty on the spokes, but otherwise it looks like one of the pictures in a book that tells you how to make it but the one you make yourself never looks as good as.

Olive green, with a white stripe down the side, and there's even a cushion in the sit-on part.

"That's better than I ever imagined," I say, with true admiration. I sit in it and Pye pulls me along the garden path, and I can steer and brake and everything. We tow the kart out of the garden gate and into the back lane that runs behind the row of houses. I'm first out of the gate, and I turn my head toward the sound of running feet, just in time to see a figure turn the corner at the end and disappear.

Macca. Has he been watching us? What has he seen? I can't tell.

"What's up?" asks Pye.

I take a deep breath. "Nothing." And then I turn and head back toward the house. "Hang on," I call back. "I just want to say goodbye to your dad." Pye smiles and shrugs.

Grandpa Byron's sitting at the kitchen table with Hypatia next to him holding a deck of cards that's far too big for her little hands. She turns them faceup one by one on the table, and he's calling the names before he sees them.

"Ten of diamonds, six of spades, jack of spades—oh hello, son. What can I do for you?"

I hesitate, not quite sure what to say. Grandpa Byron waits patiently while I find the words.

"Um, Mr. Chaudhury? Byron? You know this fireworks display you're doing?"

"Aye, what about it? It's not till October, mind you."

"Erm . . . will you have the fireworks on a sort of metal platform thingy?"

"A pyro rig? Aye, I daresay."

"Oh good. Can I just say, erm . . . they're kinda danger-ous, so will you make sure you check it's secure and every-thing?"

He screws up his eyes and sort of half smiles. "Er, yes, I daresay we'll be doing that." I can tell he's not taking me all that seriously.

"No, I really mean it. Please, please check all the bolts on the pyro rig. It's just . . . I've heard of someone who didn't and it sort of went wrong."

"All right, bonny lad, I'll check them."

"You won't forget? Check them yourself. All of them?"

There's a longish pause while he looks hard at me to see if I'm serious. When he sees that I am, he nods slowly and grins. "I won't forget. I can remember anything I want. For a lad who likes chai and knows about Kali I promise I won't forget." I can tell he means it.

"Thanks. Bye."

"Bye, Al." Hypatia echoes him in her little-girl voice: "Bye, Al!"

I turn to go, but something makes me stop for a second. I check that Pye can't see me from his position at the end of the garden. I turn back and throw my arms around Grandpa Byron in a big hug. He's startled, I can tell, and I know it's a strange thing to do, but as I squeeze him, and at last breathe in his smell of *beedis* and hair oil, I feel his arms go around me and he hugs me back.

I'm embarrassed now, and I let him go, but before I hurry out the back door, there's one more thing I want to do. Fishing my phone out of my pocket, I switch it on, hold it at arm's length, and crouch beside them.

"Look at my, erm . . . calculator and smile," I say to Grandpa Byron and Hypatia. Before I can see if they're doing it right, I snap a selfie, then hurry out the back door and up the garden path without looking back.

As I leave, I hear Grandpa Byron saying to Hypatia, "I haven't a clue, pet."

CHAPTER SIXTY-FOUR

"Where are we headed?" I ask Pye.

"Let's go down the slipway to the beach! You can build up a good head of speed."

"I know—we could go on the path down to the small bay? It might be faster." Pye looks at me doubtfully. Culvercot's beach is cut into two bays, where a low cliff juts out and divides the beach. The smaller bay has a smooth, tarmacked path leading down to it. Perfect for homemade go-karts, in fact.

Except in 1984, it isn't yet tarmacked. We stop at the top and look down at the rough, pebbly surface. "That's lethal, that is," says Pye, and turns immediately to walk over the cliff top to the other bay.

The tide is higher than I've ever seen it, and the steel-gray waves are pounding the seawall and splashing over the promenade below.

What we call the slipway is a long and steep path with grass on either side and a wide curve leading from the cliff top down to the beach, where today the sea is high enough to cover the sand. About halfway down the path, on the arc of the bend, it joins up with the grandly named promenade, which is really just the top of the seawall with two or three benches where old people go to sit.

So this, I think, *is the path that killed my dad.* It's an odd thing to think, I grant you, but that's what is going through my mind, as well as a nervous calculation about what will happen next. Just then, a weak shaft of sunlight pierces the thick cloud, which I take as a good omen, and I start to feel better and better about the whole day.

I'm going to do this, and I'm going to do it right.

We stand at the top, Pye and me, and plan out the ride. It's pretty straightforward: a steep bit at the start, then into the curve, which will take a bit of braking and steering but not much, and then the gradient levels off a bit so that by the time you reach the beach, you're going a bit slower and the sand will stop the wheels anyway.

"Who's going to go first?" I ask.

"Not me. I've done it loads of times. It's got to be you."

So I sit on the cushion, one foot pushed against each front

wheel to stop the kart from rolling forward, and it so wants to go. It was made for this. The wind is strong, and the waves are loud, and the blood is pumping in my ears, so when I take my feet away I get a cold rush of air, which I gasp at as the kart picks up speed on the first steep part.

It's a smooth ride, and *fast*! I'm applying the brake well before the curve, and tugging on the right-hand rope to turn the front axle, and my hair is blown by the speed and the salty wind as I go round the curve. . . .

"Ha haaaaa!"

I'm slowing down a bit now, and off to the left of the path I see it: the brick that Dad crashed into. It's toward the side of the path, not the middle as he had said, but it's there all right, and definitely dangerous if you hit it at full speed. By the side is a small, rusty supermarket trolley. It all fits. It's just as Dad said.

Then I'm slowing down with a shudder as the pram wheels hit the soft sand, bringing me to a stop. I leap out and pull the Lean Mean Green Machine out of the way of a gray wave that's creeping up the beach, and start running back up to the top.

On the way I stop at the brick and throw it well out of the way, and wrench the trolley out of the sandy soil it's half buried in, away from the path, and rejoin Pye, who opens his arms and shouts, "Yaaaay!" before throwing them around me and squeezing really hard so that I'm gasping and laughing.

"How was that?" he says. He is hopping from one foot to the other with excitement.

"Pretty awesome, but man, it's steep at the start. Don't forget to brake!"

"I won't." Pye stops. He's looking over my shoulder. "Is that who I think it is?"

CHAPTER SIXTY-FIVE

Coming toward us from the other side of the promenade is Macca. He's holding what looks like a bunch of sticks in his arms. He waves an arm above his head and shouts something, but it's indistinct under the noise of the wind and the waves.

"Oh terrific. What does he want?"

He stops on the prom and waves for us to come down and join him. I point to him, then to us. "No!" I shout. "You come here," but he shakes his head, holds up the sticks, and waves us toward him again.

Pye says, "You go and see what he wants. I'll ride down in a minute. I just want to shorten the string a bit." He kneels down and starts untying the steering rope from the front axle. I figure it's safe to let him ride the kart. After all, I've got rid of the brick and the shopping trolley now.

When I get near Macca, I see that he is placing the sticks

of three huge fireworks rockets into a hollow tube he's shoved in the ground, and he's got the same mean grin on his face as he had the very first time I saw him.

"All right, boyfriend? You'll never guess what I've got." He gurgles a manic-sounding laugh and bares his yellow teeth.

I don't know what to say. They are so obviously the rockets from Pye's shed, and Macca just doesn't care. He's stolen them, and what can I do about it anyway? Report him? Fight him? He knows I'm powerless and it enrages me.

"Those are *ours*! Well, Pye's," I hear myself shouting over the wind.

"What? These? Nah, man, they're mine, left over from last Bonfire Night." He's lying, obviously, but so brazenly that he just carries on without a pause. "Look, I've taped them together wi' Sellotape." So he has, and the blue touchpapers of each rocket have been twisted together too. "And it gets better."

Out of the pocket of his thin zip-up anorak he brings a jam jar filled with liquid. Opening it up carelessly, he spills half the contents on his sleeve as he pulls from the jar a long string that has been soaking and chucks the jar on the ground.

"It's lighter fluid," he explains. "And *this* is the extra-long fuse." He twists it round the blue touchpapers and trails it across the ground. It's only about a meter long, so I don't really see the point, but what happens next changes everything.

Honestly: *everything.*

"Now for the masterstroke," says Macca proudly. "Get yersel' a look at this, man."

He turns the rockets around so that for the first time I can see the other side, and taped onto them is an empty toilet roll with one end flattened down and stuck, so it's a tube with a closed end.

"It's going to be the first . . . ," and he says something that I don't catch because just then a big wave crashes into the seawall and sends a fine spray over the two of us. "Here, steady!" he shouts at the sea. "Don't get me rockets wet!"

"The first what?"

"This is *ace.* It's the first rat in space."

Out of the other anorak pocket he takes Alan Shearer. "I found him in our bunker." He's holding him far too tightly, and Alan Shearer bites him. "Ow! You little bleeder, you deserve what's comin' to you!"

"That's not a rat, that's my hamster!"

"*Your* hamster? How come? How the hell can it be yours? Don't be such a moron—it's a rat with a deformed tail.

Vermin, runnin' around my bunker, and this is what we do to vermin, specially ones that bite—OW!" Alan Shearer bites him again as Macca shoves him headfirst into the toilet tube.

"No!" I shout, "You can't!" I try to reach out for the rocket contraption, but Macca shoves me away, then turns to grab me, one hand gripping my jacket and the other grabbing a handful of my hair. He puts his face close to mine and I can taste his spit as he shouts.

"I bleedin' well can and I bleedin' well will!" He practically picks me up and marches two or three steps up the grass bank before throwing me hard on the ground so that all of the air in my lungs is forced out. Just as I'm managing to draw in some oxygen, Macca delivers a brutal, vicious stamp with his boot on my stomach, and I think I actually black out, just for a second or two, with pain and breathlessness. When I regain my senses, I can see Pye fiddling with the string on the kart, but he hasn't seen our confrontation. He's just getting into the kart, preparing to set off.

Macca's back at the rockets now, bending over the fluid-soaked string and trying to coax a flame from a cigarette lighter, but the wind is too strong. What happens next is something I can remember in every detail. I wish I couldn't, but I can.

CHAPTER SIXTY-SIX

The thought of what Macca is about to do to Alan Shearer forces me, gasping, to my feet at the same moment that the lighter flares up, and almost instantaneously a much bigger flame whooshes up from the pool where the jar had spilled. No more than a second later, and the sleeve of Macca's jacket is alight. To begin with, he glares at his burning sleeve angrily, and then he's *laughing*. Not a funny laugh, though; more a sort of crazed cackle.

With a desperate effort, I lunge forward at the rockets and push them out of the way, and at that moment I see a green shape in my peripheral vision heading fast toward us. The Lean Mean Green Machine is coming straight down the path and misses the curve, instead hurtling onto the promenade, Pye's face frozen in silent, open-mouthed fear.

Pye is careening directly toward Macca, who is still cackling and waving his flaming arm around. One side of his hair is alight now, and he can't see Pye heading toward him. In fury at his cruelty, I push Macca hard, away from me, and he staggers toward the seawall edge. Holding the rockets and the toilet roll, I roll out of the way, and Pye and the go-kart smash into the back of Macca's legs.

At the moment of impact, I'm facing the ground, and I don't actually see them enter the water, but I hear the splash as they hit the sea. There's no scream, no big noise—just a fairly small splash, and then a big booming crash as another wave hits the seawall.

I've run to the edge of the seawall now, just as the biggest wave slams into the concrete with another slap and smashes the go-kart in two. Carried up on the wave is Macca, his face contorted with terror, and then he's down again, over the back of the wave. I'm looking for Pye, but I can see nothing but boiling white surf, and then I hear a cry. Not "Help!" as you might expect, but just "Aaaaa!" and it's Macca again, much farther out now and waving with one hand. It has only been about ten seconds since they hit the water, and already the combination of the waves and the current has carried him far from the shore.

I'm still trying—desperately—to see Pye, but there's nothing. In fact, I haven't seen him since the blur of the go-kart entering the water. For a moment I wonder if he's been washed up on the beach farther along, and I run toward the tiny strip of sand that's being pounded by the waves.

"Pye! Pye!"

I'm soaked with the sea spray, hair sticking to my forehead, and I'm screaming.

"Dad! Dad!"

Nothing.

"Daddy!"

The waves continue to bash, and the wind dies down a little, and it's ages before I think about the lifeboat even though I know it's useless. All I can do is just stare at the spot where the kart and Macca and Pye entered the water. Two or three people have gathered on the cliff top, and they're looking and pointing at the same place.

At one point I think I see Pye's head, but I can't be sure, and then another minute goes past and I'm sure I see Macca's arm waving, but he's way, way out by now. And then I'm just staring, staring at the pounding gray-black sea.

I slump to the ground and pick up Alan Shearer, and I might have stayed there forever, but a couple of the people on the top of the cliff have started scrambling down toward me, so I start walking back the way Macca came—back along the promenade—and my walk gets faster, and when I've rounded the corner I start to run. I run and I run and I daren't stop, because if I do, I think I'll start to sob, and if I start crying, I really don't think I'll ever stop, so I'd better keep running. Looking back, I see the flashing blue light of a police car, so I keep running till I'm staring down the long stretch of beach north of Culvercot that goes on for about two miles, and I want to run along that too but my chest is hurting and my legs are aching, so I just sink down onto the sand beneath an overhang of cliff where I can't be seen.

Then I hear the maroon flares go off, summoning the Culvercot lifeboat men: two loud bangs in the air.

That's when I start to cry. I don't know for how long. Between sobs my gaze is drawn out to the wild sea again and again, and I blink through the tears, hoping (I think) that Pye will suddenly be washed ashore on one of the waves. But really, I know he won't.

Eventually, I stop. It's like all my crying has been done in the last night and I've used it all up. There are no more tears left, and it feels safe and dry in my little semicave. I hear more police sirens on the road above me, but I just sit there on the damp sand staring out at the gray and white breakers, still trying to see a head or a raised arm in every movement of the sea.

And I sit.

And I stare some more.

I don't know how long I sit there. Maybe for hours. Eventually I give a huge sniff and pull on my red T-shirt and spare jumper in case someone recognizes me as the kid who was running away from the scene, and I head back to the school.

The Grandfather Paradox

Some very clever people have said that time travel cannot be possible because of the grandfather paradox.

This states that if you go back in time and murder your grandfather before he has fathered your father, then that means your father never existed, which means YOU cannot exist.

And if you cannot exist, then you cannot travel back in time to murder your grandfather.

Therefore, time travel cannot exist.

You know what? Not so long ago I would have said that made sense. Time travel can't exist because it's logically impossible.

But now I know that some things *don't* add up, yet exist anyway.

CHAPTER SIXTY-SEVEN

Logically, then, I should not be alive, because my dad died in a drowning accident in 1984—long before my dad even met my mum.

Yet here I am, walking, living, breathing, aching from Macca's stamping, sick with sadness and, for some reason, very, very hungry.

I've taken the back roads and have sort of come in a circle, and I'm quite near Pye's house. I go past a pub called the Foxhunters on the corner of DeSitter Road, which in my time is a supermarket. Opposite there's a corner shop with a stall of fruit outside, and I'm now going to add to my crimes of breaking and entering by becoming a thief, because the ten-pound note I have in the inside pocket of my backpack for emergencies has a totally different design and would arouse suspicion straightaway.

The fruit's easy. An apple and an orange go straight into

my pockets, and inside the shop is almost easier. The shop stretches quite a ways back from the front, and there are two rows of shelves running up the center. One guy in a turban is manning the till, and another young guy is stacking shelves. I make sure I'm out of sight of both of them, and see what I can get on the shelves near me. It's the dairy counter, so into my backpack go a pint of milk, a packet of cheese slices, and a six-pack of yogurts.

My heart is beating fast, and at any time I'm expecting to be stopped, but no one comes near me. The shelf-stacker guy has come round the corner, so I pick up a pot of cream and examine it, then replace it before heading round the other aisle, where I manage to put a packet of custard creams into my bag (careful . . . the packaging's noisy), and I figure milk, cheese, yogurt, biscuits, an apple, and an orange—it's hardly a feast, but it might fill me up.

It's when I'm nearly at the door that the young guy who was stacking the shelves steps in front of me and folds his arms.

"What the hell do you think you're doing, Pye?"

I'm so stunned that I say nothing. He pulls the backpack from my shoulder and opens it roughly. The man with the turban is standing next to me now as well.

"Pye Chaudhury. What in the name of good God Almighty has got into your head?" He's not shouting; in fact he doesn't seem angry, just really shocked.

"I was—I was . . ." I don't really know what I'm going to say, but I feel I should say something. "I was . . . hungry?"

"Hungry? And you thought you would *steal* from me? How many times have I given you food, mm? How often have you sat in that back room and eaten *dal bhat* with me and Tarun here, mm? Why, Pye, why?"

"I . . . I'm not Pye. I just look like him. My name's Albert. Al."

They both laugh at this: a cold, forced laugh.

Gently, but with a hard edge to his voice, the man wearing a turban says, "How about we let your father decide whether you're Pye or not?" and strides over to the counter and picks up the phone.

I don't understand the conversation because it's all in Punjabi, yet at the same time I understand it completely, for what else could he be saying:

"Byron? Yeah, Shop Guy here, hi. Listen, Byron, I've got Pye here and I've just caught him trying to steal a load of stuff, right under my nose. . . . Yes, stealing, Byron. Tarun saw him, and the stuff's in his bag. Oh, and he's saying he's not Pye, he's someone else. . . . You're coming round? Good, see you in a minute, my friend."

He comes back to face me. He bends down and puts his face very close, and I can smell the cloves on his breath and the soap on his neck.

"Pye Chaudhury. Let me tell you this. Our families have been friends for many, many years, and I'm going to let your father deal with this. But until he does, I have my own way of dealing with thieves like you." He nods to Tarun, who is standing behind me, and grips me hard by the upper arms. The man wearing the turban's hand draws back and he slaps me across my cheek with the full force of the large man he is. My head is jerked to one side with the strength of the blow, and I hear whining in my ears. As if from a long distance, I hear his voice:

"Don't you ever, ever, *ever* steal from me again, you disgraceful little *gaandu!*" The pain in my face and the shock of the blow have stung my eyes with tears. Tarun is still gripping my arms and the other one is pulling his arm back for another slap, when the bell on the shop door tinkles and in walks Grandpa Byron.

He takes one look at me and says, "That's not Pye."

I look defiantly at the shop owner. "I told you. My name's Al."

"But, Byron. He . . . surely . . . that's Pye—"

Grandpa Byron smiles broadly, interrupting him: "You telling me I don't know my own son, Baru? His name's Al. Singh. Just moved here, apparently. Father's a Maratha Singh. You know them?"

And I look at Grandpa Byron, and I want to run to him, and hug him again, and breathe in his smell of *beedis* and incense, and watch *Mind Games* with him and make hot sweet chai and tell him I'm sorry again and again and again until he believes me.

Only just then, the bell on the door tinkles again, and a policeman enters the shop: an old-fashioned-looking policeman, with a pointed helmet and a proper old uniform. He looks at the scene in front of him: Tarun gripping me by the arms, my face red from the slapping, and two other men gathered around me. He pauses a moment, and Tarun slowly releases me.

"Evening, Baru. Evening, Tarun," says the policeman slowly, looking at me instead of at them with a puzzled expression on his face.

"Good evening, Glen," they say in reply, together.

The policeman looks at Grandpa Byron. "Mr. Chaudhury?"

"Yes, that's me."

"Your little girl told me you were here. I'd, er . . . I'd like you to step outside with me, please."

He has a very serious expression on his face, and I catch the two shop guys looking at each other.

"Is something wrong?" asks Grandpa Byron.

"Just, er, come with me if you don't mind, sir."

The policeman and Grandpa Byron go out the shop door and I know what he's going to tell him, and I just can't face Grandpa Byron and what's about to happen, so I take my chance to push past them and run as fast as I can, clutching my backpack in my hand.

No one follows me.

CHAPTER SIXTY-EIGHT

There is a television in the tech lab, which I have plugged in, and I'm watching the local news. On the screen are pictures of people on the seafront.

REPORTER: "Lifeboat-men and worried passersby wait above the beach at Culvercot for news of a twelve-year-old boy still missing several hours after being swept out to sea. Named locally as Pythagoras Chaudhury, he and at least one friend were on top of the seawall this afternoon when it is thought they were hit by a massive wave. One boy was rescued about five hundred meters from shore and was taken to North Tyneside General Hospital, where his condition is described as critical."

DETECTIVE INSPECTOR JOHN CALVERT: "We are very pleased at the rescue of one of the boys. He has been officially identified as Paul MacFaddyen, age thirteen, from Culvercot. The search for the second boy was abandoned this evening as darkness fell and will resume in the morning."

REPORTER: "Police say they would also like to talk to a third boy who was seen running from the scene shortly after Paul and Pythagoras entered the water. They stress he is not under any sort of suspicion, but they need him to come forward to help establish what happened.

"The tragedy has prompted renewed calls from locals for a safety barrier to be erected along the top of the seawall. This is Jamie Bates in Culvercot for *Tonight Live.*"

I'm swallowing milk, cheese, custard creams, and yogurt, but every mouthful tastes of literally nothing. My stomach is getting fuller, and hurts less, but I just can't taste the food. I feed bits of cheese to Alan Shearer and he twitches his whiskers, but it doesn't make me smile like it usually does.

As well as being totally sad, I am totally scared, and I don't know what to do.

I *pushed* Macca. People saw me. It's not murder, because he's not dead, at least not yet, but the police are definitely looking for me. They'll want to know where I live, who my parents are. And as for Pye, well, barring some miracle, he has drowned. My dad is dead, and it's my fault, pretty much.

Pye's dad, Grandpa Byron, will want to know who I am, the boy who was—at any rate—*involved* in his son's death, even if I didn't *actually* kill him.

I can't stay here in 1984, that's for certain. I need to go back to my own time, and I must ensure that all traces of my time traveling are erased.

But is that even possible?

Assuming I could go back to my own time, what will happen when I get there? Will I exist? Can I exist? I have no father, after all.

If I'm to go back to my own time, I need the zinc tub that, at the moment, is still in the MacFaddyens' bunker, and their house when I passed it at a distance earlier was swarming with people: reporters, sympathizers, police. . . .

For a long time I just sit there, unblinking, my mouth turning sour from the cheese and milk I've been eating, and a pain in my chest, which could be from the running, and the tension, and Macca's stamping, but which could just as easily be a broken heart.

It's dark outside now, and the sadness inside me is like the heaviness you feel when you've eaten too much, and I feel breathless and exhausted. But one thing has changed: there's now an idea in the back of my head.

Wearily, I turn on the six computers and then head to the caretaker's storeroom. There's a stack of metal buckets. They're made of zinc. They might just get me home.

I also need some matches, or a lighter. Surely in a caretaker's storeroom there are matches or a lighter?

Not in this one.

It's my dad who helps me out this time. Not his ghost, and not a time-traveling version of him from some distant dimension. Just his voice in my head, but it's as clear as anything, like a voice-over in a film. I'm wandering up and down the aisles of shelves, moving stuff in an increasingly frantic attempt to find *anything* that'll create a flame, when I hear him.

"Shhh. Slow down, pal. There you go, easy does it. That's what you need right there: it's in front of you."

I've stopped now, and I'm looking around me, trying to obey Dad's soothing voice.

"No, there! In front of you."

"The wire wool?" I say out loud, because I'm looking at a box of it—steel wool pads used for rust removal.

"Yes. You remember? In the kitchen?"

My breathing slows and I remember every detail, and I close my eyes and I'm with Dad in the kitchen doing one of his mad experiments. I do remember, I do.

I smile, and grab a box of steel wool.

CHAPTER SIXTY-NINE

Back in the tech lab, the only problem remaining—apart from, that is, whether this will work or not—is the code that will be left on Pye's supercomputer.

If I leave evidence of time travel in 1984, the risk is that someone will find it and piece it together, and the results of *that* could be catastrophic.

A self-destruct program would be perfect: I run the supercomputer along with the self-destruct program, and it gets me home and then wipes the disks. Only I don't know how to write such a program. Wouldn't know where to start, in fact.

The only other option I can think of, then, is setting the whole lot on fire.

In the storeroom are several tins of creosote—the brown wood preserver used on fences—and some steel wool.

Twenty minutes later everything is rigged up: Pye's

supercomputer is connected with electrical cable, via the black box, to two zinc buckets arranged to touch each other on the floor, and more electrical cables, with wires exposed at the ends, form the improvised handgrips. The shiny black box is in one of the buckets, and is connected with wire to the handgrips as well as the supercomputer. Alan Shearer is in a box slung around my neck with string, and the laptop (minus its battery), along with everything else I brought, is in my backpack. I tighten the straps on my shoulders. The laptop battery is in my jeans pocket. I pat myself down, like a commando going on a raid.

Picking up the tins of creosote, I splash it around the perimeter of the tech lab, watching it form into pools, then pour a single line of the sticky liquid from one of the pools to near the buckets.

Along the corridor from the tech lab is a locked office. By now, what I do next is becoming almost normal. Grabbing a fire extinguisher from the wall, I smash it repeatedly into the door handle till it gives way.

I'm staring at the phone on the desk. It's one of those old ones, with the rotary dial on the front. As soon as I make the call, there is no going back, and I dither and stare for what seems like ages. My palms are moist and my breathing is shallow, so shallow that I don't think I'm going to be able to speak on the phone.

I swallow hard and pick up the bit you hold. Without hesitating further, I put my finger in the hole labeled "9," drag the dial around, and release it. I do this twice more.

Almost immediately, my call is answered.

"Emergency. Which service do you require?"

"Fire. Please."

"Please hold the line; I'm putting you through now." There's a short wait, and then another voice says, "Fire Service. May I take your name and number please?"

The number is written in the middle of the dial, so I read it out: "I'm, er . . . Jamie Bates, and the number is Culvercot 212232."

"And where are you calling from?"

"46 Chesterton Road." A lie, but I'm guessing they won't find out until later. And besides, lying—among all the other crimes I've committed—is hardly worth worrying about.

"Where is the fire, caller?"

"I've seen smoke and flames coming from Culvercot Secondary Modern. Ground floor, what they call the technical lab."

"Are you in any danger, caller?"

"No."

"And are there any people present in the building?"

"No. At least, I don't think so."

As soon as she says a fire engine is on its way, I have about three minutes, because the fire station is on this side of town, and it's a straight run. But I need the flames to take hold and destroy the computers before they put the fire out.

Arson—another one to add to the list.

Back at the lab, and it stinks of creosote. I stand in the buckets, one foot in each; I've got the wire handgrips ready and I just . . . freeze.

I just cannot do what I need to do.

I don't know how long I'm standing there, but when I hear the sound of the fire engine at the top of the road, I'm snapped out of my daydream. The siren is going full blast, and I now have only seconds.

I quickly copy the line of letters and numbers from the top of the black box onto the screen, and add the coordinates for time and place.

I've got the laptop battery in one hand and I'm holding the steel wool in the other with plastic tongs, and I bring the two together, so that the steel wool bridges the gap between the battery's contacts and . . .

POW!

There's a spark, more than one, and the wool catches fire for a few seconds.

That's all I need. I crouch down and spark the wool again, and this time the creosote catches fire, but much, *much* faster than I had expected. There's a burst of flame in my face as I'm bending over, and I can smell my singed eyebrows. The fire dances along the trail of creosote and seconds later has reached a big pool of the flammable liquid, which bursts into flame with a *whoomph* and ignites all the rest of the creosote around the room.

I've barely had time to stand up again and already the flames are surrounding me, getting hotter by the second. I've got the wires gripped in each hand, and I reach out for the "Enter" button on the keyboard, but in my panic, I knock the keyboard off the table, where it dangles by its cable.

Now, as well as the light from the flames, there's a flashing light of the fire engine that has pulled up only meters from the windows, and I hear a voice shouting, "Sarge! There's a boy in there! A boy, in the room!"

I'm groping through the thickening smoke for the swinging keyboard, and I'm coughing and coughing, and crouching down with my feet in the buckets, because the filmy, wobbly bubble seems smaller than ever. When the window smashes, there's an even bigger ball of flame as the inrush of oxygen from outside feeds the fire, and I'm sure I can feel my skin burning, and I'm stabbing at the keyboard with my fingers, hoping to hit "Enter," and that's when I collapse and don't feel anything more at all.

CHAPTER SEVENTY

I've never remembered this conversation before, I don't think, or maybe I've remembered it and didn't understand its significance.

Did I mention that my dad was a bit weird in the days before he died? If I didn't it's because of a kind of loyalty, I guess. I want you to think the best of him, like I do, and I don't like remembering how he made me feel.

My dad hugged me, sure. But in the last couple of days he hugged me longer and *harder*. Like, really hard, so that it hurt a bit. And he took to kissing me, which I know loads of dads do, but mine didn't really, not since I was very little. I did mention that, yeah.

Anyway, a couple of nights before he died, he came into my room when I had gone to bed and I asked him to tell me a story, and he went very quiet.

"From when you were little."

He shook his head. "Not tonight. Tonight it's a made-up story." I didn't really mind, even though Dad's made-up stories were a bit rubbish usually. It was just nice having him there. And this story was one that sounded like he'd planned it. I mean, Dad's stories were normally full of hesitations and stuff, because he was making them up as he went along, but this one wasn't.

"There was once a young man who lived in a village next to the mighty Ganges, and one day he was visited by the goddess Kali, which in Sanskrit means 'she who is death,' and she is a very, very scary goddess with a blue face and a necklace made of the heads she has cut off. . . ."

"Gross," I say.

"Yep. Completely gross. And she said to the young man who was called . . . um . . ."

"Trevor?" It was part of the fun with Dad's Indian stories to give the characters names that were as un-Indian as we could think of.

"Yes. Trevor. Trevor O'Sullivan. And she said to Trevor O'Sullivan, 'I shall give you the gift of clairvoyance, O Trevor. . . .'"

"What's clairvoyance?"

"Seeing the future. And he said, 'O Great Kali. Thanks

very much!' And he went down to the Ganges and peered into the water, where he was told he would see his future, but nothing did he see. And verily he summoned Kali thus: 'Oi Kali, come 'ere!' And Kali appeared before him and said, 'What do you want, Trevor O'Sullivan?' and he said, 'I can see no future,' and Kali said, 'Funny, that,' and sliced off his head and strung it on her necklace."

"Oh, that's nasty!"

"Indeed it is. And the moral, Al, is if ever you are offered a look at your own future, never take it. The future will look after itself, without any help from you."

And he hugged me hard and kissed me.

CHAPTER SEVENTY-ONE

When I come round, I'm not even sure that I have come round. My head is hurting really badly, especially at the back, like I've fallen backward and banged it. My eyes are stinging and I daren't try to open them, and there's something cold on my cheek, which I take to be the floor. There's also something around my neck, tight.

Yet—*so far so good*—is the first thing I think. Then: *I'm going to open my eyes soon, and I'll be back in my room shortly before this whole thing started.*

I open my eyes dead slowly. Am I in my room? The cord of Alan Shearer's box has twisted round my throat, but I can loosen it, and Alan Shearer's unharmed, which I'm relieved about. But still . . .

I am in my room. I know I am because I am staring upward out the window and I recognize the tree in next door's garden and the line of the roofs opposite. This is the room I left, with Mum pounding on the door, and Grandpa Byron's face in the window as I disappeared. I sit up and rub my eyes and do that thing when you ask yourself if you're in a dream just to make sure you're not in a dream.

I am not in a dream. Also, this is not my room after all. The door's in the same place and the view out the window is the same, but the bed is along the other wall with a different duvet on it, the rug is different, there's a poster for a band I've never heard of on the wall. . . .

So whose room is this?

From downstairs comes the sound of a television, and from the next room the sound of a shower. Removing my feet from the zinc buckets and standing up, I go to the window.

"Oh my God," I mumble to myself. "This *is* my room." Outside is the little back garden I look at every morning, the house next door—everything is as I had looked at it last from this position.

I look around the room again, just to check, and at first I think Carly must have moved into my room while I was away in 1984.

But I set the return time to exactly when I left. By rights, Mum should be thumping on the bedroom door, Steve should be shouting at me, and Grandpa Byron's mouth should be forming an astonished O.

Then the bedroom door opens, and in walks Carly in a dressing gown, toweling her hair dry, and she doesn't see me at first.

"Hi, Carly!" I say. That's when she does see me. Her eyes widen and she emits a shriek: a long scream of absolute terror.

"Hey, it's OK, Carly; what's up with you?" I ask.

"Who—who are you? Get out. Get out. Take what you want. Take it, just don't . . . just go." She's trembling and her voice is shaking. I stay by the window.

"Where's Steve? Where's Mum?"

"My boyfriend's downstairs and my dad'll be back any minute, really, he's just gone to the corner shop. He'll kill you. Jol! Jolyon!" She's shouting really manically.

"Carly! Stop it, why are you being . . ."

At that moment things get really hairy, because I hear pounding footsteps on the stairs and into the room bursts Jolyon Dancey, who looks at me in puzzled anger. "Who are you?" he snarls. "What are you doing in Carly's room?"

"It's me—Al," I say. "You know—Carly's stepbrother?"

TIME TRAVELING WITH A HAMSTER

Then—desperately—"The hamster fancier?" His face screws up in utter incomprehension and a kind of wariness.

"Get him, Jol—do your karate on him!" Jolyon immediately adopts a weird martial arts stance: feet apart, legs bent, hands aloft. It's almost comical and I expect him to go, *"Hi-yaaa!"* but he doesn't. He just stands there with a tough expression on his face, and that's how we stay for the next few seconds until Carly says, "Well, go on then, Jol—get him!"

"Shut up, Carly!" I yell at her, and it seems to do the trick. She stops and just stands there, her bottom lip wobbling, tears welling up in her eyes. "What have you done to my room?" I ask her.

There's a pause while Carly looks at me, pleadingly. "Just go, please!"

The fear in her voice is genuine, and I'm scared that Carly has gone a bit off her rocker, and when people go a bit crazy there's no knowing what they might do—they're unpredictable. She was always heading that way, I suppose—teenage angst and all that. I try to slip past her and get to the door, but Jolyon blocks my way, still waving his hands around, trying to look menacing. "I'm a green belt. You don't want to tangle wi' me."

He is right—I don't—but the way he's standing, with his legs wide apart, gives me a chance. I turn my head to look out the window, then point and say, "Oh my God!"

It works. They both turn to look, and in that instance I draw back my foot and deliver a swift, hard kick right between Jolyon's legs. The sound he makes is horrible: a high-pitched squeak and a breathy gasp at once. I feel sorry for him as he keels over sideways, clutching his groin and retching. I have plenty of time to pick up Alan Shearer's box, take the black box from the bucket, put them both in my backpack, and leave through the bedroom door. Carly looks utterly terrified and I feel bad for that.

The stair carpeting is different. It's the one that was there when me and Mum moved in, but then Mum and Steve had it replaced a short while later. I crane my head to see if Mum's watching telly, but she isn't and I guess she'd have heard the commotion.

It's the same house, all right. But so many things are slightly off, not just the stair carpeting. Things are arranged differently. The picture of Mum in a frame on the hall table isn't there, and the coats on the rack are different.

Halfway down the street I see Steve coming toward me,

carrying a bag of groceries. He's grown a goatee in, like, a day, which doesn't suit him.

"Steve! Steve!"

Steve stops. He looks at me with a half smile. "Hello."

I stand in front of him and take on the same half smile, and say, sort of conspiratorially, "Um, Steve, I think Carly's going a bit y'know . . . I dunno . . . cuckoo?"

Steve squints at me quizzically. "What?"

"Carly. She's just screamed at me to get out of the house."

Steve shakes his head. "Sorry, son, but, erm . . . who are you?"

I give a little sigh.

"Steve, man—c'mon. I'm really . . . I've had a mad time lately, and I don't want to do this." Steve has started to walk on now, and I keep up with him. "It's just Carly was being all weird with me, and well . . . I just . . ."

"Are you a friend of Carly's? Have you been round our house before?"

"Ste-eve!" I'm getting bored with this now.

"Look, I'm sorry, son, I don't have a good memory for Carly's friends. What's your name again?"

"Stop it!" I'm truly impatient now, and I snap the words out.

"Hey—watch your step, son." We're outside our house now, and walking up the front path. "You wait, and I'll tell Carly you're here."

"Steve! Stop it!" I'm shouting now, and really upset. "Where's Mum?"

Steve turns to face me now, with his back to the front door.

"I think, son, you need to go home."

"What do you mean? This is my home!"

Steve stares at me for a moment.

"Go on, son. Off you go. You've had your fun. Go now."

"What? *No!* Where's Mum? Is she working late? Is she out with Annika?"

"This is your last warning. Now. Piss. Off." He's not shouting, but his voice is menacing, and when he turns to let himself in the door, I'm left standing in the middle of the path, blinking hard and gulping and holding a box with a hamster in it.

CHAPTER SEVENTY-TWO

I've got the tiniest bit of power left in my phone, so I call Mum.

"The number you have dialed is not available. Please check the number and try again."

So I do, even though the number is in my phone memory as MUM MOBILE.

"The number you have dialed is not available. Please check the number and try again."

I'm about to give it another go when the phone dies. I get a sick feeling in the bottom of my stomach. This is not going the way I had hoped. Mind you, the way I had *feared*—not so long ago, when I was back in 1984—was a lot, lot worse and basically involved me being dead or never even existing, so I'm kind of stuck between dread and hope, and it's not a nice feeling. Perhaps Mum's changed her mobile. Perhaps the "network is down," whatever that means. More likely there's a problem with my phone caused by traveling through aeons of space-time.

Grandpa Byron would put things right. He's never let me down.

This is what I'm telling myself on the walk to Grandpa Byron's house. But I'm not convincing myself, however hard I try. For in my heart, I know that something has gone very, very wrong.

You see, by rights—according to the grandfather paradox—I should not exist at all, because my father died in a tragic accident when he was twelve and could never have fathered me.

But here I am, so clearly that bit of time travel theory is rubbish. The thing is, I'm scared about what else might be happening.

As soon as I walk up Grandpa Byron's front path, my fears increase. Where is his moped? Why is the front door painted a different color? Where are the wind chimes tinkling by the side door?

I ring the doorbell anyway, but when a lady I've never seen before answers, I just mutter, "Sorry, wrong house," and quickly walk away.

It's getting late and dark. I'm feeling weak with hunger and thirst, and almost dizzy from trying to piece together what's happening.

Don't get me wrong. I have worked out the basics, as— no doubt—have you. In case you haven't, here's a neat list. (Incidentally, a "neat list" is just about the absolute opposite of how these thoughts are arranged in my head. Even "arranged" is wrong. What's happening in there is total chaos— thoughts and fears colliding and contradicting and the "what-ifs" forming a noisy queue, trying to cancel each other out. But anyway, here goes.)

1. When Pye drowned, a lot changed. (OK. A nice gentle start. Hang on for a bumpy ride.) So:

2. Pye didn't grow up to meet Mum and become a father to me. Which means:

3. He didn't die four years ago, so:

4. Mum didn't meet Steve and move in with him and me and Carly.

Yes, I've worked *that* out. But there's a fifth thing that is nagging at my mind and that is:

5. Grandpa Byron didn't then move from Culvercot to Blyth.

And there's a sixth thing as well, but I hardly dare allow myself to think it, or write it, but I'm going to have to, so here it is:

6. If Pye died when he was twelve (and he did—I was there), then he wasn't alive to be on the beach with Grandpa Byron and the other Indians the day that Mum nearly drowned.

In other words—quite apart from the fact that I don't understand what I'm doing here, in some weird space-time bubble where I have no parents or home, and by rights should not even be alive—I may also be the direct reason, more or less, that my mum died sometime in the midnineties by being the direct reason, more or less, that my dad died ten years before.

And *this* is why I'm wandering the street muttering to

myself, blinking hard and trying to create some order out of the traffic jam of confusion in my head. Sitting down on a wall, I take off my backpack and take out the box that holds Alan Shearer. Letting him run over my hands and up my arm always makes me smile, and I put him down next to a little puddle so that he can take a drink. He then circles around a bit and licks his tiny hands. (I should say "paws," really, but if you look at a hamster's paws they are just like hands, so that's how I think of them with Alan Shearer.)

It's the distraction offered by my hamster that clears my head. You know when sometimes in a traffic jam there's a gap ahead, and once you're there everything speeds up and suddenly all the revving and honking is behind you? It's like that.

Putting Alan Shearer back in his carry box, I turn down the street that leads to the coastal road and the buses to Culvercot, and I start running—partly because the bus is approaching and partly because I suddenly know where I need to go.

CHAPTER SEVENTY-THREE

It's proper nighttime now, a warm early-summer night with the faint taste of seaweed hanging in the air, and I'm on Sandview Avenue in Culvercot, the tiny semidetached houses—some with loft conversions—now thirty years older, with bigger trees, and cars now lining the street all the way down to the seafront.

The bamboo wind chimes are still there, but soundless in the still air. There's a moped parked on the road outside. I check it for damage to the side, where I scraped it escaping from the police. There isn't any. Of course there isn't. How could there be?

I stand in the street for a few minutes, staring at the front door, willing myself to ring the doorbell. My feet have taken me up the path, but my arm won't lift to press it. I don't know how long I've been standing there, but it must have been a while—someone inside has seen me and I can see a shape approaching through the bobbled glass, and my heart is beating so hard that it feels like there is someone inside my chest thumping to get out. Now the door chain is rattling, and I can make out details on the shape behind the glass, and it *is* him, I'm sure it is, but I dare not believe it, and then the door opens.

It is him.

Grandpa Byron.

And he just kind of leans forward a bit to get a better look, and his mouth starts moving but no sound comes out except for a croaky "P . . . p . . . ," and I'm thinking, *to hell with this staring at each other,* and I cross the door threshold and fling my arms around him, and breathe in his smell (different from what I expect, but still him), and smile a huge smile of relief to myself as his arms encircle me and he hugs me back. A few seconds pass like this; his voice becomes clearer and I hear what he is saying over the top of my head as we embrace.

"Pye. Pye. Pye. How can it be you? Oh, my boy, my Pye. How?"

Oh dear. I didn't expect that.

There we are, in his front doorway, and he hugs me harder, and he keeps repeating, "How?" and "Pye?" and I hate myself for it, but I start to become slightly uncomfortable because I know that I have some explaining to do, and whatever I say is going to disappoint him because I'm not Pye. I uncurl myself from the embrace and stand in front of him as he continues to stare at me. There's no good way of saying this, so I just say it.

"I'm sorry. I'm not Pye." There's a long pause while Grandpa Byron just looks intently, his eyes flicking to my hair, my ears, my mouth, my hands, and I add, as gently as I can, "How could I be?"

Grandpa Byron's blinking hard. I can't tell if he's blinking back tears, or what. Then I say, "I'm Al. Al Singh? Do you remember?"

Grandpa Byron's eyes move up and to the left, then back at me. He shakes his head.

"Come on," I encourage. "You remember everything! In the shop with the Sikh guy, they thought I was Pye and . . ." Still he looks blank. "I came here, to this house. The day that Pye—"

He finishes it for me. "The day that Pye drowned. You came here. Then you were in the shop. With Baru and, and . . . the other guy. His son." As the memory comes back to him, he starts nodding slowly. He puts his hand on my

shoulder and brings me into the house, shutting the door behind him. "Come on in, bonny lad," he says.

But there is no lightness in his voice. It is as if I have
sucked all the energy out of him. Very slowly, feeling terrible,
I follow him.

CHAPTER SEVENTY-FOUR

OK. Think about this for a second. How would you even begin to explain to Grandpa Byron what had gone on?

I don't know either. In fact, the first thing I say as I sit at the kitchen counter is "Is there anything to eat?" He gives me a glass of milk, which I down in one gulp while he heats up some *aloo chaat* in the microwave; then I eat and eat and eat. I take Alan Shearer from my backpack, and the look of incomprehension on Grandpa Byron's face is replaced, briefly, by a smile, and he gives him a Brazil nut and a saucer of water and seems to relax a little. It's good: I think my hamster has given him something else to look at apart from me, and the tension I have felt since the doorstep lessens slightly. Grandpa Byron pulls a stool up to the counter and sits opposite me while my hamster and I eat.

Having my mouth full means I can't really talk, so I look around a bit and am surprised to notice that he doesn't seem to have tidied for a while. It's not that his kitchen is dirty, it's just messy. Grandpa Byron's house was always full of stuff, but he had an amazing ability to keep it all neat; he must have been too busy lately, or something. I notice another thing as well: his long plait of hair isn't there. There is the beginning of an uneasy feeling in me, which isn't helped by the following exchange. I clear my mouth of spicy potatoes and say:

"Grandpa Byron, can I ask . . ."

"What did you call me? *Grandpa* Byron?"

"Oh. Yeah. I'll explain in a minute." This has kind of thrown me, as you can guess, but I press on. "What is the capital of, ooh, I dunno . . . Greenland?"

Grandpa Byron squints at me. "Gree . . . ? I've no idea, son. Why do you ask?"

And then we start talking. I won't tell you everything. It goes on for hours. I'll give you an idea, though, of what it is like from my side. Imagine trying to explain what a book is to someone who doesn't know what reading is, like someone from some ancient jungle tribe centuries ago.

I guess it could be worse. At least he doesn't assume I'm crazy, or lying. He just lets me talk and talk, asking occasional questions, trying to keep my story on track, but it is hard, and I keep thinking at any point that he will say, *"All right, bonny lad. That's enough, and this is ridiculous. Either you tell me the truth, or I'm phoning the police. You're a young boy in my house, I don't know who you are from Adam and Eve, and it's the sort of thing that could get a fellow into a lot of trouble...."*

And so on. But he never does. Because here's the thing: *I think he believes me.*

It's because of things that I can tell him, like:

1. Grandma Julie. I know who she is, and how she dies, and that "Without You" by Nilsson was number one when they got married.

2. I know why he came to England in the not-so-swinging sixties, because of fighting in Punjab.

3. Most of all, though, I know about Pye. What he looked like, how he talked, his blue satin bomber jacket, his little head bob . . .

When I talk about Pye, Grandpa Byron sits still, shaking his head, drinking in every word like a thirsty man. "My boy," he keeps saying. "My poor, poor boy."

Then I do something that almost—*almost*—proves my story to Grandpa Byron. I plug in my phone and give it enough charge to revive it, and there are the pictures I took, just a few days ago for me but thirty years ago for Grandpa Byron: me and Pye on the beach, and me, him, and Hypatia. "Do you remember this?" I ask him, and he does a slow, sad head wobble.

"I think so. Sort of. My memory's . . . well, it's not what it was, shall we say?"

We sit in silence for a bit, and Grandpa Byron gazes at the picture on my phone before saying, quietly, "Why did you run away after the—the accident?"

I find I can't really answer, and when I lift my eyes I can see he's looking intently at me. Not harshly, or angrily, but he wants an answer to something that I can see has been tormenting him for thirty years. And I hate myself at that moment, because all I can do—and I *know* it's pathetic and childish and unworthy—all I can do is look away, turn my mouth downward, and give a half shrug, and say, "Dunno."

There's a long pause as I squirm inside at my own wretchedness at giving such an inadequate answer. Looking back, I wonder if it was in those few seconds that Grandpa Byron's attitude to me shifted slightly. From that point on it has felt as if he believes my story, but also that he blames me for Pye's death, and for not facing up to it at the time; for running away like a coward and leaving him to grieve, unknowing, for thirty years.

All he says, though, is, "It's late, son. Shall I take you to your room?"

"My room?"

"Well, you look tired—and where else are you going to stay?"

The small bedroom was Pye's old room. It's got a bookshelf crammed with science books, a wallpaper mural of Earth seen from space, and a model of the solar system dangling from the ceiling. There are even still some schoolbooks on the desk and a pot of pencils.

"I haven't been able to change it since he . . . since Pye left us."

But it's not actually as creepy as it sounds. There's something nice about feeling this close to Pye.

"I like it," I say, and I give him my best smile, but he's just looking through me, a bit vacantly. Hard to blame him, really. I don't think this was how he was expecting his evening to turn out.

Then it hits me. I knew there was something else about him that was different, and it's his arms—both of them straight and strong—and I ask him, "Do you remember me asking you to double-check the bolts on your pyro rig?"

His eyes roll up as he searches his memory, and then he nods. "Aye, I suppose I do remember you sayin' that. Why?"

"I see you kept your word."

I'm sitting on the bed and he kneels down in front of me and starts taking off my shoes.

"Come on, son. You must be most cream-crackered. . . ."

(It's rhyming slang: cream-crackered = knackered = exhausted. I haven't heard him use that one before, and I smile.)

Then he pulls my socks off and he's about to turn away when his head snaps back like it's on a spring or something and he's staring at my feet, like *really* staring, and he reaches his hand forward nervously toward my foot. He's doing this odd goldfish-gaping thing with his mouth, and I could swear he's gone a bit pale. The *old* Grandpa Byron, the one from before, obviously knew all about my webbed toes. This one, though, looks horrified, and I try to put him at ease by wiggling them at him humorously (if that's possible, I don't know; he didn't laugh).

"Yep—'syndactyly,' it's called. It's pretty rare! Have you ever seen it before?"

He nods. "Once." But he says nothing else apart from "Sleep well" as he backs out of the room. He smiles, but there's something going on behind the smile, and although I'm super-tired I don't sleep, because I can't stop thinking about Grandpa Byron's confused smile and his over-the-top reaction to my pretty insignificant toe thing.

CHAPTER SEVENTY-FIVE

Well, obviously I do sleep because I wake up under Pye's *Doctor Who* duvet. Everything—my clothes, my bag—has been tidied up from where I left it on the floor. There's an old-fashioned digital clock on the dresser that says 14:02. I have slept for nearly twelve hours straight and still don't feel exactly as fresh as a daisy, but I get up nonetheless. On the desk is a cardboard box with low sides containing a saucer of water and some muesli, and some torn-up newspaper with Alan Shearer curled up underneath it, all of which Grandpa Byron has done while I've been asleep.

It comes back to me, hazily—me waking up in the night and seeing Grandpa Byron sitting on the bed. It was dawn, but his eyes were glistening in the bluish light that came through the thin curtains, and I could tell he'd been crying. I turned on my pillow and gave him a sleepy smile.

"Oh, Pye, son," he murmured, "I've missed you."

I was about to say, "I'm not Pye, I'm Al," but I found as I opened my mouth to speak that I didn't have the heart to spoil his dawn daydream.

Instead I said, "I'm . . . tired," and I rolled over back to sleep.

On a chair is a set of clothes, but they're not new, and I know straightaway that they are Pye's, including the shiny blue bomber jacket that he had on the first time I met him. When I put them on they smell like they have been in a drawer for ages.

I carry my hamster and his box downstairs to the kitchen where Grandpa Byron is tapping at the keyboard of a laptop. In front of him on the breakfast bar is the framed photo of me, my dad, and my mum, which he must have taken from my backpack while I was asleep. As I walk in and see this, his hand defensively lowers the screen of the laptop a little, prompting me to ask, "What are you doing?"

Instead of answering me directly, he looks with a sad sort of smile at me standing there looking exactly like Pye, wearing his clothes and everything. He gets up and goes to the front door. "I need to tell you something," he says as he pulls on a pair of wellies and tucks his jeans into them, indicating a pair for me to put on too.

Outside, he's walking fast toward the beach, and I have to almost jog to keep up with him. And then we're on the seafront, on the big, grassy headland that has the double bay of Culvercot on one side and the yellow-white stretch of beach toward Tynemouth on the other. There's a long, sandy stairway down to the beach, and before we get to the bottom, Grandpa Byron has already told me that he was up all night on the Internet. There's a cool fret in the air and it makes me shiver a bit, but I don't care because I'm listening to the story he told me.

It was 1994, almost ten years after Pye had died, except this day was warm—one of those days in the northeast in early summer when the fog has been burned away by a hot sun—and there was a queue, the first of the year, outside the Culvercot fish and chip shop.

The sea was calm enough in the bay, where it was sheltered by the two curved piers, but round the headland, on the long beach, the waves were beating the sand hard. Not many people were swimming: farther along toward Tynemouth the warning flags were up, but there were no lifeguards this early in the season, and even the surfers—who I've seen out there in the winter—had given up.

On the first Saturday in June for the past few years, the

Indians who lived in and around Culvercot (mainly Punjabis, and there still weren't many of them in 1994) had met for a beach party. There was the guy from the shop—his name was Baru Bakshi—whose beachwear was an old brown suit, a sleeveless jumper, and a tie. His tiny round wife, who was wearing a sari, was struggling through the soft sand with a cooler. There was Tarun also from the shop, now married to a woman from Amritsar, via Middlesborough, who was in jeans and a T-shirt, and their little girl in a yellow dress decorated with sequins. There were others as well, maybe a dozen or so. And there was Hypatia, nearly fifteen, and of course Grandpa Byron.

"Your turn this year, Byron?" said Baru Bakshi, handing him a ceremonial garland of orange and yellow marigolds strung together in a long loop.

("I thought Sikhs and Hindus had different ceremonies?" I asked Grandpa Byron, when he was telling me this. By now we had crossed the dry sand and were walking along the edge of the long, gentle waves.

"So they do, bonny lad, so they do. But we don't mind mixing it up now and then. This was more a social thing, anyway. And besides: I'm not that much of a Hindu, to be honest, and Baru's a pretty free-thinking Sikh. Now let me get on with the story.")

And so Grandpa Byron walked down to the water's edge ("Pretty much exactly here," he said, looking up and down the beach), followed by most of the others, near a group of young women in their teens and twenties wearing swimsuits, who had been playing in the shallows.

Baru Bakshi's wife had been around the group giving everyone the red forehead dot—the *bindi*—with her fingertip and red paste, and they stood there knee-deep in the water. Baru Bakshi had rolled his suit trousers up; the ladies' wet saris clung to their legs. Grandpa Byron drew his arm back and flung the garland into the waves, and then there was a shout from farther out in the sea.

The group of young women were pointing at another young woman who was not that far away from the shore, still not even out of her depth, struggling against the back draw of a retreating wave, pushing the water aside with her arms to try and stay upright; and then her head disappeared under the water as another wave began its buildup.

"Sarah! Sarah! Swim!" screamed one young woman on the shore when she saw the head reappear, and she started to go into the water before being pulled back by a friend. "No, Ava, no! You can't!"

But already Grandpa Byron was undressed and striding naked into the sea before diving under the next wave and driving his strong arms, one after the other, into the water, getting closer and closer to the drowning woman. As he reached her, her head went under again, and Grandpa Byron—still just able to stand, but knocked and buffeted by the rocking sea—duck dived beneath the surface at exactly the moment that the waves settled between surges. In the lull, the only sound was the group of young women wailing, "Ohmigod, ohmigod, ohmigod!" as they held their hands, prayerlike, in front of their mouths, and Hypatia shaking her head and saying slowly, "Oh . . . my . . . God."

There was no sight of them for about ten seconds. One of the young women started crying, and another had flipped open a big old mobile phone and was calling 999.

("Twenty seconds, Al. It doesn't sound like long, but try counting it: it's an age if you're waiting for someone to reappear from under the water."

At this point Grandpa Byron stopped telling me the story, realizing what he had said. He looked down. "I know," I said, but no more words came out, because I think I knew where this story was headed and my mouth was dry with fear and nerves and . . .)

And then someone shouted. "Look! Over there." About thirty meters down the beach, struggling out of the waves, was Grandpa Byron, holding up the young woman, who kept stumbling over in the waves. When they got to waist deep, she convulsed and threw up a bellyful of seawater; then Grandpa Byron bent down, gently scooped her up, and carried her out of the sea.

He set her down on the dry part of the sand and her friends gathered round her. Grandpa Byron stood to one side, hands on his hips, face lifted to the sky, panting and spitting salty water. And then the women's attention turned to him. Baru Bakshi sidled up.

"Well done, *Byron-ji*. But I am thinking you might want to, ah . . . put your pants on."

(I think Grandpa Byron has told this story before. Honestly—he paused with a comedian's sense of timing before he said that last bit, and then looked at me, waiting for me to laugh. I was not really in a laughing mood, but I managed to force out a little noise so he could continue.)

"I climbed into my pants and stood smiling at the girl I had just saved, and she wiped a stream of snot from her nose and smiled back at me. And then she was spreading her feet out in the sand, showing that two of her toes on each foot were fused together. And she told me her name was Sarah."

We stayed there for a while on the sand, the two of us, letting the waves lick around our wellies.

Sarah.

Mum. She's alive.

"A boy needs his mum," says Grandpa Byron, with a kind of finality. "And we're going to find her."

CHAPTER SEVENTY-SIX

Which is how, later that day, Grandpa Byron and I end up
in Blaydon, fifteen miles up the Tyne from the coast, and I
tell you: fifteen miles on the back of a little moped is enough
punishment for anyone's bottom.

Grandpa Byron's been telling me that when he first came
to the UK, Blaydon was a coal-mining village, but there's no
mining here now: just street after street of neat, redbrick
houses, and a supermarket, and a garage, and it's just like
everywhere else really, except it's up one side of a valley and
in some places you can see right down to the River Tyne and
across the other side, and that's pretty cool.

And that is where my mum, Sarah, lives, on a wide road
outside of Blaydon. Grandpa Byron's already phoned her to
tell her he is coming. They stayed in touch for a while after
her near drowning; she invited him to her wedding (to Roddy,
a policeman) but he didn't go, and then they kind of drifted

out of each other's lives. But, as Grandpa Byron pointed out, it's difficult to hide these days unless you really want to, and it didn't take him long to track her down.

The trouble is, of course, that my mum is *only* my mum in another—and I'm sorry, I'm going to have to get technical here—space-time dimensional thingy. She's not my mum here: a fact I'm not completely sure Grandpa Byron has understood (and who can blame him?). Quite what he's thinking I don't know. I don't actually think he's worked it out beyond *"A boy needs his mum."*

Now we're outside her front door, and even though Grandpa Byron has told me to be calm and not to freak her out, when she opens the door, she is exactly, *exactly* my mum, even down to the way she's wiping her hands on a tea towel, and something in me just pulls me forward, and before anything else happens or any other greetings are exchanged, I just say, "Hi, Mum!" and wrap her up in my arms, and I just *know* at that moment that the most powerful force in the universe—a parent's love—will make her see the truth, and she'll *know* that I am her son, and she'll fold her arms around me, kiss the top of my head, and say, "I've missed you, Al. All my life, I've missed you, and now you're here," and everything will be all right.

Except she doesn't. And it isn't.

It is awful. She kind of gently eases herself out of my arms, and holds on to them, and looks into my face and says, "Er . . . OK?" and I say, "Mum?" and I know I've blown it.

She's totally freaked out, though she's kind enough not to make it obvious. Her eyes flick to Grandpa Byron; she's still holding my arms at my sides so that I can't hug her again.

"This is, ah . . . ," begins Grandpa Byron. "This is my grandson, Al Chaudhury."

Mum lowers her head, looks in my eyes, and says, a bit slowly, "Hello, Al. Nice to meet you."

Of course. She thinks I have some sort of mental disability, and why wouldn't she?

So begins the most awkward, uncomfortable fifteen minutes of my life. Or—to adapt the hot stove/pretty girl analogy of my namesake, Professor Einstein—"fifteen minutes in the presence of someone who both is and is not your mum, along with her suspicious husband, feels like a lifetime."

We go through, me and Grandpa Byron, and we sit in her tidy front room, and her husband, Roddy, who's now an inspector in the Northumbria Police, brings tea and a juice box for me, like I'm five or something. She and Roddy and Grandpa Byron talk adult small talk, all the how-have-you-beens and everything, which lasts a few minutes, and I learn that she and Roddy have no children, but several nieces and nephews that they're very fond of, and they moved here about eight years ago, and Roddy built the conservatory himself, and blah blah blah . . . but then it starts to get a bit tricky, because all this while I have said nothing and there are some big question marks hanging in the air. Who am I, why did I call her "mum," and so on.

Mum says to Grandpa Byron, "Did you say Al was your grandson? By your daughter, Hy . . . er . . ."

"Hypatia. Yes."

"Didn't she move to America, or Canada, ages ago?"

"Ah. She, er, she came back."

Then Roddy chips in, "And he has your surname? Chaudhury?" Perhaps it's just me, perhaps it's just because I'm on edge and he's a policeman, but there's an almost-silent suspicion in his voice.

"Yes. We wanted to keep the name in the family," says Grandpa Byron, airily. Too airily, if you ask me, because there's still something going on in Roddy's eyes.

And me? I'm sitting there, saying *nothing at all*. I mean, I can't, can I? What can I possibly say? It just can't get any worse.

(By the way, whenever anyone says that to you, remember that it will get worse. It did for me, and it was all my fault.)

I'm on her shiny black sofa, and there's one thing I can do to show her that we have a connection, that might persuade her that she is my mum, and that's my syndactylic toes. I wait till Roddy's left the room for a moment, and then without saying anything I quickly take off my shoe and sock and say, "Look!"

(Another tip: if you're in strange company and want to convince someone beyond a doubt that you are deranged in some way, taking off your shoe and sock and saying "Look!" is a good way of doing it, I now know.)

Mum barely glances at my foot, but smiles indulgently and a bit nervously, and her eyes look at Grandpa Byron, sort of pleading for help.

"My toes!" I say. "Syndactylic! Like my mum's."

"Oh yes!" says Mum enthusiastically, but it's not her real voice. It's the voice that people who don't have children use when they talk to children. A bit too singsongy. "Did your Grandpa tell you I have that too? You probably know how rare it is! How unusual! You're very *special*, Al, aren't you?"

Special.

Mum's smiling at me, but it's not a real smile either. It's a sympathetic, synthetic smile, which might be all I will ever get from her.

It's time to go. I can't stand it anymore, and I quickly put my shoe and sock back on and stand up as Roddy comes back into the room.

Mum says, "From your mum, you say?" Then to Grandpa Byron, "I don't remember you saying Hypatia had syndactyly?"

"Ah . . . he's confused, bless him. He means his dad. Anyway, nice to see you again, Sarah, Roddy," he says, and it's like we can't get out of their house fast enough. I know I've been acting oddly, and there's just this look that is *still* on Roddy's face as he and Mum say goodbye and "Please come again!" and all of that. I know I have messed up, but still I try one more tactic.

"Say hi to Aunty Ellie for me!" I say, and Mum gets this shocked look on her face as Grandpa Byron practically pulls me up the driveway.

Back on the moped, we are a little ways up the street, and I crane my neck back to see Roddy turn to Mum. He purses his lips and shakes his head, and it's at that exact moment that I can see what's coming, and I know what I have to do.

CHAPTER SEVENTY-SEVEN

Remember how I told you that Grandpa Byron can remem-ber pretty much every single day of his life? Now that I think about it a bit more, it's easily the most impressive thing he does.

Some of what he remembers are big things, like getting married—which everyone remembers—but some can be tiny, like having a particularly nice lunch or what he wore that day.

So far it adds up to more than eighteen thousand bits of information he can call up when he wants to remember, say, where he was on a certain day, or where he was living, or who was with him, or what he ate. None of it's written down, of course, so there's no way I can check whether he's right, but I trust him.

A date might be mentioned on the radio, and he'll close his eyes and say, "Ah, yes! Twelfth of March 1977. That was the day me and your Grandma Julie walked along the beach and there was the most jolly terrific hailstorm: great big hailstones as big as peas," and sometimes he can do added details like who else was there and what they were wearing, but not always.

Anyway, we are back at Grandpa Byron's house, stiff from the moped ride, and I need to check something. We have hardly said a word on the way back, mainly because it's virtually impossible to talk over the whining of the engine and the wind in our faces, and besides, there's not much to say that doesn't involve me saying sorry for having messed it all up.

"How are the old memory palaces, Grandpa Byron?" I ask with what I hope is a casual voice, but I wasn't to know the reaction this would provoke. He goes very, very quiet and scowls, and I honestly don't think I've seen Grandpa Byron scowl before.

"Requiring a little maintenance, I'd say."

"OK. So what were you doing on, ooh . . . September second, 1980?"

His eyes look up to the left for the longest time. "That was, erm . . . like I say, they are requiring a little upkeeping."

I am disappointed and can't help showing it. "Oh, come on—what about January twenty-fourth, 1996?"

Grandpa Byron snaps at me, "Don't! I am not a performing flippin' monkey."

But I don't give up. "You wrote the book, though! *The Memory Palaces of the Sri—*"

"I know what I did, and so do you, apparently. Everything about 'me.' Except that it seems to be some other 'me,'" and to emphasize what he's saying, he makes air quotes with his fingers. His voice is quite loud now. "I have never seen that book in years, I have never seen you for thirty years, and now you are expecting me to be someone else? Think about what you are asking, Al. I'm going to the shops. You stay here. I'm not wanting you to walk the streets. It's not safe. And afterward we need to work out what to do with you."

What he means is it is not safe for him. I get it. A man cannot suddenly have a young boy live with him without people wanting to know why.

The front door slams as he leaves, and that now makes *two* rows I have had with Grandpa Byron within about five days, or thirty years, or oh, I don't know . . . take your pick. I've pretty much given up trying to work it out.

I hear Grandpa Byron's moped coughing down the street, and I have to act fast.

The thing is this: I have come back to a world that has

changed in a billion unknowable ways as a result of what I did. Mum doesn't know me (other than meeting me once and thinking I'm "special"); Grandpa Byron's just . . . well, he's just not the same. I worked this out on the journey back from Blaydon when I remembered what Grandpa Byron (or who I am now beginning to think of as "the old Grandpa Byron") told me:

"Don't dream of a different life, Al. Love the one you've got."

Does that mean I can't try to change the one I've got? I have decided that it doesn't. From my backpack in Pye's bedroom, I take out the scratched and battered black box and the cables. The string of numbers and symbols that I so laboriously typed into Pye's supercomputer is still on my key ring memory stick. I'll need to borrow Grandpa Byron's laptop. I'll need to find a zinc garden tub from somewhere.

I am going to use the time machine one last time.

And I mean it. One. Last. Time.

I am sick to death of time travel.

CHAPTER SEVENTY-EIGHT

Grandpa Byron's only been gone two minutes, and I'm down in the bottom of the garden in the shed where, in a different world, he kept his fireworks and Pye had his go-kart. If I had more time, I'd feel emotional; I'd breathe in the smell of the shed and remember Pye and all that.

But I don't. I've just got to find a zinc tub, and all the way down the garden path I have been telling myself that there won't be one, because there never is in situations like this, is there? You never find *exactly* what you're looking for.

Except I do. At the back of the shed, filled with canisters of weed killer and old plastic plant pots and bamboo canes, is a zinc tub—and it's huge. I can't even feel jubilant owing to my nervousness. I've brought out all the rest of the stuff: the laptop, the black box, the cables, my memory stick, and my hamster (of course), and in just a couple of minutes I've got it all rigged up, and the numbers are scrolling up on the screen faster and faster, and I'm beginning to feel a bit sick with anticipation and . . .

At this point I suppose I should tell you what my plan is.

It's to go back One Last Time to 1984 to a few days *before* I last arrived, so that I won't/can't meet myself. I will then break into Pye's shed and disable the Lean Mean Green Machine (I can't destroy it—that would be heartbreaking; I'll just take the wheels off or something), and then, to be doubly sure, I'll go down to the slipway and move the brick *and* the supermarket trolley. *That* will prevent Pye's first accident, and it should also prevent him from going out on the go-kart for a couple of days until he's fixed it—just in case there is some weird "fate intervenes" thing going on that means he's going to steer his go-kart into the sea regardless. I tell you— I've thought of all of the possibilities.

That is, except for one thing that I suddenly notice.

The time machine seems to be losing power. The numbers have stopped scrolling, and the blurry film that once formed a big bubble-like dome over the zinc tub now looks a bit like a wobbly liquid surface coming halfway up the sides of the tub. There is, quite simply, *no way* I could possibly fit in there, let alone get back.

Should have thought of that. I tap the "Esc" button

on the laptop, the program stops, and I start to think this through.

After a moment, it comes to me. I won't physically travel back in time, and I won't personally move the brick and the supermarket trolley. Instead, I'll send my dad a letter telling *him* to do these things. And I'll send it with Alan Shearer so he doesn't ignore it.

OK. A letter. This can work.

But as I keep thinking, a second problem arises, and this one's even bigger.

A white cursor is blinking on the screen demanding that I input the string of letters that were written on the black box. The same black box that has been in and out of every dimension as well as my backpack, wearing off the pen marks. The writing on it is illegible. The string of letters now looks like this:

WM . . . GGGG . . . 7 . . . 5E8 . . . , and then a big smudge containing a G.

WM . . . what came next? S? D? There were some numbers too. A three? A two?

I can't remember the password.

Which means I can't send a letter back to 1984.

I've left all the time machine stuff in the shed, and I'm

coming back up the path to the back of the house with Alan Shearer cupped in my hands, feeling totally defeated, when I hear Grandpa Byron's moped buzzing up the front driveway. And something wonderful happens in my memory:

The sound of the moped makes me remember being on it earlier in the day, and how my bum hurt after fifteen miles. . . .

And I was aching worst when we passed the road sign saying BLAYDON when we came into the town. . . .

And remembering "Blaydon" makes me think of the song "Blaydon Races." . . .

And whenever I think of the song now, I think of that rhyme to remember the kings and queens of England that Grandpa Byron taught me.

That's the one that goes:

Willie, Willie, Harry, Steve,
Harry, Dick, John, Harry three,
One, two, three Eds, Richard two,
Harrys four, five, six, then who?

It was the four *G*'s in the remaining smudged letters that made it click. "Geordie, Geordie, Geordie, Geordie, William and Victoria" was always my favorite line, and I knew now I had the password, starting halfway through on the chorus bit of the tune:

William and Mary, Anna Gloria,

Geordie, Geordie, Geordie, Geordie, William, and
    Victoria

Edward seven's next, and then,

George the fifth in 1910,

Ed the eighth, then George, Liz second,

Charlie, Wills, and George, it's reckoned!

In other words—WMAG GGGGWV E7G5 E8GL2CWG.

Imagine: I used to think of them as Grandpa Byron's "memory tricks," like they were something trivial.

CHAPTER SEVENTY-NINE

Back in Pye's room, I take a long look round. I'm not sure I'm aware of making it a "last look," but that is how it's going to turn out.

I look at all Pye's bits and pieces—the science books, the model of the solar system dangling from the ceiling, his clothes in the wardrobe, his clothes (jeans, T-shirt, bomber jacket) that I'm *wearing*. On his desk there are more books and a slim box labeled JUNIOR LETTER-WRITING KIT with envelopes and paper decorated with pictures of spaceships and planets.

Sitting at the desk, I remove from its frame the picture of me, Dad, and Mum. I fold it in half, put it in an envelope, and address it to Mum. Well, not my *real* mum—the one in Blaydon, the one married to Roddy.

It's a going-away present. It's like I want her to have *something* of me.

Next I write on a sheet of paper, "Please read this and remember me. Thank you, love from Al." I put it inside my copy of *The Memory Palaces of the Sri Kalpana* and leave it on the bed.

Finally, and my hand is shaking slightly when I pick up the pen, I start a letter to Pye. I don't know if you've ever written an important letter? Texts and emails don't seem quite the same somehow, but this has to be spot-on, and when I start to write the words they just come straight out with no hesitation, no crossing out, as if everything I know and everything I need are contained in the pen, and all I'm doing is holding it and kind of squeezing it onto the paper. I fill one sheet, then another, and my wrist is aching, and just as I'm near the bottom of the last sheet in the box, I realize I have finished saying what I need to say. I don't need to reread it. I know it's exactly right. I fold the sheets and cram them into an envelope, writing on the front, "FOR PYE CHAUDHURY. READ IMMEDIATELY."

I stand up, flexing my wrist, and shove the envelope in my jeans pocket.

The doorbell rings, and I hear the front door open and voices downstairs. Out of the bedroom window, I can see a police car is parked outside.

Grandpa Byron's voice comes up the stairs: "Pye. I mean, Al. Come downstairs, please."

In the hallway are two police officers, a skinny man and a fat woman, and I immediately get what has happened.

Roddy. Roddy seemed suspicious. It was the way he shook his head at Mum as we left. It's like he was saying, *"Something's not quite right here,"* and he followed his policeman's instincts and made a couple of calls, and here they are, two police officers, being polite and everything, because there is no reason for them not to be as they are just following up inquiries.

"This is Al, is it?" says the man police officer. "How are you doin', son?"

"I'm fine, thanks," I say, and give a wary smile.

"I've just come to ask you and your granddad a few questions, son. It's nowt to worry yourself about, but we've got to follow certain procedures. You go off into the kitchen with my colleague here"—he nods his head toward the woman officer—"and I'll be in your front room with your granddad. Then we'll swap around, OK?"

I shrug and follow the policewoman's swaying bottom into the kitchen. I suppose they want to question us separately to check out our stories, and seeing as we don't even have a story (other than the true one, which no one would believe), I can see Big Trouble ahead. Arrests. Investigations. Accusations. Care homes. Court orders. DNA tests. Press reports . . .

The plan I had devised, with the letter to Pye and everything else, could happily have been enacted in a day or two, once I had built up the courage and thought through the details.

No time for that now. Now I am under kitchen arrest by the unsmiling policewoman, and I must act immediately.

It's early evening, round about the time that Alan Shearer first wakes up, and I can hear him scrabbling in his cardboard box. I go over to him, pick him up, and take him over to the police officer, who just melts. Her eyes go soft, and a soppy smile makes dimples in her cheeks.

"Awwwwwwwwwweee!" she says (really—it goes on for ages and ends in a squeak). "He's *adorable*! What's his name?" I tell her and she giggles. I let Alan Shearer run over her hands and she loves it. So far so good.

Now for the next bit. "I'm just going to put him back in his box," I say, making sure she has heard, and I take him from her. With my back to her, I head to the shallow box with Alan Shearer in my right hand. With my left I pull open the pocket of my bomber jacket, and as I bend over the box, I make the actions of putting the hamster into it, but instead slip him into my pocket.

"There you go, matey!" I say, and I even move my head and pretend to follow his movements.

As casually as I can, I say, "I'm just going to the toilet," and I sort of stroll out of the kitchen—dead natural—down the hallway, and into the downstairs bathroom.

I have only got, I figure, about two minutes—probably less. Here is what is going to happen in the kitchen. The policewoman is in love with Alan Shearer. She cannot resist going over to his box and checking him out. He won't be there. She'll look in his bedding and under the little box that's in there for him to play with, and she'll assume he has got out using the plastic ruler as a ladder that I deliberately left leaning up against the inside edge of the box, and seeing as she was left in charge, she'll start looking for him, desperate to find him before I get back from the toilet.

Two minutes? Tops. Anyway, I have already opened up the tiny toilet window, which I reckon I can *just* squeeze through. Trouble is, I'll squeeze Alan Shearer as well.

Moving quickly, I take off the toilet roll that's hanging on the wall and tear off a long strip of paper. I twist it into a rope, tie it onto the cardboard tube, and pop my hamster inside, shutting both ends with a ball of paper. Poor Alan Shearer! But it's only going to be for a few seconds. Holding on to one end of the paper rope and standing on the toilet seat, I lower the toilet roll out the window and onto the ground outside.

I'm next. I have to go through feetfirst, which means standing on the sink and getting my legs through the small window, and I'm just about to push off and out when there's a knock on the bathroom door.

"Al? Are you OK in there?" It's the policewoman.

"Ah . . . yeah. Nearly finished," I say from my position halfway in and halfway out the window.

"It's your hamster. I think he's got out of his box."

"Oh no! Could you go in and look on the floor? He usually goes behind the fridge. Perhaps you could pull that out? I'm nearly finished." I can tell my odd position is making my voice sound strained, so I add, "Bit of tummy trouble!"

I hear her footsteps move away and I drop out the window, pick up Alan Shearer, and release him from his cardboard tube. Holding him in my hands, I run down to the garden shed and open it up. Now, the shed *can* be seen from the kitchen, but I just have to trust to luck that she doesn't look out the window and that she is presently trying to move the fridge to find Alan Shearer, who is instead happily in the garden tub along with the rest of the time machine stuff.

Carrying a garden tub is tricky at the best of times, as I discovered that time with Carly. There are handles on the side, but it's just the size that makes it unwieldy. It's virtually impossible to run with it, as I'm now trying to do, down the back alley that goes down to the seafront.

But I'm going in the other direction. I'm going back to Chesterton Road, back to the "jungle"—the patch of wasteland in front of my old house, number 40. Back to where this all began.

It just feels right.

CHAPTER EIGHTY

Dear Pye,

With luck you will be reading this on the morning of August 1, 1984.

Sorry I didn't turn up at the beach like we agreed.

It's a little difficult for me to know exactly how much I can put into this letter, but if this all works then things will become clearer, I promise.

Meeting you has changed my life, changed my world, but don't be scared by this. It's a good thing. Mostly.

There is just one thing I want you to do, Pye. Or, rather, NOT do.

PLEASE, Pye, do not go out on the Lean Mean Green Machine today.

That's all. I can't really tell you why, but you must believe me.

(And—for good measure—next time you go down to the promenade, there's a brick on the path that you should move.)

While I'm here, though, a couple of things occur to me.

1. Macca is bad news. (I think you have already worked that one out.)

2. If you become a dad, call your first son Albert Einstein Hawking. After me.

3. Never, ever mess with time travel. Ask your dad about it. He knows a better way.

Got that? If you don't do anything else, just trust me on the go-kart thing. Don't use it today.

Trust me like you have never trusted anyone before in your life.

To show you how important this is to me, I am trusting you with something of mine.

Please look after Alan Shearer. He's the best hamster ever.

And I REALLY hope I see you again sometime in the future.

Your true friend, Al

I've made it to Chesterton Road, hauling the zinc tub and everything else, and I'm dripping with sweat. It's not that far, maybe a mile, and I've gone down back roads when I can and generally tried to be unobtrusive.

That is, as unobtrusive as a boy running and carrying a huge garden tub can be.

From a few streets away I hear a quick blast from a police siren. I guess they're patrolling the streets looking for me by now, but it's hardly a full-scale emergency. Yet.

It's a warm evening, and the air is a bit salty from the sea. The trees that line the street cast long shadows, and I can hear birdsong and a lawn mower. Not that I'm noticing it much. I don't think you would, either, if you were going to do what I am going to do.

So I'm jogging down Chesterton Road with the tub and everything, past Mr. Frasier's monkey puzzle tree, across the alleyway that leads down to the seafront, and then I'm at the "jungle," among the scrubby bushes and dried-up litter and bits of twig.

I don't know why, but I choose exactly the spot where Carly did her mirror-and-candle thing. Like I say, it just feels right. It's as if I'm carrying out some ritual.

The battery on the laptop is charged, and I carefully place the cables and the handgrips over the edge of the zinc tub so that they are touching the bottom. The black box (which I never did find a proper name for) is connected to the laptop, and the memory stick is jammed into the side when I turn it all on and it begins its start-up.

You know, I think at a point like this it is typical to say that my heart was "beating like a hammer" or something like that, but mine isn't. My mouth is a bit dry, I suppose, but that could have been from the running, and I'm sweating because it's a warm night, but my heart? Nah.

I think it's because I simply have nothing left to lose, and nothing more to give.

From my jeans pocket I take the letter to Pye and place it with both hands, sort of ceremoniously, in the tub as well. I pick up Alan Shearer and hold him close to my face. His whiskers twitch and I give him a little kiss on his furry back.

"Good luck, matey." Into the tub he goes. He seems happy enough, and sniffs at some food I've put in the tub.

The numbers have stopped their scrolling and the blurry sheen has appeared, by now much less than halfway up the side of the tub, but still well clear of Alan Shearer's head. There are just the coordinates to enter. Cautiously, I open up the folder labeled "map." I've only opened up this folder once before and it looks scary: right now it's showing a stark bird's-eye view of the streets around Culvercot in green and black, like Pye's old computers in the school. (I think it's been adapted from Google Earth or something, and laid over with a kind of grid.) Using the touch pad, I pinpoint the exact spot where Grandpa Byron's shed is. When I click, up pop the coordinates for me to enter. That is where—all being well—Pye will discover a zinc tub, a letter, and a hamster.

Then the date and time: just *before* my hamster and I first went back to 1984.

And then the password. I hum "Blaydon Races" to help me remember.

WMAG GGGGWV E7G5 E8GL2CWG.

I have told myself on the jog here that the most likely thing is that *nothing* will happen. It's because of the doppelganger thing. I'm not traveling anywhere; I'm staying put, right here, so I can't meet my own double. But I am *hoping* that my letter changes the past. I'm *hoping* that Pye will live, and go on to meet Mum, and have me . . . and then what? Will I have somehow slipped under the barrier of space-time, broken its rules, and come face to face with the "me" that up till now has been living an unremarkable life with Mum and Dad? I'm *hoping* not . . .

But I can't be certain.

So with all this going on in my head, finally, with—with what? A trembling finger? Nope. My heart in my throat? Nope again—I just press "Enter."

Just like that.

Like I say, I have nothing left to lose.

CHAPTER EIGHTY-TWO

I turn away from the zinc tub. I don't even want to see whether it works this time, or what happens. I turn away and crouch down with my head on my knees. And before I cover my eyes, I see that walking toward me is the policeman, his radio crackling. Behind him, getting out of the squad car, is the policewoman.

"All right, son. Don't move. Just stay there, son. Just stay there."

He's talking in a calm voice, and he is holding his hands out, palms up. He is really close now, and as I contemplate the failure of my mission, and at such a late stage, I've just got nothing left. My shoulders slump and my head droops and I'm suddenly more exhausted than I ever thought possible, and I just kind of fall forward.

CHAPTER EIGHTY-THREE

There was this game I used to play with Grandpa Byron. Well, I say "used to," but it was probably only once or twice. He called it Kim's Game, although who Kim was I've no idea. Perhaps a friend of his. Anyway, what he'd do was put a few random objects on a tray, like a spoon, a tea bag, a pepper pot, a pen, a ring . . . anything that was lying around. I'd then have a minute to look at them, and after that I had to look away while he removed two or three, and I had to tell him which objects were missing.

Obviously Grandpa Byron was brilliant at it. He could do it even if you didn't remove any objects, but just swapped the positions of a couple.

And the reason I'm telling you this now is that Kim's Game comes to mind when, after a minute or so of crouching and not looking up, I lift my head and the policeman is not there.

Has he driven off? The police car isn't there either. I didn't hear it drive away. I look around for signs that things have changed.

The first thing I notice is that the garden tub has gone, along with its contents. All that's left are a smoldering black box, and the laptop with its screen black and burned out. The cables have been severed (melted?) at the point they entered the tub, and that is the sorry end of my dad's time machine.

So *something* has happened. I'm just not sure whether to be pleased or not. If anything, it just makes me more nervous than I was before. But, like a bad player of Kim's Game (me), I hadn't really paid much attention to my surroundings in the first place, so it's hard for me to tell what—if anything—has changed.

Slowly, I walk over the road to number 40, our old house. There is a car in the driveway that I don't recognize. It's not Graham and Bella's Škoda. The house's front door is dark blue, like it was when I lived there before, but . . . so what? What color had it been when Graham and Bella lived there? I can't remember.

Now my heart is beating fast. Or hard. Or loud. Or all three, I can't tell, because I know for sure that in the next few moments I will have the answer to whether my experiment has worked. I push the doorbell.

Who will answer?

Graham? Bella? Somebody else?

And the door opens, but before I can see who it is, she turns away and stalks briskly back down the hallway.

"For heaven's sake, Al, how many times? Take your key!"

I know the voice and my heart feels like it's racing, and my throat is still dry so I can just about croak:

"Mum? Mum!!"

She stops. She turns.

It's Mum. In our old house. Not Steve's house.

"Well, what are you stand— Al? What on earth are you wearing? *Oof!* Hey!"

I have rushed into the house and thrown my arms around her with such force that we almost overbalance, but we don't. Instead I just stand there squeezing her and kind of making sure that it's really her, and all the while she's saying, "Are you OK, Al? Is something wrong?" because I'm sort of half sobbing, half laughing.

In hindsight, that must have been pretty weird for her.

So we're like that in the hallway and by now Mum is hugging me back because (she tells me later) for a mum, a hug from your son is always welcome, and while I'm hugging her, I'm checking over every inch of her—her head, her hair, her hands—and I'm just grinning because everything's how it should be. Then she kisses the top of my head. "All right, Wonder Boy. Let me go."

From the front room is the sound of the television, and another familiar voice.

"Lithuania! Oliver Cromwell! Sodium chloride!" and then a chuckle. "Easy peasy lemon squeezy!"

And then Grandpa Byron's in the hallway too and everything looks right there as well. I hug him, and he smells right, and his right arm is twisted, and even *that* seems right.

Everything is right.

Mum says, "Supper in ten minutes, boys."

"What's for supper?" I ask, a little warily—because probably for the first time in my life I *want* it to be one of Mum's experiments.

"Chicken korma," says Mum, and I get the beginnings of an uneasy feeling. "Only there was no chicken in the freezer so I've done it with pig's kidneys. It'll be a bit of an experiment. And, ee, Al—where did you get those clothes?"

Behind her back, Grandpa Byron wobbles his head in amusement.

Everything is right. Everything. Apart from the one thing I need to know.

It's the one thing I cannot bring myself to ask.

I try telling myself that just staying like this forever would be good enough for me, and if I don't ask then I won't get the answer I'm dreading. But it isn't.

I have to ask.

"Where's Dad?"

Mum looks at me like I'm crazy, and I can hardly breathe. "Your dad?" she says, frowning. "Where do you think?"

CHAPTER EIGHTY-FOUR

I try to think, but I can't.

"He—he's alive?"

Mum screws up her face in puzzlement.

"Alive? Of course he isn't alive." She looks hurt and con-fused, but then her mouth starts to turn up at the corners and I just *don't know what to think.* "Did I not tell you? He was shot dead in cold blood by a gang of trained weasels." She pauses. "He's in the bunker, silly lad, where he always is. Go and tell him supper's nearly ready. Honestly, Al . . . ," and she walks off into the kitchen shaking her head and smiling.

It's at this point that I actually wonder if I can stand any more uncertainty and anxiety, and I feel like I'm going to throw up as I leave through the back door and go down the steps to the bunker. The old metal submarine-type door is gone, replaced by a normal door, and there's a smell that is both strange and familiar. I step through the doorway and try to take it all in at once, but it's very hard.

And there he is, with his back to me.

He hears my footsteps and turns, and it's definitely him. And for some reason, I don't rush forward and hug him; I just stand there and he says, "Hello, matey," without really looking at me.

I want to rush forward and hug him, but I can't. I can't move. Instead, I look around me. One wall of the bunker is lined from top to bottom with small wire-fronted cages— there must be forty of them—with water dispensers clipped on to the front, and each contains one or two hamsters: brown ones, gray ones, big ones, small ones. One or two cages have rosettes tied on with wire, and there are framed certificates above the desk, and a bookshelf, and I immediately spot a copy of *Hamster Fancying for Beginners* by Dr. A. Borgström, and I'm just staring at all this in delighted wonder when Dad comes up to me with his hands cupped.

"Look here," he says, and he opens his hands to show me a tiny brown baby hamster. "This is Alan Shearer. Here, take him."

I can't say anything, and even if I could it would only be something stupid like, *"Wha? Eh? Huh? How?"*

"He's the great-great-great-great-great-great-great-great-grandson of the hamster I found in my shed when I was twelve," he says, counting off the "greats" on his fingers. He takes the baby hamster back and puts it in one of the cages.

And still I haven't said anything. Dad turns to me and looks at me, a little quizzically.

"Are you OK?"

I nod. Then he checks out my clothes.

"Nice jacket, Al. I used to have—" Then he stops. And he's just staring at me and blinking, and I stare back, and it's as if thirty years melt away in the space between us, there among the hamsters.

Eventually, after the longest time, he says:

"Al Singh."

I nod.

And *that's* when we hug. The longest, hardest, most intensest hug of all time.

"You trusted me," I say into his chest.

I feel him give his little head nod and say, "Like I've never trusted anyone before."

After a few minutes, or an hour, or thirty years, he looks at me closely and smiles. "You and I have got a *lot* of catching up to do."

And that's great. Because my dad is hugging me. And I'm not going *anywhere.*

CHAPTER EIGHTY-FIVE

And that is pretty much it.

Did I change the world? Well, I changed mine. And Dad's, and Mum's, and Grandpa Byron's.

I've told them all everything, but only Dad really understands. He dug out my letter from a drawer of his old stuff, and we all looked at the selfies on my mobile, and even then, there were still loads of unanswered questions.

For example, the night it all happened, I had left the house (this house) for about an hour without saying where I was going. That was the "me" that had been living with Mum and Dad up until then (not me), and then the other "me" (me) sent the letter with Alan Shearer, and that world changed. . . . I say "and then" like it was a linear progression of time, one incident after the other, but as I now know (or think I do), that's not how it works. It's all very confusing.

For a while I was worried that the other "me," my

doppelganger, was going to return from his walk and stroll back into the house, which would have been totally awkward, but it seems like that's not going to happen after all.

I often wonder where that "me" is—or the Grandpa Byron with the bad memory—or the Mum married to Roddy with no children. Do they exist in some parallel dimension? Or did they cease to exist when I delivered that letter and Alan Shearer to a twelve-year-old Pye and this world became reality instead?

I hope it's the last one, but I guess I'll never know now. And maybe that's for the best.

Anyway, I'm pretty confident that the whole thing will be our family's secret.

Aunty Hypatia still lives in Canada, but she seems to be much more a part of our lives than before. I mean, before I had only met her the once, and Grandpa Byron hardly ever mentioned her. Now she's on Skype all the time.

It was a long conversation with Mum, though, and I know it's been hard for her. I think she's OK with it all, but she doesn't really want to know any of the details—any of the time travel stuff. "Ee, honestly, it does my head in," she says, and I can't blame her, really.

But I think she's pretending about being confused. This

morning she got a package from Amazon that contained a fridge magnet. The background was a starry sky, and the words were this:

Time present and time past
Are both perhaps present in time future,
And time future contained in time past.

T. S. Eliot, *Four Quartets*

Which, actually, is kind of what Dad was saying all along. (She tried to get me to read the rest of the poem, but it's, like, pages and pages long. I'll probably read it when I'm older.)

I have tried to tell her about Steve and Carly and my life with them, and her, but she doesn't want to know, at least not yet.

And now there is only one thing niggling at me, really, and it's Carly. I keep thinking of the high five we exchanged in the taxi on the way back from the Graham and Bella episode. It might not seem like much, but compared with the open hostility that had preceded it, that high five was like a peace treaty after a war. Then I think of the terror on her face when she found me in her room the other day. For that matter, I even start feeling sorry for kicking Jolyon Dancey in that way (but only a bit, if I'm honest).

I want to change all of this, and ignoring it won't help. I remember Grandpa Byron's words during our last-but-one (and one of only two) rows. *"Escaping is not changing."*

I have an idea.

Well, I say "idea" like it's something special, but all I do is send her a text. I thought about going to her Facebook page and getting all mystical, but I figured I'd exploited that "spiritual" (ahem!) side of her before, and I feel a bit different toward her now anyway.

Remember the picture of Carly I took the night we did the séance, cross-legged behind the mirror-and-candle arrangement? She said she'd send it to me, and the first time I charged my phone, up it popped like a strange echo of another dimension. I can easily send it to her. I add the message: *You won't remember this. But I do!* And then, because I don't want her to think I'm all stalky or anything, I add, *My name's Al. I'm not a stalker.* And I add ;) and then change it to :) to be a bit friendlier than a wink.

It's going to be quite interesting for Carly (or "frea-ky!" as she'll probably say) to receive a very recent photo of herself doing some kind of goth ritual that she can't remember. I hit "Send" before I can think too much about it.

Then there's the little matter of school, which starts again next week after the half-term break.

I know. It's far too soon, and I feel sick with nerves about it, but there's no getting out of it. It's a different school for me, at least—I'm going to Culvercot Secondary Modern, which I set fire to (in a parallel dimension) and is now called the Sir Henry Percy Academy. It's a lot different now. Apparently there's a new gym and a science building, and Mrs. Spetrow, who's now the "senior administrator" (and probably close to retirement), has a big new computer, as do all the classrooms, and there's dozens in the ICT department.

It's going to be a bit weird at first, because there'll be kids there that I know from primary school, but I won't know anything about the last four years. I'm not sure how to handle that, to be honest, but if I keep my head down for the first few weeks I should be OK.

I'm thinking of concocting some sort of story of a brain injury or something that has left my memory affected.

Massive memory loss would be believable, just about, and Grandpa Byron thinks it's hilarious.

OK now, here's a funny thing. Remember Grandpa Byron's copy of *The Memory Palaces of the Sri Kalpana*? The one he gave to me, right, that I then gave back to the *other* Grandpa Byron with the note left on Pye's bed? Well, Grandpa Byron—the real Grandpa Byron in this reality—*still has his copy*!

How does that work? How many copies are there? How many Grandpa Byrons are there?

And, come to think of it, how many me's are there? It's just been the one me all the way through this adventure, and I know *that* because I can remember it.

"Our memories make us who we are," says Grandpa Byron, when he agrees to teach me his method for memorizing every day of your life (and I tell you, he is *so* pleased to be asked!). "Choose one moment in every day that is worth cherishing. Welcome that moment into your memory palace, nurture it always, and it will never leave you."

On warm spring afternoons like this one, I often go down to the promenade. It's a proper promenade now, not just a level bit on top of a seawall. There's a railing I can lean on and look out over the sea, and remember a boy called Pye and his new friend Al who had a hamster called Alan Shearer.

And then I pick up my pace and head home, because:

1. Mum has made lasagne;

2. Dad'll be back from Pet World with a new Hamsterdam;

3. My phone has just pinged with an incoming text from Carly; and

4. Grandpa Byron will be waiting for me to watch *Mind Games.*